home

also by matthew costello

vacation

home

matthew costello

thomas dunne books
st. martin's press ❧ new york

To Ann Costello, wife, collaborator—and my trusted friend
who knows the real value of a good home

THOMAS DUNNE BOOKS.
An imprint of St. Martin's Press.

HOME. Copyright © 2012 by Matthew Costello. All rights reserved. Printed in the United States of America. For information, address St. Martin's Press, 175 Fifth Avenue, New York, N.Y. 10010.

www.thomasdunnebooks.com
www.stmartins.com

Design by Anna Gorovoy

ISBN 978-1-250-01273-9 (hardcover)
978-1-250-01348-4 (e-book)

First Edition: November 2012

10 9 8 7 6 5 4 3 2 1

prologue: the plan

Paterville Family Camp, 10:17 p.m.

Christie walked beside Jack as their children—Kate, a girl just a few years from being a young woman, and Simon, a boy—walked ahead of them.

He held her hand. And they each held guns.

As did their daughter, who also held her brother's hand without protest.

Something almost unimaginable.

And they walked quickly—making their way through the woods, avoiding the paths filled with other campers, some who would easily attack and try to kill them.

Making their way to the lot where their car was parked while mayhem filled the camp.

Mayhem created by Jack. He had turned off the power, shut down the electric fence so the Can Heads outside could enter at will.

Into this camp.

Where—they knew now—the people were as dangerous . . . as deadly as the Can Heads outside the fence.

Jack leaned close as he spoke to her.

Speaking so low, whispering into her ear as they walked.

Telling her the plan.

And all she could do was listen.

The too-dry pine needles and ancient skeletal leaves cracked under their feet as they moved quickly, still taking care not to make the kids run in the dark, worried that they would trip, slow them down, expose them.

As Jack spoke, he kept looking over his shoulder.

"I have the keys to the Blair's car—"

"They—"

"Gone, Christie. *Gone.*"

She didn't ask any more.

"Okay."

"They'll be dealing with the fences being down, the Can Heads roaming around. Might keep them busy, but God—"

His voice caught.

She gave his hand a squeeze.

"They can't let us out. Not with what I know. What I saw."

He hadn't actually described how he escaped the kitchen—the charnel house where they had kept him prisoner. And he hadn't told her yet what he saw there.

So she had to ask.

Had to know the horror.

"What, Jack? What did you see?"

And though he had been keeping his voice low as they raced through the woods, he leaned even closer.

"People who come here. Like us. The Blairs. Some don't leave. Some—"

Another halt.

He picked his word carefully.

"Some . . . they slaughter."

She nearly moaned at that. This place they had come to, a family camp. A massive trap.

For people . . . to trap people.

Was that the only way these people decided they could survive?

Living off their fellow humans?

"God, Jack."

"Now listen—"

The car park—well away from the Grand Lodge—lay just ahead.

Only minutes to explain.

"They'll be busy, but they won't let us get out. The main gate—they'll be waiting."

She shook her head, hearing where he was going with this.

"No. We can't—"

"Listen!" He squeezed her hand. "I'll drive our car out. I'll go fast. I'll shoot my way out if I have to. You wait."

"What?"

"Five minutes. Enough time for me to get to the gate, then you drive up the service road. To the exit at the back. Just keep driving, don't stop for anything."

"And we'll meet—?"

"Yes. Keep driving. I'll stop at the first small town we get to. Not far from here. We can all meet there."

But she knew . . . *knew* . . . what he wasn't saying.

The word he didn't utter.

If.

"Do you understand?"

Then to ensure she knew what was at stake, why it had to be this way.

"You have to do this—for Kate . . . Simon. Do you understand?"

And she did.

Until they were at the car, their SUV, Jack's guns on the seat, gun-shots still filling the camp.

She watched Jack place a blanket in the back over some bags, making it look like his family might be huddled in the back.

"Okay—"

Not wasting any time.

He gave her a hug. A crushing hug. A deep kiss that ended too soon.

Then to the backseat of the other car, the Blair's Honda Accord.

"Kids—hang in there. We're almost out of this place."

He looked at Kate, his beautiful daughter who had shot one of the Can Heads only minutes before. Then at his son, his baby.

Then: "I love you. Love you all."

He turned and got into the car.

Last words to Christie.

"Five minutes?"

She nodded.

Then, almost silently, back to him . . .

"I love you, too."

The wait eternal, sitting in the locked car. Checking her watch over and over, the time crawling.

"Mom," a voice in the back said.

And Christie so obsessed with the timing, with what she had to do that she not only didn't answer.

She didn't for a moment even know which kid it was.

Until, one more glance at her watch—

Five minutes.

Like Jack said.

He was racing out the main gate, drawing them away.

That was the plan.

Now she turned the ignition.

And though it started immediately, there was still that horrible moment of fear.

What if it didn't start?

But it did.

She put it into reverse.

"Hold on," she said. Then, using her kids' names, "Simon, Kate . . . hold on."

The car curved backward, nearly smashing into one of the other parked cars.

A quick flip into forward.

And then—

Then . . .

The mad drive up, and out of the parking area, through the hell of a Paterville under attack, driving through that hell, over and into the bodies.

The screaming from the backseat constant, like it was part of the sound of the engine.

Not stopping. The moments insane as Christie floored the accelerator to drive through anyone or anything that might stop her.

Telling herself as if it might make it fact:

Nothing will stop me.

Until—

Just as she burst through the gate to the road outside, the narrow country road that led away from Paterville, she heard . . . an explosion.

Muffled.

Like fireworks from a distant town.

But big enough, *clear* enough so she knew it had been a large explosion.

And she knew then.

(*Of course.*)

Jack.

All his tinkering in the garage with their SUV.

Making them safe.

And if anything should happen. If ever they should be caught.

They never spoke about it.

But she had long ago guessed what he had done to the car.

You didn't live with a man, a cop, for ten years and not know things.

And in the darkness, on that road, nearly losing control since she still kept the pedal down to the floor, she began to sob.

Feeling.

Knowing.

That she'd never see her husband again.

That with the sound of that explosion, the SUV blowing up, he had saved her.

Saved the kids.

And now, it was all up to her.

After muffling her own crying, the kids sobbing quietly in the backseat, she let herself cry.

For now.

Soon enough she'd have to be strong . . .

the road

1

A Gate

Christie stopped. Her hands locked on the steering wheel, like they had been for the past few hours.

Though she felt so achy, a fatigue deeper than anything she had even felt before, her eyes were open wide, her breathing fast.

She kept staring at the gate ahead, linked to the twelve-foot fence that cut off the Northway from the rural mountainous Adirondacks it cut through.

She thought: *Where is he?*

The goddamn guard. To let us in, open the goddamn—

"Mom."

Kate. Her voice quiet, hollow. Because she didn't want to awaken her brother? Or because that was the only voice she had now, could possibly ever have after the night they had been through?

After everything that happened.

Christie struggled to push that thought away. With all its images of the events of the past day.

What had happened. What had been lost. What was now changed for them forever.

"Mom. What's wrong?"

Christie wanted to turn back to her, turn to her daughter and answer.

But she didn't trust herself to do that. Not to look into those eyes now. Not when eventually there'd be so many questions, and such terrible answers.

Christie told herself . . . *I can't look at her right now.*

Can't risk that I'll start crying again.

Not for the first time this night . . . she ordered herself to hold it together.

As if by merely thinking the words would have some effect.

"Kate, I don't know. There should be someone here. To let us in."

Christie nodded as she said this. A perfectly sensible sentence. Said in a steady, rational voice. A reassuring voice, she hoped, even though something seemed wrong here.

And if there was something she knew now . . . when something *seemed* wrong, it most certainly could be wrong in ways that defied human imagination.

"Then . . ." Kate started, a hesitation, maybe thinking she shouldn't ask any questions. Not now. Not yet.

"Where's the guard? Why is there no one here?" Kate's voice had lost some of the sleepy hollowness, raising just a notch in volume, tone. Concern. After what they'd been through, Kate had every reason to be worried at every moment, at everything.

After all . . .

After all . . .

It wasn't too long ago that both kids had been screaming, that there was so much gunfire, and blood, when even Kate had to shoot a gun.

Her sweet girl, her firstborn, forced to *shoot*, to actually kill one of them and then watch it fall dead at her feet.

She can never be the same, Christie thought.

"Maybe he's asleep. Maybe—I dunno, Kate . . . maybe I should blow the horn."

"No," Kate said. Then: "Don't make noise. It's still dark."

Christie nodded, suddenly aware of the stupidity of her idea and of the newfound wisdom of her daughter.

A wisdom born of terror and loss.

She looked in the rearview mirror. She couldn't see Kate in it, but she did see the shadow of Simon's face, no pools of reflected light coming from his eyes still—thankfully—shut tight.

Then, with the car horn removed from the options, Kate said: "What are we going to do?"

We.

That's it now, isn't it? We. *Because we're in this together.*

"Maybe—just wait a bit."

But again, as the words escaped, Christie immediately knew that that was a bad idea. To sit here, like bait. Waiting until something noticed and came to investigate.

No—sooner or later—she'd have to do something.

Please, she begged something, somewhere.

For what seemed like eternal moments, she sat there, hands feebly locked on the steering wheel, both she and Kate silent, with only the sound of the car's motor, this car that wasn't theirs, the hum unfamiliar.

A car the belonged to a family now dead.

Slaughtered.

Another thought to be pushed away.

And then—from within the white light of the booth of the gate, a head popped up, slowly, eyes easily as wide as Christie's, the head rising like a human periscope.

As if it might have to duck a bullet. Or a rock.

Until the man inside was fully standing.

The gatekeeper.

The man who controlled the fence.

Standing there, looking at Christie, the car.

C'mon, she thought.

Open the gate.

For the moment, the man did nothing.

The man kept staring at Christie as if he could stare at her long enough and make her drive away.

Christie looked down to the headlight controls, and gave it a pull, flashing the light. Then again and again, and now the man looked away. She watched him look around. The sky beginning to brighten to the east, still a deep purple darkness to the west.

A thought came to Christie, one she wished she hadn't had.

Something happened. Something happened here; the man saw something and now—God—now he's scared.

And then:

Maybe I should ram the gate. Just floor the goddamn accelerator and blow right through the gate.

But was that even possible?

Then finally the man turned to the door of the small booth beside the gate. He walked out, his head still looking around. Christie had the car heater on, but she could see from the condensation on the front and back windows that it was chilly out. Fall comes early to the mountains.

The man's expression didn't change as he walked up to the car window. Christie hit a button and the driver's side window slid all the way down. The cool air rushed into the car as if eager to escape the outside.

It seemed as though the gatekeeper, wearing his Highway Authority shirt and faded jeans, was waiting for her to begin the conversation.

"Can you . . . open the gate?"

She resisted the temptation to say *goddamned*, or *fucking*, or some other word that would put emphasis on her desire to get the hell off this country road and onto the safe highway.

Another thought . . . *safe highway?*

Safer maybe. But safe?

The man licked his lips. Another darting glance left and right.

"I need to see your papers." His voice cracked as though he hadn't said any words for a long time. He cleared his throat, and squinted.

Bundle of nerves.

Christie opened her mouth.

She hadn't thought about the papers. They were in their car. With Jack. Forgotten.

Jack, who always thinks of everything. Somehow, in his plan to get them out of Paterville Camp, he forgot.

And he thinks of everything. How could—

No.

He thought *of everything . . .*

When he was alive.

The papers permitting them to use the highway, with their approval to travel the protected highway from their home in Staten Island to the mountain resort of Paterville, were—were—

Gone.

Destroyed.

And Christie immediately felt a jab of fear.

Not having those papers . . . it could be a bad thing.

"I'm sorry. But we seem to have lost them. I can show—"

The man had already started shaking his head. In a moment, she was sure, he would start back for the booth, and Christie would be stuck there, waiting.

He allowed a few more words to escape his mouth.

"You *need* to have the papers. Can't let you on the highway with-out—"

"Listen," Christie said, cutting him off but also attempting to reach his wrist, for a pat, or perhaps to hold him there so he didn't scurry back to the booth.

"I told you—we did *have* them. You can check. You still have computers, don't you? You can—"

More head shakes. "They've been down. Hours. Something wrong. Downstate."

"Right. But if you could check, I mean—"

Christie fumbled in her small blue rucksack that served as a purse for the paperwork for this trip, this supposed vacation.

She dug out her crimson wallet, now filled with mostly useless cards from companies that didn't exist or banks that had vanished.

Gotta prune it, she told herself so many times but never did.

Like that world would never come back.

She went to the side pocket and pulled out her driver's license. She quickly extended it to the man.

"Look. You can see. We—"

Christie nodded her head in the direction of her two kids in the back.

On cue, Kate said, "Mom? Mom, what's wrong?"

Such good timing, Christie thought. Kate to the rescue.

And:

We're in this together. She knows that. The two of us. Can't expect Simon to understand, to do anything. We'll have to watch out for him, protect him.

The man hadn't taken the license.

"Go on. Please. Take a look." Still no snatch of the ID. Only the man's turkey neck, turning left and right and left again.

Guy's so damn scared standing out here.

"Please."

Another lick of the lips. The man took the license.

He looked at it, too quickly, Christie thought, to take in the address . . . the location . . . *Staten Island.*

He handed the ID back, taking care not to get too close to the open window.

Is he afraid I'm going to grab him, pull him into the car?

Is that the world we live in now?

"You see. *Staten Island*, says it right there. And, and—" She fought to stay in control. So many times driving here she was so close to losing it. To begin sobbing, howling, the tears erupting.

And she had to tell herself—order herself—to hold it together. For Kate, for Simon, for sanity, for survival.

Finally—because it's what Jack would have wanted.

It's why he did . . . what he did.

In those moments after she knew Jack was gone, she had sobbed quietly at first, while the kids slept, then letting the grief come in waves, feeling as if her mourning would never end.

Now this first barrier, this first test . . .

To hold it together.

She looked up at the man as she took her license. "We've been through a lot. It's been a bad night, back there."

"I heard things happened," the man said.

Was it just hell in the Paterville Camp tonight, or—like the trees turning a fiery orange, back when there used to be so many more deciduous trees—was the madness they faced in the camp spreading?

"We were nearly killed. And I have to get my . . . *babies* . . . home. You can understand that, can't you?"

The man appeared unmoved. Jack had always said how important it was to have the right papers.

Then: "Okay. Since I can't check. Since you have that there license." He took a breath. "You look scared, lady."

So do you, Christie thought.

Another turret head look around.

"I have to open the gate by hand. Got power in my booth but not the fence, not the gate."

Now it was Christie's turn to take a breath.

"That means the electric fence . . ."

The man nodded.

Christie felt her stomach drop.

"How far? I mean, how far down is the fence off?"

The man shook his head. "Dunno. So—be careful."

He walked back to the booth, passing through it to a back door that led to the other side of the fence. He attached an iron bar to something that, in the scant light, looked like a kind of gear mechanism.

He began cranking, and the gate sluggishly began sliding to the right.

The cranks and car engine the only sounds in the chilly near-dawn.

Until Christie hit a button and the window rolled up.

And when just enough space had opened for her to get through, she hit the accelerator and flew past the man, still hunched over the crank, but already turning it in the other direction.

And she thought:

We're that much closer to home.

2

Gas

The road . . . deserted.

Christie hoped she'd see the occasional car heading north, others passing her heading south. But she was alone on the highway, and that aloneness kept her on edge.

That aloneness and, as she started watching the fuel gauge as she drove a near rock-steady 55 mph toward the Albany area, she had something else to worry about.

Gas.

There'd be people ahead as they got to Albany, she knew. Cars. Maybe the occasional Highway Authority helicopter.

Maybe only an hour away.

Close.

But this car, this nearly decade-old car that belonged to other people, was a guzzler. Not like their SUV Jack had worked on, playing with the engine, adding an afterburner, checking the fuel lines every week so they could stretch every bit of gas they had.

Christie imagined that she could almost see the gauge's needle slipping lower and lower to the left even as she watched.

She looked up at the mirror. Simon still slept.

At first, she thought that was a good thing.

He's getting some rest. He needs sleep. It's good . . . he's sleeping.

But the truth that Christie had to admit to herself was that Simon—curled up, eyes locked shut—wasn't just sleeping.

He was in shock. Had to be.

Christie took a breath. She had never felt so alone in her life.

Alone, and yet with this now crushing responsibility for her two children.

Our two children. She corrected herself. Jack and mine. We brought them this far together.

And now it's up to me alone.

At that moment, another thought: *I can't do it.*

And another . . .

I don't know how *to do it.*

But her only defense now was to push the thought away as best she could.

Go!

Get the fuck out of here. Like when she was barreling out of the camp, shooting the attacking Can Heads, their bodies flying onto the car in a desperate attempt to stop her.

Thoughts were dangerous now. They could immobilize. Paralyze.

And despite having had no sleep. Despite whatever shock she knew she had to be feeling (and yet couldn't let herself feel), she had to be as sharp and alert as possible.

She reached up and moved the mirror. To see Kate.

Kate, face turned right, eyes glued to the rolling hills outside. With the gray light of dawn, Christie could now see that face. The dried blood spatters on her daughter's beautiful face.

Need to wash that face. Take a wet face cloth and get her all cleaned up.

As if removing those stains might somehow remove the memory, the *reality* of what had happened.

She had watched her daughter kill one of them.

Shoot it, squarely, right in its head.

Could any of them ever be the same?

Christie thought she might say something to Kate. About the night. In a quiet voice so as to not awaken Simon.

But her daughter looked zoned out. Perhaps suspended somewhere between sleeping and awake.

What was the line from that decades-old song?

Comfortably numb.

Though not comfortably. But numb enough that she could just sit there.

And though there was no traffic to worry about, at least not yet, she adjusted the mirror back to its proper position.

Then, in what had become a ritual to be performed every few seconds, she looked back down again at the gas gauge.

Which now seemed to be in a mad race to reach *E* as fast as possible.

The rest stop ahead immediately reminded Christie of the last time they had stopped for gas.

When Jack had been attacked, and had said . . . *That is it. We should turn around, go back home.*

And then, Christie had shaken her head.

(*God—only days ago . . .*)

Saying that they *had* to do this. To get away. They couldn't just hide in their house. That they all deserved more.

She had taken a stand. And Jack, almost uncharacteristically, finally agreed. They would go on to Paterville Camp. They'd have this vacation.

And now—

Jack was dead.

"Mom."

Simon. Up at last.

Her eyes shot up to his in the mirror even as she slowed down to take the off-ramp.

"Mom."

"Yes, Simon?"

He didn't say anything more. She waited, chewing at her lower lip in a near terror at what he might say, what he might ask.

"Simon. Honey. You okay?"

The absurdity, the sheer mad and insane *absurdity* of that question.

After being held captive at that camp, after escaping through the night, all of them—except her sweet young boy—shooting at those things that had chased them.

Did he understand about his father? They had both become so quiet when Christie had said that she'd explain everything later. She knew from Kate's sobs that maybe she already understood.

And Simon, somehow, like some strange gift given to young boys, had fallen asleep.

But now—

"Why . . . are we stopping?"

She nearly smiled at the innocuousness of the question. So simple to answer. Not laced with any triggers to make them all fall apart.

"Out of gas, honey. Almost. Real low."

Another glance in the mirror. His eyes looked away, to the right.

She waited for another question. She wanted another question.

This silence too terrible.

Some voice inside Christie's mind said, as if a command, a massive to-do . . . *you'll have to talk to them eventually.*

Talk. Cry. Mourn.

Sooner—or later.

But she knew something else equally as well. Not now. Not yet.

She crawled to the side of the pumps, the car almost feral in the way she made it slide so slowly beside the gas pumps.

And then the pragmatic thoughts of dealing with the next moments came to her.

First, did this place even have gas? Being run by the Highway Authority, most likely yes.

She looked around. Like at all the rest stops, she saw a QuikMart.

Not going anywhere near there, she thought.

Then a look at the parking spaces off to the side.

All empty.

No one here. A ghost rest stop. And inside the small convenience store, no lights.

The man at the gate said . . . something had happened.

So they closed this place?

And if it was closed, pumps off, no electricity . . . what then?

The gas gauge hovered just a notch above the red *E*. They would have to . . . shit, get off the highway and try to find someplace open on these back roads, the sun just up but still masked by gray morning clouds.

She turned and looked at the pumps.

Begging in her mind that they weren't just dull, dark monoliths.

But she saw the small screen. The message: *Insert card below.*

Jack had given her all the cash he had. Credit cards, though, were becoming more and more useless as the last banks vanished, as the networks disappeared and the Internet for many became a thing of the past, accessible only by the government . . .

Cash became the only sure way to get goods.

That is, when goods were available.

But to use cash . . . she would have to go into the QuikMart.

Which looked dark.

She sat there, frozen.

"Mom." Kate this time. "Are you getting gas?"

She turned back to the two of them.

"Sure."

Project confidence, she thought. *Like Jack would. Be reassuring.*

Christie had the thought to smile before she realized how bizarre that would be.

To smile now.

Today.

After last night?

"I'm going to get out and—pump some gas."

They sat there.

"Yeah. Okay. I'll be . . . just out—"

Another absurdity, and again Christie thought that she was losing it, falling apart, the intact pieces of her mind that had gotten her—and them—this far, all falling away.

Then, more to herself, "Okay?"

She got out.

Cool air. Chilly. As if the past few blistering hot days—what were always blisteringly hot days—had ended. And clouds? A rarity, and even when they appeared, they rarely let a drop of rain hit the dry ground.

There was some explanation on news broadcasts, some government expert explaining convection currents and how they carried those clouds and all their moisture over the ocean where the rain fell uselessly into the Atlantic.

She finally looked at the pump.

At the small screen on it, and its suggestion to "insert card."

Teasingly . . .

Because, she thought, *I don't want to go in there, inside that damn rest stop.*

She looked at the screen.

A smiley face with legs, spindly arms, wearing a gas attendant's hat from a century ago, stood next to those hopeful words.

Insert. Card.

She held Jack's wallet in her hand, barely able to open it up but knowing that she should do this fast.

Can't stand here in the chill, thinking, waiting.

The idea again.

Like goddamn bait.

She opened the wallet, Jack's brown leather worn to soft burnished yellow from years in his back pocket.

She sucked in a breath as she flipped it open to see his NYPD identity card. Full dress blue uniform. His hat, which he never wore, sitting squarely though awkwardly on his head.

A shiver ran through her, then again the urge to begin sobbing, heaving, screaming—all at the same time.

But somehow a bit of her brain was able to send out messages, urgent, clear.

The kids are watching.

And . . .

Get the gas. Just get the gas and get going.

She slipped out one of the credit cards and with shaky fingers stuck it into the slot.

The smiley face attendant on the screen disappeared.

A message: *Card not recognized.*

Shit. Like so many cards these days. The banks, the whole connected thing that allowed the cards to be used, all screwed up, falling apart.

Again: the thought . . . she might be able to use cash, if she went into the QuikMart.

But she *knew* she couldn't do that.

Then a quick thought . . . *But what if I have to?*

What if I have to go in there?

She slid another card out and jammed it in and out of the slot quickly.

A hesitation. Then the same damn thing.

Card not recognized.

No, no, no . . . she thought. *Please not after everything we have been through.*

She took another deep breath before she slid it in slowly, as if taking her time might make a difference.

Because if it doesn't, I'm just going to have to walk into the building, hand over some cash . . .

And wondering: do I leave the kids, or take them with me, and what would Jack do—Jack always had ideas. Always could figure things out.

He was a cop. It's what he did.

A flicker of awareness hit her that she had used the word . . .

Was.

Another small chunk of acceptance that he was really gone.

With all that meant—to her, to the kids, to whatever their future might be.

The last card slid in deep and then, equally slowly, she slipped it out.

The smiley man vanished.

And then . . .

And then . . .

A new message: *Please select your grade of gasoline and press start.*

Joy. Near giddy excitement.

She pulled out the nozzle, pushed a button, refusing to let herself think that the pump might not work.

She unscrewed the gas cap and stuck the nozzle in, hurrying as fast as she could. She pressed the trigger to start the flow.

The deceptively clear fluid began shooting out of the nozzle's spout and into the gas tank.

When it clicked off, Christie jammed the nozzle back into its holder.

The smiley face on the screen now asked if she wanted a receipt.

She ignored the question and got back into the car.

Noting that in all that time, she hadn't seen another car, or a truck, or a helicopter patrolling the highway.

Like we're the only people on the highway, in this world.

She had never felt this alone. This empty.

Back in the warmth of the car, she heard Simon's voice.

"Mom. Can we eat? Is there—"

An *oomph*, and then a yell from Simon: "Hey!"

Christie turned around, guessing that Kate had fired an elbow into her brother.

Trying to tell him in her direct big-sister way that now was not the time to be thinking about food.

But they would need food eventually. Could they hang in until they got home?

And—God—water—she kept licking her lips; she seemed to have less and less saliva.

"Um, Simon—"

Her eyes were on her son, then to Kate. Both kids' eyes locked on hers.

And she saw that suddenly Simon had nothing more to say.

Was it because of how I look? My own red stains that I still needed to clean up?

"We'll get some food. Home isn't that far away. Maybe we can find a stop with—" She pulled her eyes away for a second to look around— "Some rest stop where there are people. Just . . ." A big breath . . . "Just not here. Okay?"

Simon, still silent. He nodded.

Kate's face, set, concerned.

"Okay. We're going to go now."

An attempt at a half smile.

Which probably just looked strange.

Christie pulled away from the pumps, to the ramp back onto the highway, the tank full. Plenty of gas to get them home.

That's all she kept thinking for the next few minutes.

Plenty of gas to get us back home . . .

3

Pulled Over

Suddenly, there were cars.

The emptiness of the past hundred miles changed as she entered what was called "The Capital Region" . . . Albany, Schenectady, Troy, Cohoes—the cluster of cities that tried to act as though it was the center of the state of New York.

While everyone knew, no matter what anyone said, that the center was, now more than ever, really Manhattan. The governor made no secret about living in a secure zone of the Upper East Side, and the state senate had become even more useless in these days of drought, food shortages . . . and Can Heads.

Other states, Christie knew, were far worse. Nevada apparently had fallen into total chaos. Whole chunks of Kentucky had become blacked-out zones where nobody knew what the hell was going on inside.

Jack had once said to her . . .

"If this isn't stopped. If they can't somehow stop this, then . . . I don't know where we can go, Christie. What we can do."

He immediately apologized for his words, for scaring her. It had been after a bad day on the streets.

"Don't worry," he had said.

But it was too late for those words. And they never really talked about the future again. These were not days to make plans.

Now it was all about staying safe, teaching the kids, waiting for the government, the army, some goddamned *they* to figure out what hell was going on.

And stopping it.

As she drove now, she came back to the question she had never asked but would occur to her nearly every day . . . *What if there is no* they?

It would be down to us.

And now—

She shook her head as if resisting the thought, the very craziness of the idea—

Now—it's down to me.

She saw a flashing light ahead, and slowed.

A Highway Authority patrol car blocked two lanes, leaving one open.

The squad car with its flashing lights had a line of cars pulled over . . . four, maybe five cars, all in a line.

One officer stood at the front of that line, while another stood by the side of the road, making a two-hand gesture to new arrivals to *slow down.*

Christie wondered: *What is this? What's going on . . .* as she slowed to a stop.

No one behind her.

She pulled up to the officer, who looked like a state trooper from a decade ago, except that his new Highway Authority uniform was a steely black, serious, intimidating.

Announcing . . . that they controlled the roads.

"Morning, ma'am. Checking papers."

She looked up at him. She knew both kids would be watching him carefully as well.

Should she simply blurt out the whole story, and plead for the permission to travel on?

"I—I don't have them."

He nodded. "We know that some stretches of the highway north of here have had failures. Power down, people just slipping through, trying to get out. Understandable. But I'm afraid—"

She reached a hand out to touch his arm.

"I—we live in New York City. Staten Island. Something happened—"

She sputtered on as she felt his dark eyes, hiding any flicker of understanding or empathy, look at hers, then drifting a bit, taking in her whole face, what her face must look like. Then to the back of the car, to the kids while she carried on.

She stopped herself, and also looked back at Kate and Simon.

She couldn't do this in front of them.

Not the whole story . . . not all that they had lived through.

"Officer, can I get out? Talk to you?"

A moment's hesitation, then a nod as he backed up so she could open the door.

Christie got out and walked over to him.

She reduced the story to what she thought were the barest essentials.

And only as the words rolled out did she realize how insane it sounded, this *babble*. But as if possessed and compelled to finish, with the officer still looking at her, she went on.

"We went to this camp, Paterville. A vacation. My husband . . . he is . . . *was* an NYPD cop. After a Can Head attack wounded him, after rehab, he took us there. Had a lake, boats. Food." She felt a sudden tightening that seemed to hit her nostrils, her eyes. Another word and she could easily start crying all over again.

She stopped.

"It wasn't a real camp. They—they would kill people, and then there was this place they—they—"

The Authority officer finally reached over and touched her shoulder.

"Okay. Okay. Hold on. We got a report something happened up there. Not that there was much we could do. Not with everything going on. Things happening all over. And your husband?"

Christie looked away.

My husband.

An eternity before she turned back to those dark eyes.

"He saved us."

And she thought: *Please don't ask me how.*

Now the officer hesitated.

But, his voice low, he had one more question:

"He didn't get out?"

A head shake, biting her lower lip. To stop herself.

She sniffed the air, losing the battle.

"So you see . . . you see, we need to get home." A nod to her kids. "We need to go *home.*"

The Highway Authority officer's eyes had narrowed. *Was he like Jack?* she wondered. What horrors had he seen out here?

And what does that do to someone?

He looked over to his partner, talking to other drivers.

"Most of these people, they think the city might be safer. Any city. Most—don't have papers. All pretty desperate. Some of them— well, let's just say we're not too sure who anybody is anymore. I guess—"

His eyes, in the gray morning light, seemed to radiate something new now.

Understanding? Empathy? Pity?

"—you would understand that. Better than most. Things are different. With the Can Heads. Could be—" he shook his head "—these days . . . almost anyone."

Then Christie said, a plea: "Can we go?"

The officer nodded.

"Yes. But I need to tell you something first. Okay?"

The air was still cool. The blistering sun still masked by the unusual layer of clouds. Clouds that would be vaporized in the next hour.

And then she listened . . .

"Been things happening during the past few days. Big power failures all over, and then all hell broke loose. Whereabouts you from?"

Christie looked at the officer, and felt her fear, which slowly ebbed the farther she got away from Paterville, once again building.

"Staten Island. Did it affect—"

He shook his head. "I—I honestly don't know. But it was a big blackout, hit parts of the highway system, even with all their backup power. I doubt the fence is secure as you get closer to the city. Just warning you."

She nodded.

And now what? she thought. What the hell could she do with that information?

"Is the power back up?"

"In some parts. Like I said, it's been hard for us to get information. But—"

He hesitated a moment, and Christie sensed he was reluctant to say what would come next.

"—well . . . there have also been reports of Can Head break-ins. Lots of them. And in big groups. It's—different."

"But they stopped them, right? I mean, that's under control?"

Nothing.

Which was answer enough.

"I wish I could tell you more. You're headed there. So—just a warning. It may be all right by the time you get there. Could be . . . all fine."

Or maybe not.

She wondered if she should—what? Stay here? Find some place that was safe, a place with fences working, a motel, hotel, or—

She looked over at the car. She had been out here for a while. The kids were probably worried. She saw Kate looking right at her.

A smile at them, then back to the Highway officer.

"Any place around here . . . I could stay? With the kids. Until I know more."

The officer nodded, tightened his lips.

"In Troy, I hear they have made the RPI Field House a safe place. Imagine you could go there. A few hotels in Albany with security, but I imagine they'll be full. Not even too sure how safe they are. Don't know what to tell you."

His words clarified what Christie felt.

No way in hell she could stay here. Not knowing anyone, not knowing if a place was protected.

If she was taking them home, then that's exactly what she should do.

Maybe their community was fine. Power failures don't last forever. And they had probably dealt with any Can Head break-ins by now.

Telling herself all these things.

Not knowing whether she believed them.

But knowing that she had decided what she would do.

"Thanks. I think . . . I'll just try to get back."

The Highway Authority officer nodded.

"Be safe, ma'am."

She smiled at that.

Be. Safe.

As if that was even under her control.

She walked back to the car, ready to return to the highway south.

4

The Trunk

Kate and Simon both had questions. What did the officer want? Why were they talking so long?

And then the last, eternal question from Simon . . .

"Mom? How long till we're home?"

She actually smiled at that one.

As if maybe, perhaps, some things would never change.

"About two hours," she said. "Maybe a bit more."

Then, for added assurance: "It won't be long."

In the quiet, she drove in that same steel-armed position she had held since they escaped the camp—two hands on the wheel, slightly hunched over, as if that increased alertness.

She tried to take stock of . . . herself.

First, there was the pain. A dull ache in at least four different parts of her body. Though she worked out—the government ran ads promoting the importance of being in shape . . .

These days . . .

When you might need to run, to be fast . . .

—still, her upper thighs hurt, too much sprinting, clambering. She didn't know. The ibuprophen didn't seem to do anything. (And she had to be careful—she didn't have a lot of that. She didn't have a lot of anything.)

And her arms, shoulders, all achy. Was that from the kick of the gun as she fired, or just the incredible tensing of those muscles as she blasted at the things that attempted to grab them as they raced—still a family, still together—through the woods, down to their car?

She rolled her head, a relaxation exercise, hearing the tiny cracks of the stretching muscles as she did so.

And then she asked herself a question.

And inside? Inside my head?

How is my thinking? Is it clear? What about—what the hell—how about shock. Am I in goddamn shock? Are my kids in shock?

And if I am, what do I need to do? What do I need to watch out for?

She thought of how Jack had prepared their SUV for the trip, all that armor. The weapons he had told her about, and then the ones he didn't. He did the same with their house, with the roll-down metal windows at night, the reinforced basement doors and windows. Trying to make their home a fortress even though their development was surrounded by a fence that would toast a Can Head in seconds.

The big question . . .

Can I think like Jack?

She knew one thing. Doubting herself wouldn't help. No, she needed to stay focused. All the time.

She nodded at that. That would be her mantra. *Stay focused. One thing at a time.*

She rolled her head again.

And in midroll, she heard the explosion.

The Honda immediately swerved violently to the right, into the far-right lane and nearly onto the side of the road. She quickly overcorrected, and nearly sent the Blair's beat-up car streaming into the guardrail on the left.

From the backseat, squeals, yells, and the ever-present shouting . . .

Mom!

A loud clatter accompanied the car's swerving, a *thunka-thunka-thunka* sound that now only took her seconds to identify as she began to slowly apply the brake.

"It's a blowout kids. Just a tire."

Just.

Shit.

Do. Not. Need. *This.*

Now she steered the tilted car, limping on what was left of a blown left rear tire, to the right lane. And then—the car crawling at fifteen, ten miles an hour, off to the side of the road, onto the brown crunchy grass.

She felt the tire's rim dig into the dirt as she got the car fully off the highway.

Another few feet, and she was off the road.

But she had her hands still locked on.

She reminded herself—so soon!—of her mantra.

Stay focused. One thing at a time.

And now that one thing was checking that the kids were okay.

She released her hands from the wheel and turned around.

Kate looked at her mom, and then she turned to Simon.

When she had felt the car seem to sink to the left, Kate had yelled, as if her mother had done something wrong.

Simon had also screamed and he quickly turned to her.

Turned to me, Kate thought.

As if I could—what?—protect him?

But Kate looked back to her mom, her dark eyes, looking right at them.

She looks so different, she thought.

Something different in her eyes. *She's still my mom*, Kate told herself. *But a lot of things have happened.*

Things like running away. Like killing the Can Heads that had attacked.

Kate reminded herself of one unbelievable fact.

I killed one.

I used the gun. I shot it in the head. And then it stopped.

Simple. Easy. Just like Dad taught me.

(*And I could do it again.*)

And she had this thought, though not clear what it meant . . .

Simon had seen it all too. Had seen us shooting, fighting our way out of there. My little brother had seen me kill one of them.

And Dad.

Dad.

So—if my mom's eyes are different—that shouldn't be surprising at all.

"Kids—"

"Mom. What happened?" Simon said.

Kate noticed that her brother's voice sounded different. It always used to bother her, so loud, so whiny, always wanting things. Now it seemed quiet. Just asking a question now and then again.

She wanted the old Simon back.

Mom nodded.

"Well, we just had what's called a blowout. A tire blew."

That's not supposed to happen, Kate knew.

She had heard her father talk all the time about how strong the tires were. How they couldn't get a flat.

But this wasn't their car, the one Dad had made so strong.

And even *that* car hadn't been strong enough to save him, Kate knew.

Mom had gotten them out of the camp . . . but when she heard the explosion, she knew.

They'd never see their father again. It was just the three of them.

Kate had been glad that they drove in the darkness so she could, for all those hours, sit in the back and cry quietly, hidden from her mother, muffling the sounds, the pain twisting so hard at her insides.

Now it was morning.

A new day.

"How'd it happen?" Simon asked, his voice unable to hide his concern.

"I don't know, Simon. This—isn't our car. Maybe the tires weren't that good. I—I—"

Kate rushed in to fill the gap, suddenly afraid that her mother might lose it.

"Mom, there's got to be a spare, right? We can put the spare on, and—"

Then Kate did something that felt so natural but—if you had asked her—she would say that she had never done it before.

She smiled at Simon, making her face bright, a slight smile, widening her eyes that had squinted closed with tears all night—

"We can just . . . get the spare on and get going again." Back to her mother. "Right?"

Her mother nodded.

"I'll help," Kate added. "I've seen Dad—"

That word again.

Her mother looked as though she was about to say no . . . but Kate held her mother's gaze, her eyes tight on hers.

Then a nod. "Okay—we can all do it. Just stay close."

And her mother turned to open her door. A look at the nearby woods, and in the distance, sections of the highway fence.

The door popped open.

"C'mon, Simon," she said to her brother, and they got out of the backseat.

Christie used the key to pop open the trunk.

"Now stay close. I've done this before, but this isn't our car. Just stay near me, okay?"

She looked toward the woods. Quiet. No breeze. The air warming as the sun climbed higher.

Maybe the kids would be safer in the car?

But if they wanted to help, to be part of this—maybe that was a good thing.

She looked down into the trunk.

Luggage.

(Of course.)

Three or four different-sized bags, one purple, another red, one black, one small and filled with ponies the color of rainbows.

The Blairs' bags.

She said nothing.

But she grabbed the heaviest bag and lugged it out of the trunk.

At least when it hit the grass, it had wheels, though the small rollers didn't seem too effective in the crumbly mix of dry grass and dirt.

Kate had already grabbed another one, and with a big *oomph* pulled that out as well.

And then, sweet God, Simon grabbing the one with ponies.

"Look at this! Who'd want a dopey bag like *this*!"

Christie almost laughed at . . . Simon being Simon.

The pink bag with rainbow ponies.

That belonged to a little girl who a terrible thing had happened to . . .

Simon didn't ask though.

Who's this bag belong to? What happened to them?

Some magic wall that kept him from those next few thoughts, those terrible questions.

About what might have happened to the people whose things they had just pulled out of the trunk.

Christie quickly grabbed the last bag, and tossed it to the side.

"Okay. Thanks, kids. Now, let me see—"

No tire visible; probably, she thought, under the trunk's floor-board.

The tire, the tire iron, the jack.

She looked around again. Everything so still around them. *That's good,* she told herself.

But then, why doesn't it feel good?

She leaned into the trunk and started running her fingers around the edges, digging her nails under the trunk's matting, until she made a gap and could get both hands in and pull the trunk floor mat up.

To see: a tire.

"The spare," she said.

"Doesn't look so good," Simon said. "Sure it's okay?"

Good question, Christie thought. She leaned close and felt the tire. Nice and firm.

"It's fine. Just got to—"

She grabbed a large bolt that kept the tire in place under the trunk. At first, it wouldn't budge.

Going to have to get stronger, she thought.

No man to depend on to turn and twist the hard things, to lift the heavy things, to do all the goddamn—

She stopped herself again.

The screw loosened, and spun off.

She reached in, and though the tire and rim were heavy, she could lift the spare out and place it against the back of the car.

Now for—

She looked for the jack.

Kate came and stood beside her.

Sensing something wrong.

"Mom, what is it?"

Christie leaned in again, and began feeling all around the bottom and sides of the trunk, nearly her whole body in the trunk, thinking that the car's jack had to be fixed to the side, or hidden in the back, somewhere . . .

But it wasn't.

"There's no jack," she said dully.

A quick look around.

After all—she had been rooting around in the trunk for a good minute or so.

She thought of those old nature programs, showing African animals at a water hole. How they'd lean down for a sip, then raise their heads, look left, right, then another cautious sip.

Constantly alert.

Still quiet.

"What are you going to do?" Kate asked. "Can you do it—" Christie had begun shaking her head.

"No, I *can't*. You can't get a car off the ground . . . without a jack." There was a bite to her words that she immediately regretted.

Another look.

Simon. Where was he?

But then she saw him at the front of the car.

"Simon. Back here. *Now*."

He came back.

No jack.

(*Don't cry*, she thought. *Please. No matter what*.)

Then a sound.

They all turned, the three of them standing close together, the luggage strewn around them, the sun beating down hard, the clouds all burnt away.

As a car headed down the highway . . . right toward them.

5

A Helping Hand

Christie thought of how they looked. The trunk open as she stood there with the two kids looking down the highway.

She needed help.

But did she really want the car to stop?

Did she have a choice?

She could wait there until a Highway Authority patrol car came by—but how long would that be? From what the officer had told her before, they had their hands full.

She raised her hand. A quick wave.

At the same time, "Kids—get in the car."

"Why?" Kate asked.

Christie kept her hand up, another wave.

"Kate—just do it. *Please.*"

"C'mon," Kate said to her brother, giving him a nudge.

Christie kept her eyes on the car . . . which slowed, moving from the far-left lane to the right lane near the shoulder, slowing down.

We could have been waiting here for hours and no one would have come by.

The car slowed even more, then pulled off the road just behind them. A sturdy SUV. Bound to have a jack.

Had to.

The car stopped, engine killed, and a man got out.

She saw him look around as he walked toward them, his pace slow, cautious.

Good. That means he's as worried as I am.

The man looked right at Christie.

Being real careful.

Good.

She smiled.

"Miss, you have a problem?"

Another smile as the man stopped, keeping some distance between them.

"Yes. A blowout. And somehow—" she tried to act as though she didn't understand how this could happen—"there's no jack in the trunk."

How could someone be on the road without a jack?

What the hell could Tom Blair have been thinking?

Unless he just assumed that it *was* there. People assume a lot of things.

After all, he wasn't a cop, wasn't like her husband who always assumed bad things could happen . . . would happen.

"Wow. And it's just you—"

"And my kids . . ."

Again Christie was reminded of how she looked. In fact, she wondered if the man stopped walking toward her because he was simply being cautious or because he saw her now, so disheveled, spatters here and there, the dark stains.

Maybe—we look like a family of Can Heads.

Because, in her paranoid mind, in the morning light, they now quite clearly looked like the dried spatters of blood.

"If I could borrow your jack. That's all. The spare is good, I just need—"

She suddenly realized how close she was to begging.

And wondered how close she was to scaring this man away.

He licked his lips. Thinking.

Weighing things.

Another look around by the man.

"Been trouble up and down the highway. You heard that? You don't want to be out here—"

A small laugh from Christie now.

Of course. So damn obvious.

"Right. Love to get going. Taking the kids home."

A nod.

"Okay. I have a jack, tire iron. Sure. But—" another look—"best be fast, right?"

She nodded. Then:

"Thank you."

Christie stood in place, by the trunk. She didn't want to do anything to scare the man off.

He walked back with the tire iron in one hand, the jack in the other.

This time, he closed the distance between them.

As he came closer, she felt him look her up and down, taking in what a mess she was.

"Something happen to you folks?"

She nodded. "Yes. But we—" another reassuring smile—"got away."

He nodded at this, what passed for small talk these days.

Had a problem with some Can Heads . . . yeah and except for losing my husband, it all turned out fine. And you?

"Look—let me get the car up for you. Slap your spare on. I know how the jack works. It'll be faster. Get you, and me, going faster."

"Thank you. I would appreciate that."

She stood back as the man went and headed over to the flat tire and knelt down beside it.

A look up at Christie.

"Name's Martin, by the way. Heading home myself."

He turned to the car and fit the jack into place, then the tire iron into the socket, and began turning it as the flat left rear tire began to rise off the ground.

Christie went from looking at the man working on the exchange of the flat for the spare, to scanning the road, the open space all around with not another car in sight, and then—just to be sure—a glance at the nearby fence.

It's quiet. So damn quiet . . . she thought.

The man focused on the job, hurrying. Only asking a few questions when maybe the stillness got to him as well.

"Where's home?"

"Staten Island."

"Spring Lake here. Jersey. It's on the shore. They did a real good job of making it safe. Wife, three kids. Pretty good setup there. Pretty safe. Good security. Though—"

He grunted as he grabbed the spare and slipped it on.

"—they hate it when I have to leave."

She was going to ask what he did. Why did he leave his fortress by the shore?

But then she figured—if he wanted to tell her, he would have.

He began tightening the nuts on the new tire.

"Almost done. Get you—and me—back on the road . . . no time at all."

He turned and looked around. Gave her a smile. "My good deed for the day."

"Thank you. I can't tell you how much—"

The words caught in her throat.

Because, in the quiet, with the highway empty, the still trees, most of them just dead stalks, and with the fence so close to the road . . .

She heard a *sound*.

A dry crack.

The splintering sound of wood being broken.

The man finished putting the last nut on the wheel's rim, not hearing, not noticing the sound.

Christie slowly turned from him, and looked over to where she thought the sound had come from.

Toward the fence.

When suddenly, there were so many more sounds.

The sounds came from the nearby fence—rattling, shaking as a number of bodies hit the mesh, like flies caught in a web.

That's what it looked like.

Except they weren't flies. And they weren't caught.

The Can Heads scrambled to the top of the fence so quickly, determined, moving almost impossibly fast, to the top, then over.

In those seconds, Christie hadn't moved.

She realized that she was standing there without a gun as a group of Can Heads landed on the other side of the fence, rolling crazily on the ground.

She turned and bolted for the front door of the car, even as she realized that Martin, who had been crouched by her car, had only now stood up.

Now . . . only just started running toward his vehicle.

Barely taking it in, as Christie ran the few yards to her door, and then freezing as one Can Head leaped atop the car, a crazy move that had it rolling over the top, then onto the ground—blocking Christie.

And as she stopped, the Can Head sprung to his feet, then another one came running around the back of the car, and they had her trapped.

While barely taking in Martin running to his SUV, full out.

Probably to his guns, but then seeing the other two Can Heads tackle him, sending Martin sliding to the ground, feet short of his car.

Christie backed away from the car even as the two nearby Can Heads kept their eyes locked on hers, perhaps both realizing she had no way to escape.

She thought: *The car is locked.*

The kids are in there.

They'll be okay.

And there are guns inside. They can stay in there. They might be safe.

In minutes, maybe seconds, it would end for her.

So much . . . for protecting her family. So much . . . for getting them home.

The Can Head from the front charged her, Christie's head spinning right and left, looking for the other to move on her as well.

This wasn't like last night when the crazed Can Heads from outside the camp's fence got in, and darkness made them black hulks chasing her family, attacking them.

This was daylight.

She could see them so *clearly*.

A lunge. And one Can Head's hands closed on her left forearm, the grip excruciating, then yanking her close. The smell of the thing overpowering.

She kicked, pulled back, all of it doing nothing.

When the thing's shoulder erupted in a mass of oozing red and bone.

As if something had exploded inside.

The thing released her, one of its claw hands going to the missing part of its shoulder.

Another explosion.

The other Can Head to the right fell at her feet.

And only then, did she look up . . .

6

Kate

"Mom!"

Christie saw her daughter standing there, holding the gun—

(*Holding the gun!*)

Exactly the way her father had taught her.

Arms outstretched.

("*Keep your arms straight, keep the site, the barrel, your eyes in a nice straight line . . .*")

And . . .

("*Two hands. Wrap one hand around to the other. Keep it as straight and steady as you can . . .*")

"Mom! Get in!"

Then louder.

"Get in the car!"

The sight of Kate holding the gun had stopped her, but now she moved, hearing more rattling as another batch of Can Heads hit the fence.

She ran to the front door and pulled it open.

She slid onto the seat, Kate beside her.

And a bit of her mind returned.

"Check the locks, Kate."

Christie pushed hers down, and she saw Kate double check the two back doors.

"All locked."

Thumps, as one Can Head crawled onto the hood. Another thump as one came from the back, then right on top of the car. The thumps repetitive as the one on the roof started jumping up and down.

"Mom," Simon pleaded.

The word a cry.

Christie looked back at Martin, the good Samaritan who had stopped to help them.

He lay on the ground, feet from his SUV with three of them squatting around him, picking, pulling. She saw one dig into the body, pull something out and then crazily wolf it down.

Her stomach tightened; she gagged.

That was almost me, she thought.

He stopped to help us . . .

And again: *that could have been me.*

Then:

If not for Kate.

Her daughter still held the gun in her lap.

Christie started the car, which is when another bit of crucial information entered her racing mind.

———

The car was still on the jack.

The left rear wheel, the spare tire on, had been replaced.

But the car was still tilted, *askew.*

Thump . . . thump . . . thump . . .

On the roof.

Accompanied by Simon's wails.

"Mom! Can we go?" Kate said.

That was the question.

Can we go?

Her voice quiet.

"I, I—"

In minutes, the roof might give way, or the other Can Heads could join these two and begin pounding the car as if opening a massive clam, trying to find a way to pry it open.

"I don't *know.*" Then:

"Hold the gun tight," Christie said.

She put the car into drive.

What would happen? With only one tire on the ground? Would the car careen to the right, spinning, or even roll over as the left side fell off its jacked-up perch? Or would it somehow land, and she could floor it?

Floor it.

A fast as the damn car would go.

Not a second more to be wasted with thinking, wondering.

She hit the accelerator.

The car started a spin, a semicircle as the one tire on the ground provided one-sided traction, and the car moved like an erratic firework, spinning, not going forward but *around.*

It didn't seem as if it would come off the jack, that the replaced tire would simply spin uselessly while they did circles, the Can Heads still hanging on.

But then—

The car tilted again as the jack somehow flew free, and now the left tire hit the ground and, with the two Can Heads on it, rocketed straight for the guardrail at an insane speed.

No way she could avoid hitting it. Still, Christie turned the steering wheel as sharply to the right as fast as she could.

The car—a bullet aimed at the rail—screamed as the extreme turn made the tires screech.

But she avoided a dead-on hit of the guardrail.

She had gained enough of an angle that the car hit the rail on its left side, pushing the rail free of its moorings, a metal rubber band now stretched out as it helped point the car in the right direction.

She could see out the windshield now.

The front Can Head shot out, across the rail.

The one on top, probably stopping its mad jumping and holding onto the roof, fingers dug in.

But the car was now at last aimed forward, both tires working together as it hit fifty, sixty, seventy miles an hour, racing.

Was the Can Head still above them? Somehow magically holding on, hitching a ride with them like a parasite, a human suckerfish attached to the top of the car?

Christie waited until she felt they had put enough distance between the scene of the attack, and then—

With her right hand, she grabbed her seat belt, snapping it on, asking the question—

"Seat belts on?"

Two voices, quick, a quiet "yes" from Kate, then Simon.

She stopped, applying the brakes hard.

The tires screamed, but she saw the thing clutching onto the hood go flying frontward, a human rocket shot out onto the empty highway.

That is, if you called it human.

And not a monster, a creature, a Can Head that had left humanity behind.

For a few moments, she sat there. No one said anything.

The strangeness of their life, this new world so clear that what could anyone really say?

But it was time to get moving again. If the fence was down, power off, there could be more attacks.

Christie turned back to Simon.

"You okay?"

He nodded, his blue eyes never more intense.

Then over to Kate.

Riding—what did Jack call it?—*shotgun*. Only now, with a gun cradled in her lap.

"Kate. You okay too?"

Her daughter turned to her.

Christie had the thought that she was glad that Kate sat there, beside her.

Except for one thing—

"Think you can put the gun back down, under the seat again? And make sure—"

"The safety's on? I know."

Christie heard the safety latch of the handgun being thrown and Kate slid it under the seat.

She saved me, Christie thought. My little girl. Not so little, and— apparently a damn good shot. And more—

Brave.

She acted, did what she had to. Fast, apparently with no thought to the danger to herself.

My sweet little girl.

"Okay then—let's go."

———

The closer they got to New York, the more cars they saw.

At one point, she even saw a Highway Authority chopper hovering over a section of the road.

She began to relax a little. More cars, some Highway cops, another chopper looking up and down the road.

She didn't feel all alone anymore.

And then she turned on the radio.

She hit the first two presets on the car radio, getting only static. The third brought a station, either picking it up from the Capital Region they just left, or maybe New York.

But even that station was filled with bursts of static.

She raised the volume as if that would make the few words that did escape the speaker more clear.

"—*cautioning that all travel should be curtailed . . . twenty-four hours. Anyone found . . .*

A long gap as a scratchy white noise filled the car.

Then:

"—*report all movements to any . . . do not, repeat, do not attempt . . .*"

The station dissolved into a steady stream of static.

"What are they saying?" Simon asked from the back.

"I don't know. Must be about—I guess—the problems they've had with fences. I—"

Then another question. Another unknowable.

"Will our fence be okay? When we get home?" Simon asked.

She caught Kate look at her as if wondering how she would respond to that.

"I think so, Simon. I hope so. Only one way to find out."

Christie looked up to the mirror to see his eyes dart away, and then return to hers.

She had a thought then, a new awareness.

It's not just Kate who's changed. Simon too. His questions; all about "What if?", "What do we do?"

How do we cope, how do we plan?

All good questions.

Now where the fuck were the good answers?

"What if our fence is . . . broken. What is—"

She felt a spike of anger at her son. Can't he stop? Can't he see this is not a good time for questions, not a good time at all.

(*And why is that*, she asked herself? *Because maybe you'll lose it? Or maybe you* are *losing it?*)

"Simon. When we get there, we'll see. We'll do what we have to do. To be safe."

Silence for a second, then more words from him. This time, not a question, a statement.

"I want to go home."

Christie took a breath.

"Me too, Simon, me too."

And the car became quiet as they closed the last hundred miles to the New York City border.

7

Staten Island

But even before they crossed into the New York City border, Christie knew she'd have to leave the Thruway for yet another highway.

In better times, she would have taken the Palisades Parkway, a classic highway that ran along the side of the Palisades, the monumental wall of rock that lined one side of the Hudson.

But she knew that the Palisades had become what was called an "unprotected road." Could be okay, or could have broken-down cars, with packs of Can Heads waiting to throw things in the path of a car.

It was something you didn't do.

So she took the ramp onto the Garden State Parkway, which was protected for about half its length and then—somewhere in South Jersey—ended in a final gate. You'd be on your own after that.

Since she was coming from the Thruway, she didn't have to stop and explain again why she didn't have any papers.

As they entered the Garden State, Kate said, "We're close now, Mom. Right?"

"Yup. Won't be long."

"I want a shower," Kate said. "Will that be okay?"

"We haven't used water for quite a while. So sure."

A pause. Then Kate again: "I'm tired. Maybe I'll sleep first."

Christie wished she hadn't said that word.

Sleep.

She could be okay if she didn't think about how much she ached, how everything hurt and how the weariness filled her entire body.

Sleep.

The very word was cruel.

Picturing a bed. A pillow.

Then the thought . . .

The empty bed.

Simon pulled her back.

"And eat. I'm hungry."

She noticed that Kate didn't jump on her brother. Was that gone? Had that changed, after all they'd been through?

And Christie knew something then.

That before the shower, before food, before sleep—she would talk to them.

Or—at least—start talking to them about last night.

And maybe the days and nights to come.

We're close, she thought.

And she fought to keep any other thoughts, the worries, the anxieties, the fear that swirled around her every moment . . . she fought to keep them all away, and just keep repeating . . .

We're close.

Then it was time to leave the Garden State, to take the mix of roads that would lead her to the Goethals Bridge, and finally bring them back to their home.

Gas gauge was good. Nothing to stop them.

She repeated Jack's mantra as she took the exit ramp off.

Sliding behind one car at the gate, talking to the officer, about to leave the protected road.

"Locks down."

The gate opened up.

Good. Electricity's on here.

The car left the fenced-in highway, and Christie pulled up.

The Highway Authority officer here wore a pointy trooper hat, an almost comical look, she thought.

"Ma' am," he said.

Don't ask for any goddamn papers, she thought.

He seemed to stand there and study the three of them for a moment.

"You folks okay? Know where you're going?"

Strange question, she thought.

Know where you're going . . . ?

Are people just moving around, not knowing where they're going?

"We're heading home," Christie said. "Staten Island."

The man nodded, and then—amazingly to Christie—started to turn away.

"Er, officer—are things okay there? We heard some—"

The Highway officer stopped and turned back. He hesitated for a moment as if weighing how to answer the question.

"Wish I knew, ma'am. Our communications have been all messed up. The power outages screwed that up too. Can't tell you much—except be careful."

Christie took a breath.

Not bad news, she thought.

He didn't say that anything bad *lay ahead.*

He just didn't know.

That's all.

"Thanks."

A nod from the officer as the gate opened, and they left the highway, and onto the streets that led home.

She followed the route that Jack had planned and picked for the outward journey. Sticking to the more wide-open roads, like Route 46 lined with the closed franchises that now seemed as ancient and forgotten as the pyramids of Egypt.

Lowes. Walmart. Staples.

Glass and stone monuments to another time.

Along the way, she spotted the occasional patrol car here, an army truck there, a few other people moving slowly along the road.

But no Can Head activity.

"They like the cities," Jack used to say. *"Lots of places to hide. Better for them to hunt, to trap—"*

She'd often stop him there.

Enough!

She didn't need to hear the details of the Can Heads.

Like everyone else, she wanted to forget they existed, forget that this was the world they lived in now.

Now she wished she had listened more carefully. How they act, the way they hunt . . . how to stop them.

Might just need all that, she thought.

She stayed on 278 as it turned into the Staten Island Expressway.

So close.

She used to think it was the cities that were dangerous.

Now she knew.

Not just cities.

The Can Heads were everywhere, and could do perfectly fine in the woods, the small towns, the mountains. Anywhere.

"Mom . . ." Simon said. She heard how his voice shook.

Christie turned to see where he was looking, off to the left.

She saw two figures, and as she passed, they broke into a run.

But the car—too fast—left them behind.

Can Heads? People needing help? Somebody in trouble?

Who knew?

All Christie did know was that she couldn't stop . . . wouldn't stop.

She thought of Martin, who had stopped, who had helped them. The good Samaritan.

Dead for helping someone.

I can't do that, Christie thought.

But now, as she drove past small towns close to the bridge, she looked down each side street, into each boarded-up storefront, down the alleyways, her head pivoting right and left, the tension nearly insane.

A gauntlet, she thought.

This highway's fence looking so small after the Thruway.

Though she saw no one. This, another ghost town. Everyone gone . . . somewhere.

Outside of those two—

(People? Can Heads?)

—she had passed.

Tightly gripping the top of the steering wheel, her knuckles looked like an extension of the steering wheel with its ridges. Her hands— glued to it.

Kate said something, perhaps trying to break the mood.

"I don't like it here."

Christie nodded. "Me either, Kate. Me either."

Then, with the afternoon sun turning the streets and stone buildings they passed into a blurry image of some burned-out deserted hell, the road curved, and ahead lay the Goethals Bridge to Staten Island.

"Almost there. Across the bridge. Past the toll—"

(With yet another gate. Gates . . . everywhere.)

"—and we'll be home."

The words—even as she said them—didn't sound real.

She turned left, and joined a merging road from the south, that led onto the ramp, onto the bridge, straight onto the island, this once sleepy borough that, back before everything happened, people didn't think much about . . .

While for Christie, for these desperate hours, that place, and home, had become nearly all she could think about.

8

The Turn Back

But as Christie drove over the bridge, she noticed something that made her tired, achy body stiffen, tighten even more.

Cars all going in the other direction.

Not a mass line of cars backed up, but definitely a steady flow.

And joining her, heading to the other side?

Not a single other car.

Kate may have sensed her stiffen. Or she might have simply seen the line of cars.

"Where are they all going?"

"I don't know. Looks like—" She hesitated saying the next words.

But I'm past that, she thought. *Past the time to keep Kate in the shadows.*

"Looks like they're leaving."

Kate said nothing.

Guess the implications of that are pretty clear.

Then, as she hit the high arch of the bridge and started down to the other side, to Staten Island, she saw something else odd.

At first, it looked like an encampment.

Cars parked in a near circular ring on a patch of empty land near the bridge entrance. She spotted some cop cars—NYPD.

NYPD, she thought.

Just like the patrol car Jack drove.

And a few camouflaged army trucks. Then closer, she saw soldiers, and another police car with officers standing outside, directing people to the open patch of ground encircled by the cars, and trucks.

As she got closer, she saw an army truck ahead, blocking her path forward, and a soldier with a gun slung over his shoulder making a steady gesture for her to pull off the highway, to cut across the lanes, and head to the circle of cars and trucks.

"What are they doing?" Kate asked.

A deep breath. Then: "I don't know."

She slowed as she entered the area.

It wasn't a cop or a soldier who walked over to her, but a man in a flannel shirt, a bushy moustache. A baseball cap with a patch. NRA. A member in good standing apparently . . . his gun over his shoulder.

He walked up to the car.

Of course, these days everyone had a gun. *That* battle was over.

"Afternoon, miss." A look in the back. "Kids . . . hi." He smiled, his walrus moustache rising high on his face with the smile. "Where you folks going?"

Christie wanted to ask him what the hell this was all about.

"I'm—we're going home. We don't live far from here. What is this?"

The man started shaking his head. Then scratched the back of his neck as if that was part of his process of forming ideas, words.

"You see all this?" He gestured at the cars parked in the open space, drivers standing out, talking to cops, to other people. She saw that some of the people had maps out, opened on the hoods of their cars.

Everyone depending on maps, as if GPS had never been invented.

GPS. Useless technology these days.

"Yes. What's going on?"

"Guess you haven't heard. The power failures, the outages? What they did? People getting out, that's what this is. Some of us helping the cops, the army . . . trying to make sure people have some damn idea where they're going."

He leaned close as if sharing a secret.

"Not that anyone has a good goddammed idea about where a good place is to go."

He looked back at the kids. Then: "Pardon my French. Bad habit. Still, we're trying to keep things calm. Give the people what information we have. Roads to avoid. Towns to steer clear of. And any good places we've heard of. Safe places. I'll get someone over here to talk to you in a few—"

"But . . ."

She looked over at Kate. Then Simon. Both watching so carefully. They had one parent's voice to listen to.

One person . . . in charge.

And that person is me.

"But we're going to our home. I don't know where else to go. It's a safe development, protected—"

The man interrupted. "Not too many people in the city believe in that word. Not after the past few days."

She thought of Paterville. The madness there.

This was supposed to represent a return to sanity.

(*And*—she thought—*home had other things. Needed things.*)

"Look ma'am, this is still the United States of America. You can still go on. I'm just sayin' . . . maybe you want to think twice about that."

She looked at Kate.

Counsel. That would be good.

Advice.

And not from a volunteer.

"Can I talk to one of the cops?"

"Sure—and you can see, we have this area guarded. Men, few women, too—with guns all around. It's been quiet here. So—get out, stretch your legs. Talk to one of them. I'd just say—take your time and think about it."

The man backed away, the late-afternoon sun making his orange shirt turn golden, the light also catching all the gray in the wisps of hair popping out from under his cap.

"Okay."

"Come on, kids," she said. "Let's walk around."

They followed her as she opened the door, and for a moment, they stood close by the car. After the attack on the highway, the car represented an island of safety.

Christie looked at the other people walking around . . . the mood tense, but a lot of them talking, some pointing at the large folded maps while young soldiers nodded, cops talking on radios.

The whole scene—surreal.

But Christie knew that surreal was . . . the new real.

Better get used to it, she told herself.

The place looked safe enough.

"Okay—I'm gonna find someone to talk to, all right? You two . . . stay near here, near the guards, the other people."

They nodded. Neither moved.

She walked away.

———

Christie went up to a cop on a walkie-talkie.

He nodded as the voice on the handset speaker said things, words not clear to her at a distance.

"Okay, roger that. Just tell them . . . we need those damn lights soon. Real soon."

The cop put the handset back into the car.

"Excuse me," Christie said.

The cop turned. She saw his eyes, a deep blue but surrounded with dark, puffy patches. Lack of sleep? His lips tight. No smile, no human warmth.

Then Christie remembered what she looked like.

Not just from fatigue. Not just the hours and hours of driving in the predawn night, this long day.

The flecks of blood that dotted her clothes.

If it shocked the officer—

(*Officer Ramirez.*)

He showed no sign.

"A man told me . . . I shouldn't be going home."

The officer said nothing.

She repeated her description of her development. The fence. The fortified houses.

Unlike the volunteer in flannel, the cop said nothing sarcastic. No reaction at all.

Only when she finished, when she stopped and there was a pause, did the cop finally unlock those pursed lips and talk.

"You can do that. Don't recommend it. People are leaving. They thought they were safe. Maybe—" he looked away—"maybe . . . they're overreacting. Hear that things are getting under control. In some places."

Then those blue eyes on Christie.

"Maybe where you are—"

He paused for a moment.

"—maybe it's okay. But maybe not. You have someplace else to go? Other people? Family?"

Family?, she thought. *There was no one. Some aunts, uncles somewhere. But families . . . especially the extended family . . . became an early casualty of this—*

(She thought of a word. First time she thought of it like that. With all these trucks, the soldiers.)

The word.

War.

She shook her head.

Officer Ramirez didn't have any words of advice. He broke eye contact. If there was someone more tired than she was, it had to be this young NYPD cop.

She wanted to tell him that her husband had been a cop. That he probably did the same kind of things.

But for some reason, it suddenly seemed so irrelevant.

He did look back for one more question.

"You tell me . . . the name of your development, the address . . . we have some reports. Places we know are still in bad shape."

She told him her address, and Ramirez dug out a fat notebook, with the pages bulging with scribbled notes. He flipped through it.

"No. Not seeing anything here. Could be—" his eyes up—"could be okay. Or—"

She knew then that she'd have to take her chances.

She didn't have to convince the cop it was a good thing to do.

But it was her kids that she needed to speak to.

She stuck out her hand. An odd gesture. But the cop took it, his hand cold despite the day's heat.

What kind of night has he been through?

His startlingly blue eyes on her again.

"Whatever you do, miss . . . get some rest."

As if in that shake he could gauge her total fatigue, the ways even her knees wobbled as she walked.

She released his hand.

"Good luck," she said to him.

Because—today, now, this world, this moment—if you didn't believe in a creator watching and deciding who lives and who dies, luck was about all you could hope for.

And Christie went looking for her kids.

9

A Second Decision

Christie saw Kate talking to a girl who looked near her age.

She stopped for a moment, thinking.

It's almost normal. Two teenage girls, traveling with their families, talking.

That is, if you didn't know that one family was running away, fleeing the city. And the other—

What are we going to do? Christie thought.

But then she looked around. Where was Simon?

Kate stood there by the car, but *where was Simon?*

She ran over to Kate.

"Kate!"

Her daughter turned.

"What?"

A bit of old Kate's "bite" in her question.

"Where's Simon? You were supposed to—"

Kate raised an arm and pointed. Simon, by a nearby car, talking to a kid as well.

"He's right *there*."

"Sorry," Christie said quickly. "I couldn't see."

Kate nodded. Then:

"I need to talk to you." Christie looked over at Simon. "Both of you."

Did she really mean that? Was Simon part of decisions being made? Just a kid?

Was that crazy?

"Simon," Christie called.

She saw Kate turn to the girl she had been talking to.

"Good luck," Kate said.

More luck.

The girl smiled back.

Simon ran over.

"I need to talk to you both. Something we need decide. Come on over to the car."

She walked away, and led them back to the car.

She said slowly . . . "We need to think carefully about what we do. You see, all these people—"

"Running away," Kate filled in.

That stopped Christie for a moment. "I mean, that *is* what they're doing. That's what that girl said. Her father says it's not safe anymore."

She saw Simon's eyes on his sister.

"That—may be true," Christie said.

It was Simon who asked the obvious question.

"What are *we* going to do?"

Christie looked around at the cars, the cops, the soldiers, their trucks, the guns . . . guns everywhere.

She'd had only minutes to think about this.

To think about the options.

"Well, they don't know where it's safe, where it isn't. Maybe— where we live is okay."

Kate: "And maybe not."

"Yes. And there's this. These people . . . they're all going some- where. Must have relatives. Friends. A place to go, people to take them in."

"And we don't." Kate again, and not a question.

We're a good family, Christie thought. *Strong. We work together, help each other.*

But we're all alone.

"I—I don't know where we'd go."

Christie looked at Simon. He knew about the world today that they lived in, but until last night . . . he hadn't really lived in it. Now— well, could he deal with all this?

How much can a kid take?

"There's another thing. At home, your dad—" her voice caught. Not even twenty-four hours. The pain ready to flash back into a ter- rible fire.

"He had things hidden. Gas. We're going to need gas. Who knows what we'll find out there. Food, a lot of food that we locked up. First- aid kits. Flashlights."

"Yeah—I got it," Kate said. "There's a lot of stuff at home."

Was Kate's own fear making her snap at her mother? Had they gone from being together in this hell, to—already—now snapping at each other?

"Yes. And guns. I mean, I—I . . . you've seen what happens. The w-way things are, and, and—"

And then—

So totally surprising.

So totally coming from nowhere, like a freak wave crashing into a shoreline, swamping everything, washing all else away—

Christie fell apart.

She turned from them, and fell against the car and sobbed.

And sobbed.

And sobbed . . .

Until she felt a hand on her shoulder. Then, another hand on her other shoulder. She had raised her forearm to her face as she cried into it, her body shaking, nearly convulsing with the crying.

But the two hands helped.

One a little bigger. One a little smaller.

She waited until she could take one, two, three breaths normally, without any more moans, or shivers.

Almost normal breathing.

And she turned back to her two kids, their hands still in place, resting on her.

Kate and Simon both had tears in their eyes, and once again she was reminded that she had to be strong for them.

I'm all they've got, she thought.

She reached up and took a hand of each.

"Okay," she said taking a breath. "I've been thinking. I made some decisions."

A squeeze to their hands.

"We're gonna go on. We're going home."

"But—is it safe?"

She looked at Kate. If anything, she needed her daughter to understand, to be with her on this.

"I don't know. But I know we can't just stay here. And how safe is it out there, wherever all these people are going? Besides—"

She lowered her voice. An instinct, she thought. And she had the sudden awareness that she didn't want anyone to hear her next words.

She labeled the feeling, accurately she hoped . . .

Paranoia.

"Like I told you. In our house, there's gas. Lots of gas. And food. Your dad, he stockpiled so much. And—"

Her voice even lower.

"Weapons."

"But . . . but we have guns," Simon said.

A smile. "Yes, Simon. We have *guns*. Some ammunition. But who knows—we may need more. And we could always trade them."

Kate added her support. "Guns . . . are a good idea."

"As I said, lots of stuff—things we might need."

She took a deep breath as if the air would help her keep standing.

"So we go. We see what's happening. Maybe our development is okay. But either way, we can get all those things."

Christie saw Kate look away, then back.

"Yeah," Kate said. "It's what we should do."

What we should do.

Like they were a team.

"But—" and now she fixed her mother with her dark blue/green eyes. "Mom. You can barely stand. You need rest."

"I—I don't think we should wait, Kate."

The word. *Rest.* The very sound of it was irresistible.

"You can't just keep going on, Mom. Especially—" she saw Kate look to Simon, measuring her words, taking . . . care.

"—when you don't know what we're gonna face."

"But I think we need to go now. If things—"

"A nap, Mom. Just a little sleep."

Kate's eyes showed her worry. The fear totally clear.

She doesn't think I can do anything more, drive, face what's ahead.

Sleep.

Can I afford to sleep?

And in this place? She'd been told that lights were on their way here, but what if they didn't make it?

"Okay, But just . . . a little sleep. Forty-five minutes. No more."

She looked up at the sky, the sun having turned the area a golden yellow.

And Christie thought: *what would it be like after just forty-five minutes?*

Will I even be able to move?

But Kate nodded. Accepting the offer.

"And you—?"

"We've slept, Mom. During the drive. We'll stay by you."

Christie slipped off her watch and passed it to Kate.

"Forty-five minutes. 5:15. Got it?"

Kate took the watch, gave the face a glance, and slid it into her pocket.

"I promise."

Christie turned back to the car and popped open the rear door.

She crawled into the backseat, pulling the door shut behind her.

A last look at the window, at Kate and Simon looking at her, then she laid back, face resting against the material of the backseat, closed her eyes, and—instantaneously—everything vanished.

10

Kate and Simon

Simon turned away from the window and started walking away.

"Where do you think you're going?"

Simon kept walking. "I dunno. Not just going to *stand* here. That's boring."

Kate hurried to catch up with him.

"Okay."

Now he stopped. "You're going to walk with me, follow me?"

"I told Mom we'd stay together."

"I'm not going anywhere. You don't have to babysit me. I'm not two!"

"I told Mom—"

He turned and started walking away quickly, making loops and curves, forcing her to follow his crazy path.

He's so annoying, she thought. *Doesn't he know I'm the big sister, and I have . . . have—*

Responsibilities.

As Simon performed his dumb loops, he kept saying things.

"You want to follow me, follow me."

Then:

"Bet you think just because you shot one of them, that makes you something special."

Kate thought about that.

It did make her feel weird every time she thought about that.

But—*weird* wasn't the word. Like she had become someone else. Like who she was before last night had disappeared.

Amidst her fear, the horrible sadness, the worry, she had become a different person.

Maybe—she expected Simon to see that.

Then another thought: maybe Simon was different too. Or perhaps he would have to become different.

She ran to catch up to him, and pulled on his shoulders.

He shook her hand free, and turned to her.

"What?"

His face looked rigid, lips closed.

For those seconds, Kate didn't know what she was going to say. And then—she did.

"Simon—Dad's dead."

Kate watched Simon freeze.

"Dad's dead—and Mom needs *us*."

And—so fast—Simon raised his hands, balling them into fists, and began pounding her, the fists landing together, pounding her repeatedly.

But Kate didn't feel them, she just kept looking at Simon's face, the tears again, his lips tight, but trembling as if they needed to say some-thing, wanted to say *something* that would make her stop . . . make her take those words back.

Then—when he had raised his hands for yet another blow—Kate quickly reached up and grabbed his wrists, taking care to use just enough pressure to hold him but not . . . but not—

(*Not cause any more pain. No. He's had enough pain.*)

And in that same move, she pulled him close, her hands freeing his arms as hers went around him.

And he sobbed into her.

Didn't pull away.

Didn't do anything but let her hold him tight as he cried.

She had this thought:

Have I ever hugged my brother like this?

And surrounded by the cars, the people milling about, talking to police, they just stood there, brother and sister.

Somehow they both knew it was done.

Kate released Simon, and when he stepped back, she could see it was over. The crying, the face so tight it looked as if it might ex-plode.

Kate spoke first.

"I'm going to go wait by the car. Till it's time to wake Mom."

Simon nodded.

Kate nodded back, and then turned away and started for the car.

To find Simon walking beside her.

"I thought you were going to walk around, explore?"

A quick look and she caught him shake his head.

"No. I'll stay with you. By the car."

"Okay," she said.

In minutes they were back, sitting on the ground.

Kate looked at her mother's watch.

And they waited.

Until Kate heard a car engine start.

She opened her eyes.

Opened her eyes!

She had fallen asleep.

And she felt Simon leaning into her, also asleep.

She dug out her mother's watch.

Nearly an hour and a half, twice the time her mother had wanted to sleep.

Kate scrambled to her feet, taking note of the nearby car pulling away. People leaving. The sky, now a deeper blue.

She popped open the door.

"Mom. Mom!"

Her mother didn't stir. Kate reached in and gently gave her mother's shoulder a shake. Then another.

She saw her mother's eyes open slowly, so reluctant to open.

"Mom. It's later than you wanted."

The eyes slowly coming awake, looking at Kate.

Kate had a thought about what this was like, now, for her mother. Only from her sleeping in the car, she *knew* what it was like to wake up and have everything different.

"What—?"

The eyes, the face, remembering as it all came back.

"What time is—?"

Kate handed her mother the watch.

And as if it had electricity running through it, her mother's look at the watch face made her sit up in an instant, moving quickly out of the backseat.

———

Christie shook her head.

Kate expected her mother to say something like . . . *"How could you?"*

Or: *"I depended on you."*

But she said nothing, and that silence was even worse.

She saw her mother look around.

"People are leaving."

Kate nodded.

"About an hour or so left of daylight."

Then her mother took a look at the circle of cars, this camp of cars and people.

Now with fewer people.

When she had finished, she turned back to Kate.

"And no lights. They said lights were on the way. But they're not here."

"Maybe they're still coming," Kate said.

She saw her mother look at Simon, following every word.

Knowing that her mother would be careful with what she said.

"Maybe. Then again, maybe not."

She took a deep breath.

"We still got some daylight. To get back. Right?"

Kate nodded.

Less light than we would have had . . . if I had stayed awake.

She tried to push the guilt away.

It happened, she told herself.

She made a silent promise to herself that something like that wouldn't happen again.

Her mother depending on her. And letting her down.

"So we go, okay?"

Kate guessed that her mother left unsaid the idea that staying here, even with police, in this open area, without lights, might be a bad idea.

Then:

"You guys set?"

"Yes," Simon said.

His voice so . . . formal.

Like responding to a question in class.

Then Kate answered: "Yes, Mom."

Not knowing whether she was *set*, or if this was a good idea, or anything.

The three of them got into the car.

Kate started for the back.

"Kate, stay up front."

A bit of that guilt faded.

And Kate got into the front passenger seat as Simon shut the back door. Her mother started the car, and joined a line of cars leaving the area.

All heading in the opposite direction they were . . . as they got back on the road.

welcome home

11

Fires

Christie stopped the car at a hill that overlooked the flat plain of their development, a once-empty space filled with wild grass and dumps, transformed into an inviting development of rows of houses, all with identical lawns and backyards, all safe behind the fence that promised not only deadly electricity but also 24/7 guards.

She stopped and looked out at the whole expanse, the curving roads, the houses—and her heart sank.

Because amidst the houses, she saw smoky plumes, some rising from homes—or so it seemed at this distance—others rising from the middle of the roads, from jumbled piles of—

What? Why would people put piles of . . . stuff in the middle of the road?

But she could guess.

There could be only one good reason you would do that.

To keep something away.

Her gaze drifted away, to the west, the sun nearly down, the sky still a cheery blue.

She thought:

Twilight. But not for long.

It would be dark in—what?—an hour. Hour and a half at most.

She felt immobilized. What to do? Where to go? How long could she just sit here, on this hill that led down to the development before—

"Mom?"

Christie turned to Kate.

"Yes?"

As if she didn't know what her daughter would ask.

"What are we doing here? What's wrong?"

The question tested Christie's decision to be honest with the kids. That decision . . . as best she could, she would let them know her thoughts, the possibilities. To discuss things with them.

"I'm not sure."

Which was true enough.

"But—there are fires. Doesn't look right. Maybe they had problems."

Again she thought: honesty.

"Maybe they *have* problems down there."

Quiet, then . . . Simon:

"So we're not going home?"

The question itself sad.

She took a breath.

"I think . . . we need to go there. Get the stuff. Your father put things there for us. The things I told you about."

Another look at the sky. Darkening even as she spoke.

"But what about them?" Simon said. "What if *they're* still there?"

Christie wished she had binoculars. All she could see were the smoky plumes, a few roads with fires still smoldering. It might be all over.

"We won't stay then, Simon. We'll know. But we can get those things."

Don't ask the obvious question, she begged.

Don't ask . . . *where will we go then?*

And neither Kate or Simon did.

"Mom's right," Kate said, turning to Simon, her voice free of any put-down, of any of the big-sister bite that had been constant . . . again, just one short day ago.

The love she felt for those two right now . . . overwhelming.

And though that vulnerability made her feel weak, defenseless— she had to think that in some way it also empowered her.

As Jack showed her—

As Jack showed them all . . .

—you do what you have to, what you *must*, for those you love.

Simon nodded at Kate's words, also accepting this new version of his sister, borne out of their shared loss and devastation . . . and—

Their horror.

"Okay. We'll go in. Get all the things we need. Doors locked—"

The words an echo from Jack.

"—windows shut. In, and out. Fast."

She took another breath, like a runner forcing the oxygen-laden air into her lungs, preparing for the sprint.

And then she started down the curved road, to the flat plain of what had once been the protected island of their home and community.

The front gate lay open.

Terrifying to see—this gate that had always been firmly closed and guarded.

Now it lay open as if someone had let the farm animals out. Though in this case, the animals came in.

The streets, though, looked normal at first, as Christie drove at a slow pace, not wanting to get caught in a blocked street that could turn into a trap.

A dead end could be bad.

No place to turn.

So moving slowly was the way to go.

While she kept looking left, straight, right.

Amazingly—everything looked nearly normal.

The house, the streets—all quiet.

Down one road, she saw a smoldering pile of junk, but the fire looked as if it was in its last minutes, and nobody—

(*And nothing . . .*)

Stood around.

Almost normal.

A fire in the road and nobody doing anything about it.

Christie reminded herself to keep her guard up, her eyes focused. That small sleep she'd had gave her only a brief recharge. But every few minutes, she needed to remind herself to keep looking, to stay alert— all this, with whatever emotion and fear-laden chemicals ran through her brain.

Until they got to a corner.

Sycamore Street and Oak Lane.

Amazing, these roads named for *trees*, in this world now with trees of all kinds dwindling, endangered, vanishing completely.

Oak Lane.

Their street.

She took the corner slowly.

Their house was just ahead.

12

Home at Last

Christie left the car running, sitting right outside the house.

She kept looking at their home, everything looking okay, saying to herself, as if she needed someone to tell her . . . *it looks okay.*

Door tight, windows all barred, metal gates down.

Just the way we left it.

Even the street seemed quiet.

No fires on this block, she thought. Maybe whatever happened was done.

Maybe it really was okay here.

Then:

"Mom—we going in?"

Reminding Christie that time was slipping away.

She turned to Kate, at the same time making sure to include Simon in the conversation.

"Okay. Here's what we'll do. I'm going to go in and start getting stuff—"

Simon groaned.

"We're not staying?"

She looked right at her son now.

"I don't know, Simon. I'm going to see how things look. I mean, you saw—"

She took a breath.

"—you saw how the fence was down? Not sure we can stay until I know it's safe."

She hoped that Kate would add some words of support, her new Kate, her new partner in this.

But Kate sat quietly, maybe also wishing that they could just go into the house, lock everything up, spend the night, and, and—

Sleep.

Sleep.

It sounded almost too good to think about. But Christie kept thinking about the fires, smoke billowing from homes.

It could be a fatal delusion to let herself even think that everything was okay.

The kids were quiet.

The sky, a sere blue. Beautiful, as if its deepening color didn't represent passing time, and what she feared the darkness might mean.

She announced the next information with what she hoped was a voice that said that there would be no more discussion.

"*I* will go in. Get the gas, the food—" a pause—"the weapons. Ammunition."

Thinking she had to say it. The guns, the ammo. They have to know how important they were.

They've seen the worst.

They know the worst.

"I have stuff I want, too–" Simon began.

She held up a hand.

"I know. I'll get some of your things, some of your toy guys, Simon, and pictures, and—"

Kate, who had gone suddenly quiet, spoke up.

Christie gave her daughter her full attention.

"And what do *we* do?"

Christie nodded.

"Right. I'm going to go in. Get those things. Fill the trunk. The back. I'll be fast." A breath. "But if you see anyone come here, then you beep the horn. You see *anyone*, beep."

She kept her eyes right on Kate's. "You understand?"

Her daughter nodded.

"Okay. No time to waste."

She hesitated about her next action. Too alarmist, was it needed? Would it only scare them more?

But she knew what Jack would do.

She reached under her seat and grabbed a gun with one hand, and—beside it—a few of the scattered bullets with the other.

Then, the words almost devastating as she opened the door:

"Love you both."

She opened the door.

She had never had an easy time opening the door to their home.

Three different keys, never knowing whether a bolt was locked or whether her action had simply relocked the door.

Needing to guess when all three were unlocked and she could do the simple human act of turning the doorknob, and enter their home.

She fumbled; Jack could do this.

But then the last key turned, and she grabbed the knob, hoping she had been successful.

She gave it a twist.

The door opened.

The first sensation, how much darker it was inside.

Should she throw some lights on? But that immediately sounded like a bad idea.

There was still enough light to see, and why alert anyone to the fact that someone was at home?

As soon as her eyes adjusted, things would be okay.

The important thing: move quickly. Lots of lifting, carrying, ferrying to the car.

No time for anything else.

Make use of the damn light while she had it.

She began moving.

She brought out the gas first, six five-liter plastic cans that took up a lot of space in the trunk.

But gas might be the most important thing to have.

Because—she told herself—if the gas stations begin to close, not just a few, but all of them, then what?

They'd be stranded.

Trapped.

As she shuttled the plastic canisters into the trunk, she saw her kids. Watching her, she gave them a smile.

Must have looked like a crazy smile.

Look how much fun Mommy is having.

Then, to the food, making choices here. Things that would be okay when opened and left unrefrigerated. Dry cereals that the kids hated, even with a ton of artificial sweetener on them. Cans of fruit and vegetable substitute, stuff that apparently never went bad.

She had a few cans of real food . . . some treasured green beans, yams, peaches in syrup.

Food to be saved for a special occasion.

She took all of them.

When Christie had finished getting the food into the car, the trunk nearly full, there were the final items on her shopping list. Guns. Ammunition.

Especially . . . the ammunition.

She looked over to the kitchen table, near the door that led to the basement and the garage.

She looked at her gun on the kitchen table.

Bring it down, or leave it here?

Her arms would be full. Especially if she found some of Jack's secret weapon stashes.

She knew he had more guns in this house than he would admit.

Didn't want to scare her.

And now, she wanted them all—if she could find them.

Leaving the handgun, she walked downstairs.

13

The Car

Kate looked at the door to the house, left open so her mother could carry things out.

She had watched her mother bring out the gas, then the food to the back.

She should let me help, Kate thought.

Then: *it's so quiet here.*

And now, as her mother gave her a smile again, returning to the house, Kate knew what she was going back in for.

More guns. And ammunition.

She wondered if her mom felt the way she did. That this all seemed too horrible to be real.

That in such a short time they were on their own, that their dad, the man they all depended on, was *gone*, and now it was up to the three of them.

"Together," her mom had said.

"We're in this together."

Kate accepted that. They all had things to do now. Even Simon was part of it, only a kid, just a boy. Someone who used to drive her crazy, but now, for a reason she didn't completely understand, she suddenly loved him in a way that she never felt before.

Stupid Simon.

With the dumb things he said, and his toys that he battled with all the time in the backseat. Always making his soldiers or whatever they were . . . fight.

Now, her brother, more than accepted.

Almost sweet. She wouldn't change a thing about Simon now.

And as to his toys, and the fighting . . . why they all now knew what that was like for real.

Even Simon.

She looked over at him.

She hadn't noticed, but he was looking out the front window, then to the side, then, finally, to Kate in front.

Their eyes locked.

"You okay?"

He nodded.

Then: "Wish Mom would hurry."

Kate nodded in return. Then words of encouragement.

"She'll be done soon. Just getting some more things."

(*Guns. Bullets.*)

Another nod from Simon.

Then he pointed out the obvious, something that Kate had pushed away even as it became so clear.

"It's getting dark."

Another nod.

"We should go. Back to that place. With the soldiers. And the people."

Simon's words triggered a cascade of feelings, growing, swelling, suddenly too clear for Kate to deny.

"I don't like it here. The street is dark. Everyone's gone, Kate. Why did they go?"

"Guess . . . when the power went out—they left. Maybe some people are still in their—"

She looked out front as she said the words she didn't believe in.

"—homes."

Simon cut through that fantasy, his voice low.

"I didn't think so."

And as Kate kept looking out front, she realized that Simon was right. Whatever light the sky had retained was almost gone. Just the merest hint of a deep blue and purple on the horizon ahead.

She thought: *we have to* go.

She wondered whether she should beep the horn. Get her mom to come.

But that was only to alert her.

If Kate beeped, her mom would be scared. She'd be angry.

No, they would have to wait.

Kate wouldn't ask Simon how he was doing anymore.

It only seemed to make him more scared.

Instead, she did what he did.

Looked out the front windshield, then to the right, then to left . . .

Over and over and over.

14

Dark

Christie grabbed the flashlight that Jack had stuck to the side of the downstairs wall, plugged in. Would it have any juice? It hadn't been used since the power had gone out.

Should be okay.

She aimed at the ground, and switched it on.

A small pool of bright light appeared at her feet.

"There," she said, the sound of her own voice calming her.

She had thought of turning the lights on down here, but Jack had filled the basement with lights, the brightest area of the house. He did that—she knew—from his fear that the Can Heads might try to get in here, as if they could get through the metal barriers that sealed the downstairs windows and the thick steel plate that served as a garage door.

No lights, she told herself.

Let's not advertise things.

She went to a metal cabinet, next to a bench with tools suspended over it. She flashed a light on the bench, the tools hanging on pegs on the wall.

Hammer, saws, pliers. Assorted screwdrivers. A sabre saw.

She remembered when Jack would come down here and work on their SUV.

Now she knew what he had been doing in the weeks leading up to their trip.

So clear now.

So obvious.

As he fitted the vehicle with explosives, a switch—his terrible secret—made only more terrible by the way she learned about it, as he told her how they would escape the camp.

What she must do.

What he might have to do . . . left unsaid . . .

Because—

(*And she knew this so clearly.*)

If he had actually told her what might happen, she wouldn't have done what he asked. She wouldn't have taken the Blairs' car, and gone out the back of the camp while all the camp people, those, those—

(Can Heads)

—followed him, trapped him, thinking that his whole family was in the backseat.

She still didn't let herself think about what might have happened if she hadn't gotten the kids out.

But she did. They were here. Alive.

She dug out the keys and unlocked what she once thought was just a metal chest.

Jack told her once what was in there, under a layer of power tools.

"If you need them, they're there," he had said.

Putting the flashlight on the nearby workbench, she searched for the key that looked as if it might fit the massive lock that kept the metal latch shut tight.

The first key didn't fit.

"Damn it," she said.

She spread the keys out. Jack had taken only the one key to the SUV. Most of the keys were for things she didn't have a clue about. She spotted another likely key, trying to imagine its serrated teeth sliding into the big lock.

She stuck that in and slid it home.

"Good."

A quick turn, and the curved *U* of the lock popped open, and she slid it out.

As Jack had told her, a layer of tools on top, a rubber mat below them. She grabbed an electric saw of some kind, a power drill, tossing them onto the workbench.

Her casual throw made the flashlight begin to roll.

Barely aware of its movement, she saw the circle of light that had been aimed at the wall begin to move—and her hand flew out to the flashlight before it fell to the ground.

Arresting its roll, she grabbed the light and pointed it into the well of the metal chest. To see:

Guns. All embedded in a foam rubber mat. Two rifles. Did she even know how to fire them? One looked like a shotgun, with twin bores at the end. Two handguns, one so unlike what Jack took to work. A rectangular handle, the gun shaped like an upside down *L*.

She'd have to figure out how to use these.

And . . . and—

Teach the kids how to use them.

Boxes of shells. She'd take all of them. Ten, maybe twenty boxes.

The insanity of the moment hitting her before she continued her inventory.

Off to the right, a smaller metal chest, with a latch, unlocked.

She flipped that open with her free hand.

Round metal tubes. Some kind of switch on the top of the tubes.

What were they?

Then she guessed—though she had never seen them before.

Bombs of some kind. Grenades. The thing on top, a switch or a timer.

Should she take them?

But a voice in her head said: take everything.

She looked around for something to put the cache into.

Over to the side, where the stairs led into the basement, she saw the table where she folded laundry.

From a million years ago.

From a life and time that wasn't real anymore.

On the floor: a laundry basket.

With water use monitored, controlled, rationed . . . laundries were infrequent.

But they still got done.

The blue plastic laundry basket would work.

She ran over to get it.

The sky turned black.

Clear, like most nights.

Stars visible through the windshield.

Kate didn't want to look at the door to the house, as if that would only delay her mother's return. On all her other trips, she had been in and out, with the food, the plastic gas cans.

This was taking longer.

Maybe—she thought—

Maybe . . .

—something's wrong?

Should she go out? See what her mother was doing?

Leave the car?

Leave Simon?

She chewed her lower lip, feeling as if she couldn't do anything but look at the house door, look at Simon, that's all.

When finally, she heard a noise.

She let herself turn to the house.

To see her mother coming out with . . . what?

Then Kate recognized it, even in the darkness.

A laundry basket. As if she had been watching her mother carry loads of laundry down to the basement, then back up.

Only there was no laundry in this basket.

Filled with things Kate couldn't make out as her mother went to the back of the car. She heard the jangly sound of metal clanging as the basket was lowered into the trunk.

The sound of things being moved around, to make room.

Then, the trunk being closed.

Until finally her mother came around to the passenger side of the car.

Not the driver's side.

Time for us to go, Kate thought.

We have everything.

Kate rolled down the window.

"Mom—we have to *go*."

Her mother nodded.

"One more thing. I'll be fast."

"What?" Kate asked.

But her mother turned away. Not answering the question, but now racing back into the house.

As Kate watched, she saw her mother turn on a flashlight as she entered the now totally dark house.

Then, the light and her mother disappeared.

In her head, Kate started counting.

Three hundred. I'll give her to 300, she thought.

That's enough.

Till 300, and then she'll be back or I'll beep.

She started.

One . . . two . . . three . . .

15

The Past

Christie ran up the stairs, aiming the flashlight at the steps as she went as fast as she could.

One last thing, she thought.

Since—this might be the last time she would be in this house.

Had to accept that, she told herself.

Things might get back to normal.

What normal used to be.

But if not, she had to be prepared for that. She had to prepare her kids for that.

At the top step, the last step to the narrow and dark upstairs hallway, she slipped, and fell. Her knee cracked into the carpeted edge of the stairs, right at the spot where her kneecap ended.

She groaned.

The flashlight slipped from her right hand, and rolled on the rug.

The gun. The gun, though, remained tightly held.

She wasted no time scrambling to her feet, even more quickly scooping up the light, pointing it down the hallway, then moving again.

Her right knee ached, joining so many other places that hurt.

She went to their bedroom.

As soon as she entered, she felt a physical wave crash into her.

Their bedroom.

The bed made. The closet doors shut. The end tables, hers with a book, Jack's with nothing. He always, always—

She stopped herself.

No time for any of that.

Turning, nearly spinning to the bookshelf to the left that faced their bed.

Filled not with books but—God—photo albums.

She stuck the gun into her belt, and with no time to examine these albums, to sift through them for what photos were indispensible, what images that she had decided to print . . . that she would now bring.

She only knew that if there was to be a future, for her, for her kids, beyond any of this, these photos were important.

She grabbed one, then another, then a third, so she had to tuck them under her arm, like oversized research books for a school project.

If she put the flashlight down, she could grab another.

A moment's debate.

Mere seconds for a decision.

She stuck the flashlight into her pocket, beam up.

And with her now-free hand, she randomly picked three more

mismatched albums, grabbing randomly at years of their life from their fourteen years together.

Precious, she kept thinking. *Precious.*

"What's that?" Simon said.

Kate had just been looking at the door, counting. Well past 300, but still she didn't beep.

Wondering where her mother was. This one last trip seemingly taking longer than any of the others.

Maybe that was just how it felt.

Simon's words in the now-dark car made her quickly snap forward.

To see the obvious.

Down the street, down . . . their block, at the end.

Two figures.

Two people walking.

She thought: maybe some of the neighbors stayed. Maybe they're coming to see what's going on.

But as soon as she thought it, she knew it wasn't true.

Neighbors don't wait until dark to come out.

A quick look to the front door, for her mother, for salvation.

Then, despite her own immense fear, a new thought.

Mom. *Inside.*

And they were coming.

She didn't answer Simon right away.

Instead, she checked for what must have been the tenth time . . . the door locks.

Buttons down.

Then her grip tightened on the gun.

"Kate, who are—"

She snapped her head back to look at Simon.

His eyes caught whatever scant light was there.

Her look said everything.

Back to the windshield.

The figures. Now more of them.

Her heart raced. She felt like she might start to cry, to whimper. But she didn't.

Instead—she leaned over and pressed down on the horn, once, again . . . and again.

The flashlight that she had stuck in her pocket made a jerky search-light hitting the ceiling of the hallway as Christie hurried, then shining above the stairs as she took care going down.

The reflected light only gave the slimmest of hints as to where a step ended, and the plunge to the next step began.

And no free hand to grab the handrail.

Awkwardly making her way down, so slowly, step after treacherous step, she questioned her decision to take so many photo albums.

But leaving those birthdays, Christmases, big turkey dinners, days at the beach when people still went to the beach—the idea of leaving that all behind had seemed impossible.

But now?

Navigating this.

Step by step.

She couldn't quite tell how close she was.

Soon, she thought.

At the front door, then out.

To the car. To pull away.

Back to a place where there would be people.

And not letting her mind wander past that point. Staying as focused as she could be.

Step . . .

Then—she heard the car horn.

———

Not two, Kate saw. But four figures.

Not moving fast, or slow, but steadily, cautiously. Walking together. There was a streetlight way down at one end, but none of the lights had come on here, near their house.

Broken? Power out?

Smashed?

Kate was frozen.

She was stone.

All she could think to do was look straight ahead, with the figures now only three . . . two houses away.

Simon vanished from her mind. She might as well be alone.

She looked to the house, the door, wondering why her mother wasn't racing out, getting to the car before they got here.

Christie moved as fast as she could.

The horn—could be Kate trying to get her to hurry up.

A dark pool awaited her at the bottom of the stairs, the dark end of the front hallway.

It would be darkest here, though the flashlight now at least hit a flat ceiling, and the reflected light let her see.

She had thought there would still be some twilight outside, enough so the open door would be clearly visible. But this black moonless night had arrived.

Had she taken that long?

She tested that she was truly past the staircase steps, moving one foot ahead, testing.

Flat. She started walking toward the door.

Again slowly. Because there were still obstacles.

A table just past the entryway, facing the living room. She couldn't see that. And a coatrack, a small bench to slip off shoes, a mirror for a last look.

So—still slowly.

But amazingly, breathing a little easier since she was only feet away.

Then—they were there.

Four of them, just dark figures.

Kate had expected them to be hunched over. Weren't the ones they saw last night all . . . hunched over?

Or was that because they had been hurt?

Because some had been shot, and—

And I shot one, she reminded herself. *One went down and didn't get up.*

Finally, Simon couldn't resist anymore, keeping his voice to the faintest of whispers . . .

"Kate . . ."

Speaking volumes.

The four figures stopped at the house, her house—a pause, seeming confused—then, still in a group, a pack . . . they moved to the open door.

16

Trapped

Christie froze.

Though the house was dark, the night a perfect black and the flash-light pointing almost uselessly at the ceiling, the scant light let her see that there was someone at the open door.

The shape hesitated as if frozen by the darkness within.

Christie took a step backward, then another.

She thought of her hands, full with the photo albums.

The gun tucked absurdly in her belt, the cool metal digging into her midsection.

If she dropped the albums, she could get the gun.

But would that make the figure hurry, knowing there was someone there?

Another step backward. Another.

The even darker kitchen behind her.

Christie's eyes locked, straight ahead.

Then—she almost gasped—another figure, slightly behind, the two
black shapes mere outlines, blurring together as one thing.

But now two of them.

They were still cautious.

The rug muffled any squeaks.

Soon she'd hit the wood floor of the kitchen. Would that be as
equally quiet?

The albums, the memories, the past—now so heavy, the foolish-
ness of coming back for them so clear.

And then another thought, as if a tremendous oversight.

The kids.

Outside. In the car.

Locked up.

Safe.

Then a more accurate thought . . .

Safe?

Another step. She felt the slight bump where the rug ended and
the kitchen floor began.

In seconds, she'd have no choice.

She heard a deep inhale of breath coming from the two dark
shapes.

An inhalation, as if bracing, as if getting *ready*.

Christie dropped the albums to the floor.

Kate quickly looked once more at the door to the house, at the Can
Heads gathered at the front door as some disappeared inside, as if
swallowed by the dark house.

She reached under her mother's seat and grabbed a gun, a small one that could fit a small hand.

She spun around to Simon, holding the gun out to him.

"Simon!" she said.

She kept her voice low and level, as calm as she could. But she also had to get him to move.

It would be bad if the Can Heads heard her.

"Take the gun."

A whisper.

He shook his head.

"Take the gun now, Simon!"

He shook his head again, but slowly reached out, his small hand almost too tiny for even this small handgun.

Kate looked at him through the open space between the front seats.

"You throw this switch here."

She reached back and gave the safety switch a flick, just like her dad had taught her.

"Then you can shoot. Just hold it up, point straight ahead, and slowly—"

She heard her father's voice in her ears.

"—slowly *pull* the trigger. Look at what you want to shoot, then pull the trigger."

Simon shook his head.

But he still held the gun.

She flicked the safety back on.

Then:

"Lock the door after me."

More shakes, his eyes watery.

"Just do it, Simon. *Lock* it."

She turned around.

Another shape had entered the house. Only one still hovered at the opening.

Three inside. A fourth on its way.

Kate pulled up the lock and popped open the door.

The albums clattered to the floor, some tumbling onto the rug, others falling behind her, making smacking noises on the wood floor.

Her hands in motion.

One pulling the gun out from her jeans, the other grabbing at the flashlight.

To aim the light first.

To see that first face.

Smeared. Cracked dark stains on it. The mouth open, teeth blackish, eyes wide trying to see—but now the light in this gloom blinding it.

She pulled the trigger.

Nothing.

Of course.

The safety.

The thing came at her as she brought her flashlight hand close and flicked the safety off with her thumb, the light swirling left and right in the room.

Then, to fire.

A bullet to the head, she thought.

But so scared, so shaky, she saw the first shot blow a chunk out of the thing's shoulder.

And as that Can Head hesitated, the other came from behind it, then around it, heading toward Christie, who raced backward, firing wildly into the darkness.

She bumped into the kitchen table, and the angle sent her flying forward, ricocheting toward the Can Heads.

She stumbled, nearly falling forward onto the floor.

Getting her balance.

Firing.

More blasts. Two, three.

How many does this gun hold?

She had put bullets in all the guns.

Did she count, did she even have a goddamn idea?

The first Can Head, so quickly recovered from its wound, crouched and then leaped at her.

All of a sudden—Christie was back at the camp.

Only now, all alone.

Cornered in her own kitchen.

And what was going on outside?

God, what was going on outside?

17

Outside

Kate popped open the door.

The one Can Head left outside the house heard the sound. She watched it turn slowly to her even as she checked that Simon had pushed the lock down.

She heard the *click*.

Good boy.

Then:

The others were in there, going after her mother.

She took a step toward the Can Head.

Just a dark shape. Like someone trick or treating, an oversized kid wearing a gory mask and knocking on a house where no one was home.

She needed to pull the trigger, but her finger wouldn't move.

Then—a shot from inside.

And that was all she needed.

She pulled the trigger, and shot the Can Head.

The thing near the door turned, moving down a step, another step, on level payment, coming right at her.

Kate's aim so off.

She wasn't even looking at the gun, the length of the barrel in front of her.

Ignoring what she had been taught.

Her eyes locked on the thing.

Another shot, hoping she'd hear a similar blast from inside.

Had her mom missed too? Were they starting to circle her?

Again, the idea—her mother trapped, and then she and Simon all alone—propelled another shot.

This time, she hit it in the chest.

Too low to kill it, and it now started hurrying toward her.

Only one more chance, finally looking at where the gun barrel was pointing, and firing—no slow squeeze this time, but a quick jerk back on the trigger.

Doing her very best to aim at the head.

After the blast, she didn't know whether she had hit the thing at all.

But it fell on the ground at her feet.

The way inside clear now, she could help her mother.

More blasts.

Thinking: *Mom's okay. Still shooting. She's all right.*

If I can just get in.

Then, from what seemed so far away, she heard the horn, honking over and over, like those alarms triggered in parking lots.

Only this was no broken car alarm.

She turned.

Kate made out Simon, who had crawled up into the front seat. Throwing his body into all those honks, over and over.

Because . . . down the street, only houses away, actually *rushing* this way.

So *many* of them, coming right toward Kate, toward the car, toward this trap.

And though she held the gun out in front of her, she knew, as much as she had ever known anything, that it was hopeless.

Shots outside. Then a second blast.

Kate, Christie thought.

The gunshots from outside seemed to make the three Can Heads grow cautious, pausing a moment as they made their way deeper into the kitchen.

Christie had moved away, and then around the table, putting the heavy wooden table between herself and the three Can Heads.

The Can Head she had wounded lagged behind. The wound enough to slow it.

With only seconds of protection, Christie picked another one to hit.

A second blast from outside.

Did that worry them, did the Can Heads in whatever crazed mental processes they had for thinking, consider backing away?

Instead, she watched one open its mouth, as if opening its jaw to loosen it, popping the joint, ready to . . .

. . . *fucking eat.*

She fired at that one, not seeing where she hit, only seeing it swerve away as if it had walked into invisible netting.

The third scrambled over the table, charging.

Crawling like a kid onto the wooden table, so fast, leaping up, hands and knees.

A human dog coming at her.

No. Not a dog. A wolf, something hungry, wild.

She swung the gun back, hoping to shoot it, but it was already too close, and the barrel hit the side of its face.

The gun almost knocked out of her hand, but instinctively she had tightened her grip just as she smacked the Can Head.

She backed against the wall, near the back door. Shut, locked, bolted.

So close—but useless as an escape.

The Can Head reared up on the table where her family had shared so many meals, so much talk, so much life.

All gone, as if swallowed by the darkness.

Kate saw them running at her.

She had wanted to save her mother, and now all she had done was make all of these other Can Heads race toward her.

She didn't even bother to shoot. Not yet, with them still houses away.

She'd be shooting at the air.

And amidst the sound of the charge, this race to get to her, she heard—again—a sound.

A *click*.

Then the door opened.

And Simon, her little brother, came out, nearly *rolled* out onto the dark sidewalk, scrambling to her.

Until he was beside her.

She couldn't say anything to him.

She didn't know what she felt.

The fear claimed everything.

She felt Simon sandwich his body next to hers.

His arm raised.

Holding a gun.

"Wait," Kate whispered.

As if it would do any good.

Moving backward gave Christie a few feet of distance from the table.

The thing on the table now towered over her as it knelt up, recovered from the smack of the gun.

It located her in the dark room.

Then jumped at her.

Christie screamed.

The sound as if coming from someone else.

Shrieking, loud, filling the room.

But even though she screamed, she pulled the trigger repeatedly, not worrying anymore about how many shots were left.

Three blasts, one after the other, as the thing landed on her, the weight pulling her down to the ground, smacking her down hard onto the wooden floor.

The smell overwhelming, her mouth, nostrils filled with it.

The smell of one of those things, the reek.

Then she felt wetness. Blood, in different spots, gushing.

And as she felt that blood, and the stench filled her mouth, lungs, something she could nearly taste, the Can Head didn't move.

Christie grunted and pushed it away.

The wounded one was nearby, but it hadn't attacked, the wound finally taking its toll as its blood covered the floor.

She stood up and bolted for the pitch-black opening that led from the kitchen to the hallway, to the open front door—

To her kids outside.

18

Surrounded

"Now," Kate said quietly.

Simon said nothing. No whimpers, no cries.

As Kate herself fought back the tremendous urge to cry, to put down the gun with them so hopelessly attacked.

She pulled the trigger, trying to aim at the figures racing toward them. Then a blast from Simon.

More encouragement: "Keep shooting. Just . . . keep shooting."

But could they hit anything in this dark, with the creatures running wildly toward them? She aimed at one Can Head only a house away, but it weaved and bobbed.

They know how to dodge the shots, she thought.

And:

We can't stop them.

Her brother kept firing.

Such a good kid, she thought.

Again she fired.

How many bullets left?

Not enough. Not enough bullets, not enough light to see and—

She stopped, not letting her mind drift to the next thought.

What will they do to us? What will it be like?

And thinking . . . only a minute left of this.

Christie rushed out of the house. She could see her kids shooting outside the car.

Why the hell did they get out of the car? I told them, told them to stay in the car, locked, and—

Then to see: the horde racing toward them.

Her heart sinking more than she ever imagined it could. The despair, the terrible fear and horror crashing into her.

Seconds.

To take all that in, and she kept running, nearly tripping as she leaped off the two stone steps that led up to the front door, moving to stand beside her daughter just as she fired.

Simon beside her.

Simon. Holding a gun.

Shooting.

The moment insane, impossible—

And when she got there, not a word.

No, because she happened to notice movement from across the street, from beyond the car.

More shapes moving.

The sick blackness of the street making them nearly invisible.

But she knew—they were *circling* them.

Were there a dozen of the Can Heads, or only a few, moving fast, cutting left and right, sailing closer? Human rats. Or wolves, circling prey.

Not human at all. Animals.

She shot at one of them that hurried around to the back of the car, closing this ring around them.

In those seconds, as the ring closed, a jolt of guilt.

I did this. I was supposed to keep them safe.

Now—what will happen now?

A blast from Simon's gun, shooting into the darkness.

A boy. With a gun.

She pulled her trigger—a Can Head only feet away, as it dodged and feinted.

She was answered with a metallic click.

No more bullets. All the bullets, and the other guns, in the car.

She thought then she whispered a word.

"Sorry . . ."

So quietly.

And the next sound . . . was anything but quiet.

A cannon went off.

Then another, a near-deafening boom that filled the night.

And she saw that one Can Head, one that was one last leap away from landing on them . . .

. . . was *gone*.

Where did it go? What happened?

But the cannon booms kept coming.

Steady, sure, rhythmic in the way they rang out.

In between the third or fourth rocketing *boom*, she heard a *click*.

Kate's gun. Out of ammo.

Christie turned to her. Put an arm around her, and then Simon, who alone still had bullets, still pulling his trigger.

They both shook under her arms, as if they had been standing in an icy polar wind and nothing would ever get them warm again, would ever get them to stop shaking.

The cannonading booms kept coming, and Christie knew that as loud as they were—so different from the blasts that their handguns made—it was a weapon.

The dawning realization: someone else was firing.

She scanned the area around them, this circle made by the three of them and the car.

To see: fiery explosions from an area just behind them, past the back of the car.

And in the light . . .

. . . made by those flashing blasts . . .

A woman. Not even as tall as Kate.

Holding a rifle, this monster of a rifle, as she kept blasting away, the blasts interrupted by the oh-so-fast click of her moving something on the gun to get the next shell in place.

A blast. More clicks, more blasts.

Until this woman, close enough now that her face, round, but with a set, determined look, stood beside them.

Raising the gun for each shot, reloading in a breath.

No one said anything.

Until—that rhythm slowed.

And finally—stopped.

And the woman, their savior, this angel with a cannon for a gun, finally spoke.

"I think they're gone . . . for now."

The woman lowered the barrel of her gun.

Christie said the first thing that came to mind, the street littered with bodies, the remaining Can Heads retreating.

"Who are you?"

The woman smiled. She took a moment to look at Kate and Simon, the smile broadening.

"A neighbor." Then a small laugh. "Remember them? Neighbors?"

And then before Christie could say anything else, the woman nodded in the direction of the house.

"How about we get off the street and go inside, to my place, hmm? I could do with a cup of tea. Maybe—"

That set face suddenly relaxed—"maybe something stronger."

Christie didn't know what to say, her arms around her kids, the three of them standing there for a moment as if nothing had happened.

And all she could do was nod.

19

A Home

The woman's name was Helen Field, and she lived just around the corner from them.

Maybe Christie had seen her before, maybe not.

But even after so many years in this development, they certainly hadn't spoken.

People stayed in their homes, their fortresses, locking out the rest of the world.

Helen took a sip of the dark tea with half a packet of artificial sweetener.

Honey would be nice. Like a lot of once common things, now not common at all.

"You all look pretty beat," she said.

Kate and Simon sat at the kitchen table as well, their eyes wide as if still on the street. So much Christie wanted to say to them . . . ask them, but for now, she felt immobilized.

Boiling the water for Helen was about all she could manage.

She asked Helen if sitting here, in her house with the lights on, was a safe thing.

"They're gone. I doubt they'll be back. Don't think they like the smell of their own kind dead. With the doors and windows locked and shuttered, about the safest place. For one night at least."

"I don't know how to—thank you."

"It's Henry that should be thanked. My husband. Died two years ago. Colon cancer. When all this stuff happened—" another shake of her head toward the world outside—"he made sure I knew what to do with a gun. Every weekend, had me out practicing. Ex-marine, so the man knew his guns."

Christie turned to her kids, their wide eyes locked on the woman.

"He was a big fan of the one I used tonight, a riot shotgun. Holds a lot of shells, and the pump action is fast. I got pretty good at it."

No one said anything, but the woman kept smiling as she put her cup of tea down.

"Look at me. Going on about my gun. And you kids—you look like you need sleep. Why not sleep here while your mom and I talk? Two warm beds, just upstairs . . . hmm?"

Taking charge, directing us, Christie thought.

But didn't they have to go, get on the road, get out of here?

"We shouldn't stay here—we—"

"Look, Christie. These two need some sleep. So do you. I'm well rested. I can stay here and make sure everything's—what's the word—"

Another small laugh.

"—copacetic."

Christie didn't know what to do. If anything, this woman's thinking had to be clearer than hers.

We all need sleep, she thought.

And having seen Helen in action, she felt amazingly . . . safe.

"Okay."

She turned to Kate and Simon.

"You two—go get some sleep, okay?"

She saw Simon's eyes on her. A question there perhaps, but one he wouldn't give voice to.

"I'll come up in a bit. Check on you."

Would have been an absurd thing to have said to Kate even a week ago, so fiercely independent, pushing away all those lines that could keep her tethered to her parents.

Now, though—

Kate nodded, stood up.

And in another moment that wouldn't have happened a short seven days ago, she reached down and took Simon's hand. "Come on, Simon."

Christie looked at her daughter. "Maybe you can wash up a bit."

All that blood. Be good to get some of it off.

"Sure, Mom," Kate said.

Echoed by Simon: "Sure."

They walked out of the kitchen.

And when they had gone, she turned to see Helen's eyes looking right at her as if she had seen a ghost.

"So. What happened to all of you?"

And taking care not to make much noise as she did, Christie began crying.

When Christie finished her sobbing, muffling it with her hands so the kids wouldn't hear, she told the story in a crazed, haphazard way, missing details, jumping ahead, then back.

"Jack . . . my husband . . . had been wounded on the job. And this place we went to . . . was supposed to be a vacation for us."

"This Paterville Camp?"

A nod. "Only Jack thought . . . something was wrong with it. I mean, right from the start."

"A good cop."

"He started looking around. And then discovered that some of these people who went there hadn't left, hadn't really left the camp, you see . . . because . . . they had all been—"

Helen reached out and put a hand on Christie's wrist, gently closing her hand around it.

"Then you had to get out."

Christie nodded, continuing the story.

"They took us to a cabin. Guarded us. We didn't know where Jack was. But he had been tied up in their—kitchen. The place they did it. He told me about the bodies in the freezer."

"Christ."

"But he escaped. Came and got us. But there was a problem."

"How to get out?"

"Exactly. He told me his idea. His plan. I wanted to tell him no, that we all stick together."

She took a deep breath. So hard to even talk.

"Maybe you should stop. For now," Helen said.

But Christie continued. The story had to be finished.

So Jack's sacrifice would be seen clearly by this woman. This new friend.

"He took our Explorer out the main gate. There were explosives in it. Me and the kids . . . we took the car belonging to these people, all dead—the Blairs. Jack had found the keys. He'd distract the people who ran the place. It was the only way, he said. I—I didn't know—"

Helen got up and came behind Christie.

"You're here. You're alive. It worked. He saved his family."

The tears again, even though she felt she didn't have any more tears.

"Look. Your kids may be waiting upstairs. Go give them a kiss. And you, you need sleep."

"I can't—"

A squeeze to her shoulders. "I'll stay up, right here. My trusty shotgun by my side—though I think we've seen all the action we're going to see for one night. Sleep, and tomorrow, I have things to tell you, to talk to you about."

The words compelling.

So much so . . . that there was really no other option.

"Maybe wash up. Change. In the morning, I'll be here."

Christie nodded, and suddenly felt as if she couldn't get out of the chair.

But somehow she was able to give that command to her body, slide the chair back, stand up.

Then standing, she said, quite simply, "Thank you."

Helen gave her a hug, released her, and then Christie turned and followed the kids upstairs, going to them, and then on to Helen's bedroom where she would, for the first time in so many years, sleep alone.

20

The Plan

Christie came down the stairs, to the hallway.

She saw that the pile of photo albums that she had dropped the night before in her house were now here, neatly stacked on Helen's hallway table.

She kept on moving, the feeling dreamlike.

Into the kitchen.

Where she saw Helen still sitting in the same chair, just as Christie had left her the night before.

Her eyes widened as Christie entered the sun-drenched kitchen.

"Well—*you* got some sleep. Good."

She nodded.

"The kids?"

"Still asleep."

"Not surprising. After all they've been through."

Helen nodded at the stove. "Got some of that coffee stuff warmed up. Just made it a while ago."

"You must be tired."

"Been worse."

Christie walked over to the stove and the coffee machine, the coffee a mixture of chicory, dried soy, and maybe even a dash of real coffee, mostly known for having caffeine and a bitter taste.

She poured herself a cup and went to the table and sat down.

"Was it quiet last night?"

"Oh, I heard some of them out there. Doing who knows what. But they stayed away from here. Guess even when people turn cannibal, they don't want their heads blown off."

"Guess so," Christie said. She even managed a smile. "Thank you. For getting the photo albums. For everything."

Helen smiled as Christie took a sip of the coffee. Then:

"Something I wondered about last night. Everyone's gone? From here?"

"Pretty much. Even had cops going through the development, recommending that people get out. Least until the power comes back on. Even now, there's only power in certain spots. My house is one of the lucky ones."

"And you didn't leave?"

"Oh, I wanted to. But some nice neighbor wanted my car. Maybe theirs broke down and my Suburban looked pretty good to them. Left me high and dry."

"You were trapped here? No one would take you?"

"Guess it's not that kind of world, Christie. Anyone near me had left already. I did talk to some people racing away. They looked at me as another mouth to feed, I guess, less space in their car for their stuff.

No one knew how long they'd be away. A few days? A week? A month?"

Helen looked away.

"Forever? Who knows."

Then quiet. The stillness of them both thinking over the words, the ideas, the fear.

Then Christie spoke:

"You can come with us."

Helen stood up, leaned across the table, and gave Christie a giant hug.

When Christie could see the woman's eyes again, she saw them glisten.

The first tears she had seen from this woman.

Then simply: "Thank you."

She sniffed as she sat down, took a breath. "Me and Henry were always pretty independent. Something he prided himself on. Semper Fi and all that jazz. And I might be able to hang here for a while. Got some food, weapons—"

Christie smiled. "You *are* a pretty good shot."

"Only pretty good?"

But the smiles faded fast.

"But sooner or later, if this place doesn't get back to normal, with no guards and the fences down, well—how long before I made a mistake and they get me."

"You can't stay." A beat. "Come with us."

"I do have someplace we can go."

"A place? Someplace—"

"Someplace *safe*. It's where I was headed. They call it 'the Redoubt.' And—"

But then the sound of steps on the stairway.

A voice. Kate.

"Mom?"

"We're in here."

And her two kids came into the room, faces washed.

Her two beautiful kids stepped into the sunlit room.

Simon ate some of the cereal out of the box while Kate, seeming so adult, poured a cup of coffee.

So far, no one had talked about the night before.

Until Simon went out of the kitchen to the front door.

Christie became alarmed.

"Simon? Honey, what—"

She got up to see him at the door, looking out the slits made by the steel bars of the outer door.

"Wh—where'd they all go?"

For a moment, she didn't understand what he was talking about.

But when she went to the window, she saw that the bodies across the street, the exploded bodies of the attackers from the night before, were gone, leaving only massive red blotches on the sidewalk and street.

"I don't know."

He looked at her, and she knew he didn't believe what she had said.

She felt a tug of her arm.

"Got a moment, Christie? A few more words?"

And Helen steered her into the dining room.

"This Redoubt? What is it?"

"A friend of Henry's, another marine. Lived near New Paltz since he liked to climb. The mountains there, Shawangunk. Really beautiful. But when things went bad, he decided to do something."

"To protect themselves?"

"Yes, and others who joined them. Like a cooperative, designed to keep people safe and alive, protected from Can Heads. There's a giant inn up there, a gorgeous mountain hotel called Mountain Falls Inn. Ever hear of it?"

Christie shook her head.

"Of course, like a lot of those places, it ended up empty, abandoned. No one doing that kind of thing anymore. So these people moved in. Brought other families in. Set up patrols, fences. Made it safe, secure. Henry's old buddy called it 'the Redoubt.' A place to make a stand."

She shook her head.

"Military men. With their jargon, their gung ho. It's where I was heading. Should have maybe gone earlier. But with Henry gone, well, you know I didn't really much give a damn about doing anything."

"It's safe?"

"Supposedly—as safe as anyplace can be, Christie. And listen, do you have another place to go?"

"No. I mean, some distant aunts and uncles down south. I haven't heard from them in a—"

Helen raised her eyebrows, sufficient comment on that idea.

Is that where we should go? Christie wondered.

Then: *I feel numb . . .*

I feel all wrong.

Helen's stare reflected back how oddly Christie must have seemed to act, to appear.

"Look, I'm going to tell you something, okay?"

She took Christie's hand.

"You got a decision to make. A big, but simple decision. Are you going to get through this?"

A pause. A look toward the kitchen.

"Are you going to get your kids through it? Because if you are, you're going to have to make those decisions. You're all they got. And not every decision you make will be perfect or right."

A small laugh.

"You may even regret inviting me to come with you. But—you need to show them that you are *here*. With them. And together, you're going to make it."

Christie felt the words register.

The meaning so clear. Their importance.

Words she would need to hold on to.

"A redoubt," she said. "And you think it's safe?"

"Yep. The Mountain Falls Inn. And we can be there by this afternoon."

"Okay. Then that's where we'll go."

Christie forced her voice, which she now realized had turned dull and leaden all morning, to become louder, stronger. She tried to dig somewhere deep inside herself to find strength, and let her voice reflect that.

Now she covered Helen's hand with hers, making a pact.

The gesture seeming official, and primal.

"Like you said, Helen. Only a bit different."

A shake of the hands layered on each other.

"Together—*we're* going to make it."

And Helen Field smiled broadly at that.

Then: "Mom—let's get going!"

the mountain falls inn

21

Leaving Home

Midday, and the silvery span of the Goethals Bridge reflected the sun, beautiful and suspended over the river.

Christie had thought that Helen would have been a nonstop talker, but after they picked up some of her things, a small suitcase, and a metal box filled with, as she put it, "you know what" as she waved her shotgun, she was quiet.

Christie had asked, "That's all you want to bring? I mean, we still have a bit of room, and there's the roof."

"I'm good," Helen had said, a bit more grimly than Christie would have imagined her to respond. "Get to my age and you learn to travel light."

As they left, she didn't look at Christie, leaving her to imagine what was going through the woman's mind as they left the development and headed for a place that was supposed to be safe.

Like . . . Paterville was supposed to be safe?

Maybe—at this moment of departure—both having their doubts.

Either way, Christie let the silence hang, and after a quick check on the kids . . .

"You guys okay? All set?"

A nod from Kate, a yes from Simon . . . the journey began.

And as she drove across the high arch of the bridge span, Christie saw the other side, where the military had previously set up camp, a place to guide people leaving the city, a place where the cars had been circled and she had heard a soldier say that lights were due to come soon.

Now, there was nothing there.

Not a car, no trucks, no police or soldiers, and certainly no lights.

Helen must have sensed something shift in Christie.

"Everything okay?"

Christie spoke low, trying to make the words she said inconsequential. Despite the long night's sleep, she ached miserably in places she had never ached before. It would take more than one night's sleep to erase both the pain and the fatigue.

"That's—" She hesitated, searching for the best way to express it.

Then: "—where we had stopped. There had been—"

She shot Helen a look as if trying to get her to read between the lines.

And what lines are those, she thought?

The emotions. The feelings.

At the very bottom—the fear.

"Lot of cars were there. Cops. You know, people leaving."

She caught Helen nodding.

"And now—all gone. I guess—" the woman said with what sounded to Christie like a lack of sincerity—"everyone who wanted to move on, moved on."

The woman sniffed.

Then added another idea that Christie couldn't believe.

"I guess—everyone who wanted to get out, did."

Thinking . . . did some not make it out?

And to seal this exchange of doubtful ideas, Christie simply said, "Yeah."

She drove past the area where the camp—the gateway for people leaving the metro area—had completely vanished.

Only, with one last thought . . .

Twenty-four hours, and it's gone.

These days—things happen fast.

Helen suggested an alternate road to the Garden State Parkway.

"The old Highway 17. Takes you past a bunch of small towns. I mean, why get on the highway until we have to, right? More options on a smaller road."

Christie nodded as if the logic of that was clear. For now, she was glad to have someone else's voice in her ear giving advice.

Could she ever get used to being alone, totally responsible for the kids?

She thought of . . . what did they call it? The stages of grief? Mourning?

Where the hell am I on it? Have I even begun?

Can I even afford that luxury?

Helen seemed to sense her getting lost in thoughts.

"Nice towns along here. Hank always said we should just find a small apartment here. But when the proverbial"—a glance back at the kids, a modification to her language—"*stuff* hit the fan, we had no choice."

A breath.

"Gotta be safe. Needed a protected development."

Christie nodded. The small towns still looked appealing, except for the stores with boarded-up windows, and then the occasional house, windows smashed, broken into.

Nobody walked around.

Places like this weren't safe.

The only thing you'd find if you did a walk-through of the town would be some dark hole where Can Heads slept during the day, waiting for dark and whatever instincts took them hunting.

It's an alien planet, Christie thought.

We've landed on a world light years away from the earth I grew up on. So very different.

"Another few miles," Helen said, "and then you pick up the parkway. Take it right to the Thruway."

Helen reached over and patted Christie's knee. The gesture seemed both odd and reassuring at the same time.

She barely knew this woman, and yet she could feel herself instinctively depending on her, liking her, then—in this guarded world, unusual—caring for her.

Christie kept her eyes peeled for the green and yellow sign announcing the on-ramp.

Then—she spotted it. But she also saw something else.

Christie slowed.

"What's that?" Helen said.

It looked pretty much like other places they had passed. Men standing guard, a barrier to the highway. Papers to be checked, questions to be asked.

"A checkpoint. That's all."

The briefest of pauses, then Helen said:

"You sure?"

And her words made everything Christie could see about it come into focus.

Yes, there was a barrier. Men standing, waiting.

Even one man in a uniform.

Another had started waving at the car even though they were still yards away.

A big-armed gesture, hand waving, then the same hand pushing back at the air.

Slow down.

Stop the car.

Still not there yet, Christie gave voice to what she felt.

"Seems . . . wrong."

But what was wrong? The look of the barrier? The fact that there was a man in a uniform, and others just standing there. They held guns—so they couldn't be Can Heads. No they had to be—

Then, a quick flash.

The memory of Paterville. That night. Where supposedly normal people . . .

Slaughtered other people.

Chopped them up and served them as food.

Her stomach turned.

She had begun to slow.

But—

Helen's voice was slow.

"If you think something's wrong, Christie—"

She paused for a long moment.

Then: "Trust your gut."

Christie felt the woman turn and look at her. After all, she was the one driving. She held the damn steering wheel, her foot on the accelerator.

Slowed a bit more.

Because—

(And this thought was clear.)

Let them think I'm going to stop.

When actually.

Closer now.

She pushed her foot all the way down. The car engine seemed to hesitate, as if pondering the command to speed up as fast as it could.

And with the men backing up, maybe just trying to keep the road safe . . .

Ready to walk over for a polite and concerned chat.

The engine roared, the car finally accelerated, and the beat-up Honda suddenly flew into the barrier, the men pulling back even farther, Christie ignoring them.

In case they were raising their guns.

In case some had guessed what she might do, and had their guns already in motion, to shoot at the windows, the tires—

"Mom!" Kate said.

And the car smashed into the wooden barrier.

22

The Talk

The wooden barrier split into two, the pieces flying left and right as the men scrambled.

Christie waited for the sound of gunshots, and in anticipation made the car swerve.

In the distance, she heard the crackling of gunfire, but her move must have surprised them, and she was well away before they took aim.

"Wow! Some driving," Helen said.

Kate's voice was more sober: "Mom—why did you do that?"

She gave Kate a look.

"Guess I didn't want to stop."

"O . . . kay," Kate said.

Helen gave her a look. They both knew why she hadn't stopped. What her fear was. How—though she might have been wrong—it was better to be overly cautious than trapped by them.

Better safe than dinner, she thought.

Whatever it takes to be safe.

After a few minutes, Helen added: "I think they're going to need a new barrier."

"Oh yeah," Christie said.

Miles down the road, Christie caught Helen as she turned and looked at the backseat.

In the rearview mirror, Christie could see Kate, eyes closed.

Still exhausted?

Simon played with some of his toys that he had rescued that morning.

Then Helen looked at her.

"You okay? Driving?"

"Sure. Still hurt like hell, probably will for weeks."

A look at the woman beside her.

"It'll get better."

Sounding more like a hope than a belief.

"I wanted to ask you about something."

Her voice lowered. Quiet. Two adults talking about boring stuff.

At least that's what Christie imagined it would sound like to Simon as he lost himself in play.

"Those others. In that camp. Something I don't understand. Were they Can Heads?"

"Hmm?"

"You said—"

Even lower.

"—they captured people. That—" A hesitation. "They—"

"Right," Christie said quickly, not wanting the next words.

For herself, for Simon?

For all of us.

"That's what they did."

Helen shook her head. "And yet—they had a fence—"

"Two of them."

"And guards, guns. To keep the Can Heads out."

"You got it."

Christie feeling annoyed now.

Why all these questions?

"Then—" A pause, as if Helen knew she was digging too deep. "So—were they Can Heads too?"

A look to the mirror. Simon still playing, oblivious. Kate not stirring. Then a glance at Helen.

Flatly.

"I don't know."

Then nothing for a few minutes. But the woman's questions had stirred something.

"Maybe this thing is changing, whatever is turning people into these things, these animals."

"Changing?" Helen said, with a shake of her head. "Or spreading."

"What do you mean?"

"Look, I used to talk about this with my husband. He was no scientist. Just a retired grunt. But he went online. He said it could have been all those foods, genetically modified foods they called them—"

"Supposedly safe."

"*Supposedly.* Like a lot of things. But I mean, what he found on the Internet is that they were creating new genetically modified organisms. Called GMOs. He thought . . . maybe that's what did it."

"I don't know."

Christie wished she would stop talking about this.

"I thought . . . maybe it was the droughts, the shortages," Christie said. "All that was some kind of trigger."

"Maybe. But here's the thing: why *some* people, not others? Why not you or me, your kids? Climate change? Holes in the ozone? Who got *it*, and who didn't?"

"Helen—"

"Okay. I'll stop."

"No. It's okay. I don't mind—"

"It's just that I haven't really had someone to talk to in quite a while."

Christie gave her a look. A half smile.

"It's okay. Really."

Then, her eyes back on the road . . .

"I never got a chance to ask Jack what he thought. About those supposedly normal people in Paterville. There was no time. And afterward—I didn't think about it. But now, listening, talking to you . . . were they any different?"

"The ones inside the fence, not outside?"

"Yeah. Is what happened at Paterville something—I don't know— rare? Were we just unlucky. Or—"

She stopped for a second as the thoughts formed in her mind. Like storm clouds coming together.

The day changing.

"Or is something like that happening all over? Places like Paterville. A new type of Can Head. Looking like us."

"But not like us."

She shot Helen a look.

"Or maybe exactly like us. Is this thing—whatever it is—spreading, changing?"

Helen's eyes had narrowed, her face frozen.

Christie pressed on.

After all, Helen had started the conversation.

Started her thinking.

"Yeah, spreading—or do you have to let it happen? Is it—God—a choice? Did those people in the camp have to *let* it happen, to become like the things outside the fence?"

Then quiet.

Christie realizing that her words scared even her.

Because if they were true . . . if they were even remotely possible of being true . . . then what was this world?

What was the future?

For my kids?

And if it was . . .

"You see, if that's true then there's the other difference."

"Difference?"

"Between the ones outside the fence, and the ones . . . inside."

"What's that?"

Now it was Helen's voice that had turned hollow.

"The ones inside could think. They could plan. They could seem like us. How would you ever tell? And one more thing."

A moment. Then, again, the question, quiet:

"What?"

"They're smart." A deep breath. Hands tight on the wheel. "They can be as smart as us."

And with that, they both stopped talking.

23

To the Mountain

The gate leading off the Thruway to Exit 18 swung wide open, and this time Christie wasn't surprised.

Something happened, and it wasn't just in Paterville, not just New York City; it didn't just happen to us.

"Little tricky here," Helen said. "You could go straight through the town. But there's a side road. Why not give that a shot?"

She made it sound so casual.

"Why not give that a shot?"

Christie could read between the lines.

Towns up here could be the least safe places, especially small ones like this with one narrow Main Street, and few side streets.

Perfect for a human trap.

"Just take the street there, and follow it around. You can pick up County Road 6, and take that all the way up to the mountain and the inn."

Christie drove at a steady pace, and she kept looking left and right as she drove, reassured to see Helen doing the same thing. Her gun lowered, barrel pointing down.

"There—this is it. County Road 6. Goes all the way up the mountain."

"We're going . . . up there?" Simon said.

Simon leaned forward to get a better view of the mountain ahead of them. The sheer cliff rising up nearly straight, hitting the deep blue of the afternoon sky. Near the top, the roofs of the inn's buildings juttted out, just below the peak.

Helen turned around to him. "That's the place. It's something, hmm? The Mountain Falls Inn."

"They built it right on top of the mountain?"

"Sure did. A Victorian castle built in 1851."

Christie looked in her rearview mirror. Kate hadn't said anything. No excitement from her. No questions.

Though awake, she sat with her lips pursed, eyes narrow.

Looking out the window.

But not at the mountain, at the great building ahead.

Christie started up the mountain road, suddenly twisting, curving, cut into the ancient granite, with only a small rock ledge at the side to stop a car from veering off.

She slowed even more.

"Only this one road up there?" she said to Helen.

"Uh-huh. Guess that's why it's a good redoubt."

"What's a redoubt?" Simon said.

"Well, the way Mr. Field explained it to me, Simon, is that it's like, well, a fort. A place to be safe. A good thing."

Finally, Kate spoke.

The word flat. Loaded with doubt.

"Safe?"

Christie saw Helen still looking at the back.

She hesitated answering. Then:

"So I've been told."

"We'll check it out," Christie added quickly.

Her eyes shot to the mirror, meeting Kate's.

Kate held the look for a moment, then glanced away, back to the windows as the car traveled the narrow serpentlike road up to the mountain inn.

Near the top, the road straightened a bit, and they passed signs.

Signs. About parking. And registration. One with an arrow pointing to a lake.

And Christie immediately felt that this was all wrong.

So goddamned familiar.

And then . . . *what must the kids think?*

Maybe this was all a bad idea. There had to be other places to go.

Though the place might be nothing like the Paterville Camp with its collection of small cottages, how could they not be thinking about it?

But before she could let those thoughts sink in, to process what she thought, to figure out what her options were, she took one last curve, and came to a small cabin beside a metal barrier.

A fence led from either side, not high, but it ended where it joined the mountain.

Certainly didn't look terribly . . . *safe.*

Men stood there with guns.

Men with guns. A constant in this world.

Everywhere. The barrier remained in place, and the men made their weapons tilt up a bit.

Christie did the only thing she could do.

She slowed, then stopped the car.

Before the first man got to the driver's window, Helen said quietly . . .
"Let me do the talking."

Christie hit a button, and the window came down.

"You folks lost?" the man said.

Helen leaned across so she could get a look at the man.

"Afternoon. Is there somebody we could talk to?"

The man smiled. Shook his head. A glance back to the others behind him.

"You're talking to me."

Christie saw Helen smile. Holding it together.

We're not exactly being welcomed, Christie thought.

"Right." Helen said. "My name is Helen Field, and these people, this . . . *family*, they've been through a lot. We were hoping that—"

The man cut her off.

"Sorry. No one gets in here without prior approval. Kind of full up. Now, to turn around—"

At that, Helen pulled back from Christie and popped open the passenger car door, and got out.

The men to the rear came forward, guns at the ready.

Helen paid no attention to them, but walked around to the front of the car, where the man she had been talking to stood.

Christie watched them talk.

Both standing in the brilliant sun.

The man shaking his head.

Helen gesturing with her arms, hands . . . in a way that Christie now expected.

It went on.

Kate spoke: "Mom, what's wrong? Won't they let us in?"

Christie shook her head.

"I don't know."

Had this all been a waste? The gas wasted, the time. Now here—and where the hell were they?

She thought of how many times she had said those words in the past days . . .

I don't . . . know.

Finally, she saw the man give one last shrug, and with the barrier still down, he walked over to the small cottage near the barrier, and went in.

Christie saw him pick up a black phone.

They have phones, she thought. *That's good. Maybe things aren't so bad here.*

Helen looked over to her. A small smile. A little widening of the eyes.

The expression said that she had given it her best shot.

And it all depended on what happened in the little toll cottage by the barrier as the man spoke on the black phone.

Finally he came out, and as if it was no big deal—

No big deal . . .

—he gave a signal and the long metal barrier began to rise.

The guns lowered.

Helen gave him a pat on his right shoulder to which he didn't react, and then quickly ran back into the car, slamming the door behind her.

"What did you tell him? We're in?" Christie said.

Helen looked first at the kids, then Christie, her tone almost suggesting that this was some kind of adventure.

Rather than what it really was—

A matter of life and death.

The woman took a breath.

"Not exactly . . ."

24

The Interview

They followed a young man—couldn't have been more than seventeen . . . eighteen—who led them into the castlelike building.

"Wow," Simon said, looking around at the mammoth main complex flanked by two other buildings.

Inside—though the overhead lights were off—enough afternoon sunlight poured through the massive front windows that overlooked the very top of the mountain, the lake, and the sheer cliff that faced the inn.

"This way," the young man said with no warmth.

"What a joint, hmm?" Helen said.

The man walked to a great staircase and started up the steps.

The inn was the kind of castle one might see in Europe; in fact, the whole setting seemed like they were in the Alps.

At the top of the stairs, the man turned, walked down the hallway a few steps, and knocked on a massive wooden door.

He stood there, his face blank, not registering anything as they waited.

The hallway also had no lights on.

Probably on a generator. Watching their fuel, Christie thought.

Someone opened the door, and the young man gestured for them to go inside, not following them, his escort duties apparently over.

Christie looked at Helen, who took the lead and walked in.

The room, an office—all dark wood, giant windows, bookcases on all the walls, and a massive desk surrounded by heavy chairs—smelled musty.

Behind the massive wood desk, a man in khakis sat wearing a green and gray camouflaged cap with large black letters—USMC—arms resting on the table, hands folded.

Christie saw someone else standing to the side. Another man, not in khakis, but holding a gun.

The man at the desk spoke first.

"Helen Field. God, didn't expect to see you up here."

"Hi, Bill." She looked around the room. "Nice digs."

Christie saw that Bill didn't react to the light tone.

He also didn't offer them seats.

She turned to see Simon and Kate still taking the room in.

"After what we heard about the city. The problems they had with the electricity, then the damn Highway Authority. Thought things had finally gone over the top."

"That's kinda why I'm here. I know that you and Henry used to talk. And when he learned about what you were doing up here, he thought, maybe, some day we should come along."

"He *should* have."

Christie noticed the use of the word *he*.

Did Bill like Helen, or was he only connected to her now-dead husband, part of a band of brothers that didn't suffer females?

And now he had three of them in his office.

Helen smiled. "Guess I wasn't up for leaving. And then when he died—"

The man looked away. "Tough thing. Sorry I didn't get down for the service—"

"Wasn't much."

A pause.

The man's eyes turned to look at Helen, then Christie, eyes boring into her.

Should I say something? she thought.

And then another . . .

Do we even want to stay here?

This dark, cold castle?

Maybe there were other options.

"Look, Bill—as you—"

The man behind the desk cleared his throat.

"Helen. Hang on a second. They call me 'the Colonel' here. Helps keep things . . . orderly. I say things, things, they get done."

Helen smiled. "Sure, Colonel, I was hoping that I, my friends here . . . we could stay. For a while. Until things settle down."

Bill—now "the Colonel"—stood up.

"Settle down?"

He seemed angry at the thought.

"You think that things are going to . . . 'settle down?'"

Simon had been wandering around, looking at the rows of books, a painting of the inn above a giant fireplace.

Now, though, he came close to Christie.

The man with the gun had his eyes on her, watching.

No, she thought. *Maybe this is all wrong.*

The Colonel gestured to the outside, a wave of his hand.

"Tell you what, Helen, just like I told Hank years ago. This thing isn't going to . . . *settle down*. It's a war. And to fight a war, let alone win it, you got to survive. Which is why we're here."

The Colonel stood up and walked under the giant painting of the inn.

"When they abandoned this place, we came in. Started making it safe. None of that electric fence crap."

Christie imagined that his language could get even more colorful.

And standing here . . .

With a couch dotted with maroon pillows only feet away.

It would be so good to just sit, lean back.

Simon's hand found hers.

Another gesture from the Colonel, a dismissive wave at the world outside.

"We set up real patrols. Boots on the ground. The perimeter guarded. Only one way up here, and we guard it. Lay in all the provisions we could. Scavenge. Recover. Get food, gas. We even found plots of ground during the summer where things grow. And thank God for that lake outside."

Helen nodded, shooting Christie a quick look. "You've done well. Hank always said—"

She kept playing the name of her dead husband, as if that ancient bond might help.

"We have. We have a *system*. Everyone follows that system. If there's a way to get through this, we'll be here. Surviving."

He finally stopped.

Then, walking away from the painting, planting himself in front of his desk, leaning back so he could rest while they remained standing, as if ready to be interrogated, the Colonel finally asked a question.

"So what is it you want from me, from us?"

Helen started to answer . . .

But Christie—on impulse—rushed to answer.

"We need a place to be safe."

She wanted to tell him what she and her kids had been through, what they lost, the horrors—

But she couldn't summon that in front of the kids. Somehow, they had to get past all that.

"We just—don't have any place to go. When Helen said—"

The Colonel put up his hand.

"Look—I have thirty-eight souls living here, under my leadership."

Souls.

There was somewhere else they used that word, Christie thought.

But where?

Souls . . .

"And keeping them alive, and healthy, and fed—I take that *very* seriously. Our resources—they're strained already. And four new people? Three of 'em people I don't even know? How can I do that?"

Helen cut him off.

"You know me, Bill."

Stopping, for the moment, the "Colonel" horseshit.

"And you and Hank were more than buddies. That is—" she shook her head—"unless the stories he told me, about you guys . . . in Iraq . . . in Afghanistan . . . weren't true. Were they, Bill?"

Brave, thought Christie as she took another deep breath, the musty air in this room now feeling even more close, more stifling.

"They were. And some you probably never heard."

Christie caught Helen's drift.

He owes Hank, and therefore . . . Helen.

But what about us? Strangers?

Then:

"Can I have a word with you alone . . ." Another small smile . . . "Colonel?"

He nodded, and the man with the gun led Christie and the kids to the hallway outside.

Simon sat down on the rug, a swirling carpet of curlicues and pear shapes, a dark rug that made the unlit hallway even bleaker.

"Mom," Kate said, "maybe we shouldn't stay here."

Christie looked at her.

They had followed Helen up here, looking for a place to be safe, even for just a while. Now, unwelcomed, this mountaintop castle didn't feel like any kind of safe place.

"Maybe—" Christie said "—you're right. I just don't know what else to do."

Simon, on the carpet, had begun tracing the outlines of the swirling dark shapes on the rug.

"I like it here. It's big."

Christie nodded at Simon, who hadn't looked up. Kate rolled her eyes.

Good, she thought. *A bit of my normal Kate.*

That's what I want back.

The Kate who complained, who bickered with her brother.

Sweet . . . normalcy.

"I'm not sure if we have much say in the matter. The 'Colonel' may not let us stay. But where do we go then? He seems to know what's been going on in the world. I think we need to know more—before we go anywhere."

Then she looked right at Kate. Not a demand but a genuine question.

"At least for a little while?"

Kate took a long moment to respond.

Then:

"Okay."

That was all. An agreement, again reminding Christie that they were now a team.

"Still, he might not—"

The door opened.

"You can come in," Helen said, her eyes on Christie, wide but revealing nothing.

25

The Rules

The Colonel had gone back to the seat behind his desk.

"Helen has explained your situation."

He looked at Christie, then down to her kids, his face set.

"Been through a lot?"

Christie nodded.

The question . . . almost stupid.

"And you kids—you've been helping your mother?"

Kate looked up at him, then a nod from her.

"So, I decided you can stay."

"Thank you," Christie said, not knowing what else to say.

Not even sure she wanted *to stay.*

"But before you agree, best I explain the rules here."

She looked at Helen. Had the woman kept something from her? How this place works, or was this going to be all new for her as well?

"You give us your weapons."

Christie shook her head.

No way in hell that was going to happen.

"Now hang on. You get to keep one each, and ammo. For your own protection. So you and your daughter can—"

"I can shoot," Simon said.

The Colonel stopped. He looked right at Simon, then up to Christie, as in—

What do you think about this?

And as if it needed repeating, Simon said it again:

"I can shoot. I need a gun, too."

"Really?" The Colonel grinned at the man standing beside him.

Was he going to embarrass Simon? Make fun of what the boy had just said?

"He can. He gets a gun," Christie said quickly.

The Colonel arched his eyebrows.

"Okay. But your responsibility. It's kept safe and away. Understood?"

"Yes."

"Then, here's how we work here. Thirty-eight souls, everyone with their jobs to do. You folks make forty-two. There will be things for all of you to do, to keep this place running, keep it safe, everyone protected and fed. Agreed?"

Again: "Yes."

"This isn't like the outside. We don't know how long we'll have to stay here. Is this 'home' or is it just a temporary place while we wait for the government—"

A shake of his head.

At the apparent ludicrousness of the idea.

"—the damn government to figure out what the hell is happening. How to stop it. Until then, this inn may be all we have."

He took a breath.

"You understand that?"

Christie looked at her kids. She wanted them to know that whatever they did, whatever they decided, they did together.

"We do."

"One other thing. And this one you're not going to like."

Now alert—Christie looked over to Helen. Her expression showed that what was coming was probably not going to be good.

"You have to give us your car keys."

And at that moment, Christie's heart sank.

Because they might as well just walk out of this cloistered office.

Giving up their keys?

That—wasn't going to happen.

The Colonel must have noticed the look in her eyes.

"Now wait. We take the keys for security."

"I've been in a place . . . we were in a place where it was all about security. Until it wasn't."

"Let me explain."

Christie took another deep breath as she let him go on.

"We take the keys since we can't have people deciding they're leaving here anytime they want, leaving us all exposed, gates coming up and down, maybe cars getting hijacked by outsiders. We have young people here like your daughter there. We especially don't want them to get the idea they can just go out."

It made sense.

Still—to give up the only thing that gave them freedom?

That didn't.

"When you decide to leave, when you *plan* on leaving, you get the keys back. You get half the gas you came with. All of that, no questions asked. Your decision. But it's something discussed, planned . . . understand?"

Should she say, "Yes, sir"?

Simon was wrong. This wasn't a castle.

It was a military installation.

She looked over to Helen for her next words.

"I don't know. Maybe this isn't—"

And Helen spoke up.

"Where would you go, Christie?" Helen said. "And this is their place, their rules. They do make some sense."

"Some?" the Colonel added.

"And what's out there? If you leave?" Helen said.

"And you are perfectly welcome to leave right now, guns, gas, and car keys intact," the Colonel said. "Helen worked hard to convince me to give you a chance. You don't want that chance? Fine. Then that's your decision. Free country. Or used to be. Here—it still is."

She looked back to Kate. A decision was required.

"I don't know," she said with Kate's eyes on her.

They still trust me to make decisions.

My job.

Back to the Colonel.

"How about we try it?"

"Sure. We'd be trying you out as well. If life here at Mountain Falls, our 'Redoubt,' isn't for you, or you don't fit in, then we part ways. Just like I said."

Christie tried to analyze the situation, to really think through the options, now with everyone's eyes on her.

Options?

Did she even have any options?

Get back on the road? And drive where?

Find someplace and wait until normalcy returned?

And when would that be?

Never?

And there was this:

She was so tired. Exhausted. Emotionally shattered, and she hadn't even begun to let all that had happened sink in.

To walk with her kids, and talk to them. About what had happened. About their dad. To help them grieve.

To help them get better.

Options?

As far as she could see, she had absolutely zero options.

"Okay. I—we—agree to all the rules."

The next, hard to say. "And thanks, Colonel, for letting us join you."

"You can thank me after you've been here for a while. When you see if you can really live here, 'kay?"

She nodded.

"Whew—" Helen said with a clap of her hands. "Glad that's settled. So now—"

The Colonel gestured to the man with the gun.

"Sam here can show you folks around a bit. Show you the place, where you can stay. Get your guns from you."

He cleared his throat.

"You can leave the car keys right here."

Christie dug into her jeans and pulled out the key ring with the metal *B.*

The initial for the Blairs.

Not even my car, she thought.

No.

Our car had exploded hundreds of miles away from here, destroying my life.

So maybe it was no big deal to pass these keys to the king of this castle.

The Colonel's right hand closed over the key ring.

Sam, swinging his gun behind him, stepped forward, smiling.

"Ready for the tour?"

Christie took her kids' hands. Helen stepped beside them.

And Sam led the way out into the mammoth inn.

26

Under the Inn

Sam led the four of them down the hallway, back down the stairs to the giant lobby.

He stopped at the bottom, turned, and looked at the four of them.

"Okay, there's a lot to tell you, but I'm guessing you people are really beat."

"That's putting it mildly," Helen said.

"So I'll get you to your rooms ASAP, and you can just sleep for today."

Why, Christie thought? *Does everything change tomorrow?*

She reminded herself that they were going to try staying here, if only for a while.

"But a few quick things to show you before we do that. The front doors here are locked after dinner. No one goes out without permission."

"Who do we get permission from?" Kate said.

She looked at her daughter. At fourteen, only maybe five . . . four years younger than the man giving them a lecture.

But did any of that matter anymore?

What *did* matter in this world?

What values, what beliefs, what hopes, what dreams?

"If the Colonel isn't in his office, someone else will be. And that person is the person in charge. There's always somebody there. To deal with things. During the day, you can go out—just tell the guards at the door where you're going."

"Can we climb outside?" Simon said.

Christie looked at her son.

Already . . . he's thinking of this as his new home.

"As long as you stay within sight of the house and a guard can see you. All the roads and trails that lead up here are guarded. The cliff on the other side of the lake is off-limits. Stay within the grounds and you're safe. Better than fences."

It worried Christie when she heard such confidence.

That kind of confidence just didn't make sense anymore.

Nobody had the right to be confident of anything.

"Now, down there—"

Sam turned and walked away from the massive entryway and staircase. The giant lobby narrowed to a dark hallway.

"This leads—" Sam said over his shoulder "—to the dining halls. We only use the smaller one. Plenty enough room for us. This inn could hold three big events at the same time. Weddings, whatever. Here you go."

He stopped and pushed open one of the double swinging doors.

He held it open, but didn't lead the way in.

Christie saw people at long tables, some carrying stacks of plates, others setting up what looked like a warming station.

"The food is simple. You serve yourself back there, carry your plates over to those other tables. Scrape, then put your plate in the plastic bins. You women will probably start out working here cleaning and in the kitchen."

He moved away and let the door shut behind him.

"The Colonel will assign you jobs. Usually everyone does a few things. Maybe work in the school—"

"There's a school?" Simon said.

"He sounds excited," Helen said quietly to Christie.

And he did, Christie knew, because a school meant other kids.

"We have about ten kids, all ages . . . from I guess"—he looked at Kate—"your age, down to some real little ones. Few hours a day, they do schoolwork."

Sam grinned. "Keeps them out of our hair."

"What's all the way down there?" Christie said.

She pointed down what looked like an endless hallway.

"Other ballrooms, dining rooms, then there are more offices, storage rooms. They're all closed up. And at the end, a locked door closes this main building off from the other buildings. When it starts getting cold, we'll just heat this main building, and even then only the first two floors."

He paused.

"And up here . . . it's going to get chilly."

He walked them back to the lobby, and they passed a large stairway that led down.

"And down there?" Helen asked.

"That leads to storerooms where we keep the food, the extra weapons, all locked up. And there's also a giant underground garage, more like a cave. Carved right out of the rock. Your car will be brought down there later, and the gas. I'll do that once you get your stuff."

He nodded.

"Down there is also, er, off-limits."

He stood there for a second as if it was important for that to sink in.

"So—let's see what rooms we have for you."

He headed to the big staircase.

The bedroom smelled even more musty than the Colonel's windowless office.

Dark-brown curtains covered the windows, and as soon as Sam led them in, he went over to the windows and pushed open the drapes.

Golden afternoon sunlight shot into the room, illuminating the floating dust in the room.

"Guess—" he said, "—it's been a while since anyone used this room. But it's got two beds, queen for you, a twin for your daughter. But the boy—"

He looked at Simon. Then he walked closer to him.

"Got a question for you—"

"Simon," Christie said, as if revealing a secret being held back.

"Yeah, so Simon—do you want to sleep on your own? Got a small room. Tiny. Big enough for you. Or I could put you with some other kids. Two older kids."

Christie wondered if she should answer for Simon. Maybe they could get a cot. Maybe he could stay right here.

She also guessed that he might not like the sound of the other kids, older kids.

She didn't have a clue how he'd answer.

"I think . . ." he said slowly . . . "I'll take the small room." Then quickly: "Is it nearby?"

"Sure is; two doors away."

"Okay." Simon nodded, the deal sealed.

Sam turned to Helen, these moments almost like checking into some kind of absurd hotel.

"And you, ma'am—"

"Ma' am? Did you grow up on a farm, John Boy?"

Sam looked confused.

"Why, yes I did."

"A place where they still say *ma'am*. Amazing."

"There's another room. But farther away. You can be on your own. Plenty of rooms in this old place—unless—"

"No. That'll be fine. As long as it has a bed. Which I think we could all use now."

"Right. I'll get some of the guys to help bring up your stuff. You can settle in. Dinner at six."

A communal dinner, Christie thought. *Just like Paterville.*

And again: *is this right?*

"Thanks," Christie said. "For the tour, the rooms."

Sam nodded, and he went away to empty the car that would then disappear in the basement labyrinth.

And then—

They were alone.

Christie, Kate, Simon.

In the big room, the curtains still open, the sunlight now making the sheen of dust everywhere look more like a hoar frost.

Helen had left, off to her room down the hall, with plans to see them at dinner.

I should have thanked her, Christie thought.

But maybe she should reserve those thanks until she saw how this all worked out.

The kids sat on either side of her on the too-soft bed.

She asked the question that she guessed they had been waiting for.

"So guys—what do you think?"

She looked at Kate, then to Simon.

No one answered quickly.

"It's strange," Kate said.

"And big."

"That's for sure," Christie said.

She had put the three guns that they were allowed, the boxes of ammo, in the bottom drawer of an old dresser with claw feet.

Her two kids knew where they were.

And where—with luck—they would stay.

"I think," Kate said, "it might be okay. Like Dad used to say—"

A spear hit into each of them.

A spear that Christie knew couldn't be avoided, that only time would make it less swift, less horribly painful.

"What's that, Kate?"

"One day at a time."

"Right. He liked that one. Good . . . for when things are bad. Or—"

a look at Simon . . .

Need to keep his spirits up.

"Or when we just don't know what's ahead."

"Right," Kate said.

"So—I need to sleep. And you guys as well, hmm?"

They both nodded, though she imagined Simon would have liked to explore.

"Then we can start to see how much we like this old mountain inn as our new home."

"Home for now," Simon added.

"Yeah. *Home for now.*"

And—for now—they all just lay back on the bed, on top of the heavy covers, the three easily fitting on the queen bed.

And even with the brilliant sun streaming through the windows, they immediately fell asleep.

27

September

That dinner, the first night, set the pattern for all the dinners to come during their first weeks at the inn.

Christie quickly saw that everyone sat in the same groups at their tables, night in and night out.

And it became obvious that she, her kids, and Helen were relegated to a smaller table with a few other women, women who all shared one thing.

They had no men.

Something had happened to their men.

Despite that isolation, sometimes Christie caught some of the men looking over at the table.

Looking at Kate . . . sometimes her. She wasn't sure. Either possibility made her skin crawl.

Her thoughts:

Just try.

The other women at the table were quiet, dour—though Helen, as was her pattern, kept up a steady conversation.

And that at least provided the first true picture of this place, the information on how it ran.

The expectations.

The rules.

The way things really worked around here . . . as one night, one of the quiet women started talking, her sad, hollow eyes revealing a pain, a loss that Christie imagined easily matched her own.

During one of those early dinners, the woman talked about the "night patrols."

She explained what they were, what the men did, and just how important they were to this place.

The hollow-eyed woman, Janna, first said the words.

Between forkfuls of food, pasty stuff, marginally edible, Helen asked . . . "Night patrols? What are they?"

"There's a system here," Janna said, almost furtively, as if she might be revealing a deep dark secret.

"A few men go out and scout places where food might be hidden. Abandoned houses with locked storage fridges, or stores with overlooked warehouses, and now—when it gets near harvest time, what used to be harvest—to check fields where things might still be growing."

"Makes sense," Helen said.

But Christie thought . . . *something strange about it.*

Kate looked bored with the conversation.

"Why at night? Isn't that more dangerous?"

Again, more darted looks, more eyes scanning the room.

"It's the way the Colonel wants it. Says there's less chance of being seen at night. Being found."

"Sounds dangerous to me," Christie said.

Helen arched her eyebrows, perhaps surprised that Christie would be so bold as to offer an opinion.

Occasionally, a burst of male laughter exploded from a nearby table.

There was no laughing at Christie's table. Not yet.

Maybe—she sometimes thought—not ever.

"So they go out, find food—?"

"Gas, too. Weapons. They find a lot," Janna said, sounding like a faithful supporter of night patrols.

Kate's wandering eyes had returned to the table, probably—Christie thought—taking in the rest of the room. The laughs, the few other young people near her age—

And Kate asked a question.

By now, the other women, all with the same expression, part fear, part some kind of emptiness, had tuned into the conversation.

"Do they all make it back?"

"What do you mean?" Janna said as if the question itself wasn't clear enough.

"Does everyone come back from these 'night patrols'?"

Kate looked at Christie, then Helen, checking that there wasn't something completely off with her question.

Christie wanted to reach out and cover Kate's hand.

A signal. Steady. *Let it go.*

Or perhaps simply . . . *not now.*

The other women sequestered at their table looked at each other.

Christie thought of a play she taught in high school. Before Jack, the house, the kids, the world ending . . .

Macbeth.

And the three weird sisters.

Witches, or simply crazy women prophesizing Macbeth's doom due to his own actions.

This group would be perfect casting, she thought.

Janna—who had somehow become the spokesperson for the others—finally answered.

"Most nights they do. Sometimes they even bring new people. Not too many lately. So yes—most nights—" a look at her other sisters— "they're fine."

Most nights.

And the others? Christie thought.

She should take her own advice.

Let it go. Enough. There would be other times, other dinners for questions.

To learn. How things really work here.

But as the evenings trudged along in their sameness, there weren't many more questions, and certainly not many more answers.

Some nights, the Colonel walked around the room.

And Christie couldn't help but think about Ed Lowe at Paterville. The camp director. Presiding over each family dinner like a king, maybe secretly eyeing the people they would single out to be taken away, to be butchered, to become part of those oh-so-tasty Paterville Camp meals—

She stopped herself.

That was *then*, she'd reminded herself on more than one night.

This is now.

The Colonel, though, would stop at a table.

Sometimes joining in the barrel-chested laughing of the men. Or crouching down to talk to one of their wives. Lord of the manor. Like Ed Lowe, king of this realm.

Some nights, he made announcements.

Reminding people . . .

"The hallways, now you all *know* this, are to be clear one hour after dinner. If you are out and about, you better have a reason. Want you all secure, hear?"

Or:

"Those of you looking to rotate into other jobs, hang in there. Working on a new duty roster. Gonna be . . . real soon."

Sometimes people applauded.

Some laughed.

Smiled.

No one—Christie saw—did anything that could look like a challenge to the Colonel's authority.

People mostly applauded when the Colonel made some men stand up, and announce what they'd found the night before. The food. The supplies captured. Soldiers who went behind enemy lines, and brought back things to keep this castle, this fort running.

Big cheers. Whistles.

And—Christie noted—no tears. No table with people crying because someone didn't come back.

She thought . . . maybe this works. Maybe me, the kids, just have to *deal*.

Though it was Kate, after the first days and evenings, all melting into each other, who first said the words that Christie was thinking.

"Mom," she said as they left after one dinner.

The Colonel had been in expansive form that night, leading the cheering for a successful night patrol, as he clapped loudly for the men, scanning the room to see that everyone else was also applauding wildly.

Christie had felt that there was no other option.

She clapped for the brave men who went out into the night to hunt for food.

To get the inn all ready for—as the Colonel reminded everyone regularly—winter!

Kate walked beside her mother. Both had done the morning slog in the kitchen and dining room, so now they were free of any duties.

To walk the halls.

When you didn't work, there wasn't much else to do.

"I don't like it here," she said.

Christie nodded—but didn't pick up the conversation until they had moved away from the others, and she felt that they could talk—quietly—about what Kate had just said.

And despite the fact that Christie felt exactly the same way, she asked the question.

"Why is that, Kate?"

Kate looked right in her eyes, as if not believing her mother could ask such a naïve question.

They were two weeks into their life here. This chilly home.

Kate eventually answered.

"All the rules. Don't they drive you crazy? You go *here*, do *this*, follow the Colonel's—"

"Kate," Christie said, hearing her daughter's voice rise.

"Right. And the guys. They keep looking at me." She took a breath.

Christie thinking . . . *my beautiful girl. My sweet and wonderful girl.*

"I don't like how they look at me."

The meaning of that left unsaid between them.

Because, despite all the rules, Christie wondered if in the world of this castlelike building, this community of night patrols, and duty rosters, and laughing men, and hungry eyes, could there be new rules?

Christie felt icy.

Was she overreacting?

Options, she thought.

What options do we have?

On cue, three men walked by, voices loud. As they walked past Christie and her daughter, she picked up bits of their conversation.

"Schuylerville. That place . . . still cherry, I tell you."

"And those fields? They can't all be bad. Bet there's some corn there."

Night patrollers getting ready. Two middle-aged guys trying to keep up with the bravado of a younger man walking with them.

Their guns slung over their shoulders.

Christie waited until they were well away.

"Listen, Kate. I'm not happy here. The stuff that bothers you . . . that worries you . . . worries me, too."

Simon, who had made friends with some of the other boys from another table, finally caught up to them.

"Mom, is it okay if I stay with the other kids for a while?"

"Watch the clock," Christie said. "Don't want one of . . . the guards . . . bringing you back."

Simon smiled.

He at least still seemed to enjoy exploring the halls, corridors, rooms, and hidden areas of the inn.

Two boys had befriended Simon, one boy twelve, another looking closer to nine.

It was a relief that Simon seemed, for now, okay.

Then:

"Kate, I don't like it. But I said we'd try it for a while."

"We have, Mom. We have."

Christie nodded.

Then she grabbed her daughter's hand, and gave it a squeeze.

She had to tell her something important.

Something—she hoped—that might buy her some time.

To think, to plan.

"Kate, I'm still—it's still hard for me." Then, in case her daughter, with those glistening blue eyes locked on her, didn't get it . . . "being alone."

Kate's eyes didn't waver.

But she did squeeze her mother's hand back.

The crisis averted for now.

And as she released her daughter's hand, she saw Helen walking down the hallway, taking in the scene.

Smart woman, Christie thought. *Bet she knows exactly what this is all about.*

And as Kate sailed on, to the staircase, to the rooms above . . .

Christie waited for Helen, who didn't ask about what she'd just seen.

For that, Christie was grateful.

28

September Ends

Those first weeks also brought a clear understanding of how the jobs in this place got done.

More of the Colonel's rules.

His *system*.

Once they found out that Christie had been a teacher, and had also been a neonatal nurse before getting her teaching degree, her duties became clear.

Or at least did to her.

The Colonel had set up a small infirmary, nothing more than a few first aid kits, bandages, nothing too major. Occasionally, night patrols would find prescription drugs and, if anyone knew what they were for, this is where they went.

The closest they had to a doctor was a young woman who had been a few years into her premed.

What would they do if something bad happened? More than a scrape and surface wound?

It wouldn't be pretty.

Christie worked a few hours in the infirmary each day, talking to the young woman, Gina, who seemed to be afraid of what might walk through the door.

And what Christie brought to the table wasn't much. Only what you might need to help a mother or a newborn.

And not much else.

The classroom was an even stranger setup. A dozen kids ranging in age from seven to sixteen, all in the same room like in frontier days.

A retired—and confused—elementary teacher tried to keep them occupied while the group of kids seemed to search for ways to drive her crazy.

That woman, Mrs. Blake, acted even more relieved than the premed student when Christie showed up.

But even with all that, Christie still found herself assigned to kitchen duties, scrubbing pots before they went quickly into giant washing machines designed to handle parties of hundreds.

Quickly—because water had to be conserved.

They also had a system there, overseen by a bullet-shaped woman who clearly relished the idea that she ruled this domain, and anyone assigned to work in it.

They let the dirty dishes, the pans, the utensils—all of it—accumulate.

"Otherwise, you waste the water," the woman said when she showed Christie how to fill the machine. "We only run when we're full. You got that? And not a full cycle! You understand?"

She asked the questions as if there might be something wrong with Christie's mental functioning.

Christie nodded, and soon was scraping plates, giving them the briefest squirting rinse before putting them in one of the inn's giant dishwashers.

Most days, she worked all over the building.

The infirmary. The classroom. The kitchen.

Busy.

And that—was probably a good thing.

And the men?

In this world of the Colonel, the men clearly had different roles.

Those who knew about things like boilers and plumbing and cars had plenty to do making sure everything stayed in good running condition.

These men, old, young, stuck together.

Like they're working on the Manhattan Project, Christie thought.

Scientists who are probing the arcane mysteries this centuries-old inn.

She would catch these men heading down the main staircase that led to the bowels of the building, the forbidden zone of the garage, and supply rooms.

Did the boiler and the cars really need that much maintenance, or did they just go down there to—what?

Hang out? Have a smoke? Maybe a drink.

Yeah.

There was no question that she smelled alcohol wafting from a group of them as they walked into the dining hall.

Guess some of the "night patrols" could bring bounty not meant to be shared with everyone.

And then there were the guards, and those groups of men who went on those patrols. There wasn't a patrol every night, and the Colonel clearly had a roster he followed or maybe favorites he liked to send.

These men *always* carried their guns as if they might have to spring into action at a moment's notice.

Perhaps that was a good thing—though those first weeks had been quiet.

Almost—Christie thought—too quiet.

All the guns, this fortress, the guards.

What was going on in the outside world as this new reality became her and her kids' entire universe?

That—was anybody's guess.

Many nights, the Colonel gave his reports.

How things had gotten worse. Shortwave radio messages about this city gone bad, another one under attack.

Or so said the Colonel.

His message clear: *you folks should be mighty grateful that you're here.*

But people still had radios, the inn's generators still kept the electricity flowing until curfew time, when they then routed power only to certain strategic spots.

Radios. A few TVs. The TVs picked up nothing.

But now and then, a radio station would come in, usually right after sunset.

And for a few moments you could hear a station, someone, somewhere.

Music escaping from a distant spot in Vermont, or Massachusetts, or Connecticut . . . wherever the signal had amazingly traveled from, also occasionally carried new reports and updates on—

(They had a name for it now . . .)

—*the failure.*

Amidst the sporadic programs, there was a report that sounded like control had been restored to the area near Middleburg.

And Christie wondered where the hell that was. Vermont? Upstate?

Then, on another night, how sections of Albany, the Capital City, had been cordoned off, "the failure" still complete there.

And people should always—please—check the status of a region before leaving to go somewhere.

The failure, it seemed, had been widespread.

The reports—snippets really—conflicting, ultimately useless.

Once, a station played a statement from a government official, an undersecretary of Homeland Security . . .

One of those reassuring messages that used to be broadcast regularly, even back when they were safe and protected in Staten Island.

How the government had made inroads in controlling the outbreak of Can Heads. And yes, there were signs that the illness—that's what they called it—was abating, even if you might not be seeing signs of it.

And the undersecretary went on, in those seconds of clear radio signal, to say after what had been a global failure of control, of security, of the basic electricity and firepower used to keep people safe, yes, soon things would be getting back to—

(The undersecretary didn't say it. No, that would have been laughable. To say *that* word. *Normal.*)

No.

She said . . . "Getting back to a place where things like food and fuel, as well as all protective services, will *start* being restored."

The hidden message: *hang in there, folks.*

The radio signal faded shortly after that gem.

The group who had gathered stood there, around the radio.

No one saying anything.

So many desperate thoughts of hopelessness filling the room.

After that, Christie thought that the radio, whatever news it carried, was probably perfectly useless.

As useless as the Colonel's pronouncements.

———

Then one day, Helen came by the infirmary while Christie sat there, waiting for a bloody nose or a finger with a gash to walk into the room.

"Hey," she said.

Helen had done a lot of kitchen work, but she had also convinced the Colonel that she—and her riot shotgun—would be good to have on one of the guard rotations outside.

She had laughed, telling Christie about it, when the Colonel agreed. "I'm one of the boys now."

Today she said:

"How you doing?"

"Okay. I'm done here in a few."

Gina, wearing a white jacket and the fear in her eyes, came into the room.

"Hi," she said to Helen quietly.

Then Helen turned back to Christie.

"You free? Bit of a walk?"

Christie nodded. "Sure. Until lunch, I'm good."

"C'mon."

With Helen now pulling some guard duty, they didn't get much of an interrogation when they went out the front door to walk around the outside, near the lake.

Staying, of course, within the approved area of the nearby grounds.

"Leaves starting to change. Wish there were more of them."

Helen pointed to the mountain face across from them, the off-limits cliff rising from the other side of the narrow lake.

"I used to love fall," Christie said. "The colors. Loved it."

"Yeah. Me, too."

They walked along the lake perimeter, leaving the front of the house. Staying on the road that led from the base of the mountain, two guards could see them walking.

They nodded at the guards.

Who nodded back.

"So," Helen said. "Like I said . . . how are you doing?"

"What? You mean here?"

"Yes, that. And . . ."

"Here. This place. It is . . ." Christie smiled . . . "what it is. Can't say I like it."

"Safe at least."

"Guess so. Can't believe *you* like it."

Helen Field acted like a woman who knew her own mind, and had every intention of speaking it.

"It *ain't* paradise. That's for sure. But maybe—for now—it's okay."

Christie sniffed the air. Chilly. The altitude making it cooler, the breeze off the lake so cold.

"Maybe. I guess you're right—okay for now. I don't know."

More steps, and silence.

Then:

"And otherwise?" Helen stopped. "How are *you?*"

When was the last time someone asked that question? And meant it?

Knowing exactly what Helen was driving at.

Thinking: how sweet of her to ask.

Christie turned and looked at her.

"Trying to hold it together. For the kids. Trying not to think too much, remember too much."

"That's the hard part. The remembering."

With that, Christie was reminded that she wasn't the only one standing here who had suffered loss.

And maybe, there was a model in how Helen acted, spoke.

The way she seemed to move on.

Yet, the idea of "moving on" seemed impossible.

Not when you had a whole life planned with someone, even in this world. And then you didn't.

She felt that anger, that hatred, those feelings that fueled what she did back at the house in Staten Island.

Blowing them away.

That's what she had done.

Blown them the fuck away.

"You know," Helen said, interrupting that memory, that sudden surge of feeling, "if you need someone to talk to, anytime, night or day, I'm here. You know that, right? About anything. Even if you want to talk about those memories."

She reached out and put a hand on Christie's shoulder.

"Understand?"

"I do. And thanks."

The hand slipped away, the human touch sealing the offer.

The sunlight vanishing from the area near the lake where they had been walking.

Time to head back.

They walked back to the inn, slowly, Christie enjoying the air, being outside, being alone with Helen.

Away from the fort.

And just before she walked past the guard at the door, she had a thought.

One that tied into the remembering, and moving on, and everything they had been talking about.

Today, she thought, *is the last day of September.*

Tomorrow—October.

Time moves on no matter what. The weather would change, the sun slip farther away.

How long would they need to stay here—*have* to stay here?

How many more months?

No way to even begin to answer that question.

And with that, she followed Helen into the great stone building.

29

The Secret

Simon followed the other two boys down the hallway.

Joe, the older kid, looked over his shoulder.

"Mrs. Blake didn't even see it! She's frickin' blind!"

The other kid, Billy, younger than Simon, laughed. Simon laughed too, though he wasn't sure that he should be laughing at the fact that Joe had stuck a piece of chalk in the old-fashioned eraser that then made a white path on the green board.

Mrs. Blake couldn't figure out what was wrong.

All the kids laughed. Even one of the teenage girls gave Joe a thumbs-up.

Still—Simon's mom sometimes worked in that classroom.

So the laughing thing, pulling tricks, maybe not so funny.

And that was another thing.

That Joe decided what was "funny," what was "awesome," and what wasn't.

After a while, Joe didn't find anything "awesome" in the old building.

They did tricks though. Like sneaking a dead spider in the middle of a pile of plates so that when one of the people serving grabbed the next plate, they'd see the spider.

That *was awesome*, Joe told Simon.

The day they sneaked down to the basement and nobody saw them.

Yeah, that too was pretty awesome.

These were the only two kids near his age, and Simon wanted to hang with them.

After all, if he didn't, what would he do here? When the dumb classes ended?

Only by doing things that they weren't supposed to could they have any real fun.

Simon let Joe lead, but he didn't like the fact that Joe treated him as if he was the same age as Billy.

There was nearly a whole year's difference.

"*You two*," Joe would say, always the leader, and Simon always lumped together with Billy.

Until—

Despite his promise to his mother, he felt he had to tell them.

That . . . *something* that would change things.

Especially today when Joe didn't seem to have any ideas.

He waited until they had turned the corner, at the other end of the long hallway from the dining hall and the pretend classroom.

Locked rooms here, nothing interesting, but it was private.

He saw Joe try a doorknob.

Joe pointed at the door.

"We gotta figure out how to get into these rooms. So we have a place to, y'know, hang out."

"Someplace secret," Billy said, always ready to support a Joe idea.

"Right, Billy boy. Secret. And maybe we'll find some cool stuff inside."

Nothing for a few seconds. Joe moved on to the next door.

Simon had the word he wanted to use.

"Y'know, I have a secret."

"What? That you're a nerd?"

Billy joined Joe in laughing.

This time, Simon didn't laugh.

"No. A *real* secret."

Joe stopped laughing. Kept his smile. Took a step closer to Simon.

"Okay, tell us, Secret Simon."

Simon felt both their eyes on him. Their faces caught some of the light from the entrance, so he could see them easily.

Simon licked his lips.

He should have shut up.

I promised Mom, he thought.

But there was no way out now, not with the two of them standing there.

"I shot one."

Nothing.

Then Joe laughed as he slapped Billy hard, getting him to laugh as well.

Though Billy's laugh didn't seem too real.

"Right. You . . . fucking—"

Even Joe didn't use that word a lot.

And again:

I should have kept my mouth shut.

But it was too late for that.

"—shot one? What a squirrel? A fucking—"

More laughs, another slap to Billy's shoulder.

". . . *bluejay?*"

Eyes still on him. Billy's lips straight but Joe still with a grin.

"No. A Can Head."

And now having said it, Simon could see that the secret was too big.

Because now—Joe took another step closer to him, so that his face was only inches away.

And Simon wished he could be almost anywhere else.

Joe jabbed at Simon's chest with a finger.

"You shot a Can Head?" A few endless moments went by. Then: "No you didn't."

All Simon could do was nod.

"Okay. How? Where?"

Billy nodded and added his question.

"Yeah. How?"

And Simon realized he had to tell them everything, or they would never believe him.

The only two kids he could be friends with, and they might turn on him.

Worse, they might even turn his secret into a joke. Tell the others.

And then—what would his mother think?

So now, he told them everything.

About the house. That night. About his sister teaching him how to hold the gun, how to undo that thing, the—

"Safety," Joe said.

He had shot a gun. Up here, maybe a lot of kids had.

But not at a Can Head.

Never killed one.

"Yes, safety," Simon added.

Then how they kept coming, so many of them, and Simon shot one, missing, then hitting, more shots until finally it fell.

He realized—in the shadows of the hallway—that he was shaking. He guessed that the other boys could see that as well.

Finally, when he was done telling them about that night, he stopped.

"No . . . *shit*," Joe said.

And Simon knew that he believed him.

Simon felt himself stop shaking. He had been breathing hard as he told the story fast, in a quiet voice.

The other kids' faces still catching the light. Billy's eyes—especially—open wide.

"So where's the gun?"

Simon could have told them that too.

That there was a gun for him. His own gun.

And that he knew where it was, how he promised his mom never to say anything about that to anyone else.

And that . . . could perhaps be an even bigger secret.

Instead:

"After that, my mom took it. She must have given it to the Colonel. It's . . . gone."

Joe nodded; it obviously made sense to him.

"Too bad. Man!" The grin again. "You *killed* one. *Really* awesome!"

Simon wanted to go back to the main hallway. Maybe see if they could play one of the board games that Joe always labeled as "dumb." Or borrow one of the other kids' handheld videogames. Didn't have a lot of games, but it was something.

Instead, Simon realized something else.

That his secret. That what he had said.

The truth of it.

That . . . it represented a challenge to Joe.

How could he be the leader?

If Simon had killed a Can Head?

Too big a secret, Simon thought.

Joe smiled.

Then said: "I've got an idea. And, after that story . . ." he lowered his voice . . . "Can Head killer, you're going to *love* it."

Kate felt a tap on her shoulder.

After an hour of stirring pots of a yellow slop that was tonight's dinner, a few real potatoes in it, but mostly giant tins of government-issued "soy product," she wanted to get as far away from the kitchen as possible.

She turned to the person behind her.

One of the young guards.

She had seen him looking at her during meals.

And he didn't look away when she noticed.

"All done in there?"

She nodded.

"Not much fun. All that kitchen stuff."

"How would you know?" Kate said.

After all, the guys with the guns never did any stuff like that. As if carrying a gun made them allergic to cleaning dishes, serving food, or any kind of real work.

"I'm just guessing," he said, his grin returning.

He *is* cute, Kate thought. But older.

"I'm Tom," he said. He stuck out his hand.

Kate shook it. Tom gave it a squeeze and released it.

"I'm—"

"Kate. I know."

Then: "Been watching you. Thinking . . . *she must be bored out of her mind.*"

Now Kate smiled. "Yeah. I am."

"Not much to do here. For fun, I mean."

"I've noticed."

He came closer. "But there are things. Places you haven't seen. If you want to get away."

"What do you mean?"

Tom looked around, making sure that no one could hear them.

"Been downstairs? To see what's underneath this old building?"

"Off-limits, right? The Colonel's orders."

"Not all orders have to be obeyed. I can get you down there. Show you around. Good place to get away."

"Get away? For what?"

As soon as she asked the question, Kate realized how stupid it sounded. Like she was a kid.

I'm not a kid, she thought.

"That'd be cool. Maybe later—"

"Maybe now," Tom said jumping in. "You're done with work. I'm not supposed to be anywhere for a while." He took a breath, grin widening. "Let me give you a tour."

Now Kate looked around.

She hoped that her mother might walk by, and take this possibility away . . . at least, for now.

But they remained alone in the hallway.

"If you don't want to, that's okay. I just thought—"

"Okay."

"Really? Sweet. Just follow me."

Tom turned around, and started back toward the dining rooms, the row of offices, to a part of the inn that Kate thought led nowhere.

But she soon saw that she was wrong about that.

The three boys huddled by a large couch covered with shiny material and legs that ended in animal's paws.

The chair looked as if it had once been alive.

"So listen—what happens when you go outside?" Joe asked Simon.

"The guard tells you where you can go. They watch you."

"Right. And where can you go?"

"Not far. Just in front of the building."

Joe gave Billy a nudge as if there was something funny about Simon's answer.

"And what fun is that? But we"—another nudge to Billy—"have been far away from this place, on our own."

Simon thought of the secret he had told them, and how he shouldn't have told them at all.

And now Joe was talking like he too had done something secret, something awesome.

Maybe—Simon thought—something dangerous.

He leaned close. "We were able to get over to that cliff. There's a path, all crumbly, has an old wood handrail. We climbed it. Nearly to the top. We could see . . ." His hands flew out . . . "all around."

Simon didn't know what to say.

Though he could feel where this was going.

"That was awesome, right Billy?"

The younger boy nodded. Then, as if expecting another elbow to his chest, he added, "Yeah, it was really—" the boy thought for a moment. Then: "—awesome!"

"Yeah."

"You didn't get caught?" Simon asked.

"Caught? No way. I came up with a plan. And it worked. Takes three kids, though. Did it with this other kid. He and his family left. Just before you came. But now—" he slapped Simon on the back— "you're here!"

Simon didn't want to ask any more questions.

He just kept thinking how he wished he hadn't told them about his using a gun, about shooting a Can Head.

Should have just stayed quiet.

"One of us distracts the dopey guard, then two of us can get away, get to the cliff, the trail. Climb it. It's amazing."

Simon looked at Billy, guessing who the two to climb the ledge would be.

"How does it work?"

Simon felt as if he had to ask.

"You in, Simon?"

Billy had his eyes on him too.

Maybe . . . hoping that Simon would say no.

Instead: "Sure."

"Good. I knew you'd be, Can Head killer."

The words stung.

"Now let me explain how we do it. Listen up, 'cause we're going to have to be fast."

30

The Cliff

Simon and Joe waited by an old clock while Billy walked to the front door.

Glass panels on either side would let Billy see out.

"Just got to be . . . patient," Joe said, a whisper.

Then he saw Billy turn and give them a wave.

"There you go!"

Joe had explained that the guard would sneak to the side of the building where no one could see him and have a quick cigarette. Every twenty . . . thirty minutes.

Just had to wait.

And when he did, the main door would be unguarded.

They watched Billy stand by the door, looking out one of the glass panels.

Then Billy went out, pulling on the great door, the wooden door a giant compared to the small kid.

"Okay—wait," Joe whispered. Then: "Okay—*now.*"

Joe hurried to the door.

Kate came to the end of the corridor, following Tom to where two sliding doors sealed off the hallway from the rest of the inn.

They've got to be locked, Kate thought. *This can't lead anywhere.*

Tom hurried to where a latch kept the doors locked together.

Kate watched him pull a piece of metal out of his pocket. He stuck it in the keyhole of one of the sliding doors.

A click.

He turned back and grinned at Kate.

"Easy, huh? Just need a little know-how."

He slid the door open.

"Now, *quick.* Don't want anyone to see."

Kate hesitated.

Yes, she was bored. But going somewhere that they weren't sup-posed to?

Actually . . . breaking in?

"Come *on.*"

Tom looked as if he was about to slide the door again, the adven-ture over.

She made a quick decision and slipped in, just as quickly followed by the boy.

Suddenly, Kate stood in darkness.

"No electricity here. So it's kinda dark. Got some light from the windows down farther."

The air here tasted even more stale than that in the main building.

For a moment, Kate turned back to the door that Tom had slid shut behind them.

"Going to lock it?"

"The door? No. No one checks it. I'll make sure it's locked when we come back."

His face in the shadows, backlit by the windows at the far end.

"Okay. All set? Follow me."

And he led her deeper into that darkness.

"Now!" Joe said, pulling open the front door to the inn.

Joe ran out first, and Simon raced to follow him. The older boy fast, easily outpacing him.

Simon looked over his shoulder.

The guard hadn't come back to his position at the front door. Still smoking a cigarette, and now with Billy talking to him, making sure he looked the other way . . .

The plan was working.

And when Simon looked ahead, he saw Joe run to the side of a path, going even faster, heading through woods to the sheer ledge that rose above the inn and the lake.

In minutes, they were out of sight of the building.

Safe, Simon thought. No one can see them here.

It was like . . . an escape.

And now, it was *fun*.

Joe slowed his run a bit, letting Simon catch up.

And as soon as Simon caught up to the older kid, Joe slowed to a walk.

He turned to Simon and put a palm up.

High five.

Simon had never "high fived" anyone.

He put his palm up and Joe slapped it, with a bit of a sting.

"Wasn't that sweet?"

"Yeah," Simon said.

"So easy to get past that guy. Sneaking his smokes. Jerk!"

They kept walking, and Simon looked ahead, to see that the sheer wall of the cliff was only feet away.

He had a thought: *that was fun. But maybe they should head back.*

He wanted to say that.

But what would Joe think?

A few more feet and the other boy stopped.

"There it is."

Simon saw a stone trail—a ledge that led up the cliff, cut right into the stone.

In front of the trail, pieces of wood thrown across it, blocking it. A sign.

Just a few words.

"Danger. Trail Closed."

Black swirling letters as if they had been done fast.

Joe stepped over the pieces of the wood.

"Coming?"

Now Simon had to say something.

"It says *closed*. Maybe it's not safe."

"I've been on the trail, *dummy*."

Simon didn't like it when Joe called him that name.

Dummy.

"Sure, it's closed. No one's supposed to even be over here. But here we are. So let's get climbing."

Simon came closer to the wood pieces, the dangling metal sign. The words of warning.

He put his hands on one of the wood pieces blocking the path, and raising one leg, climbed over to the other side.

Another door, and even darker.

"Wait. I can't even see," Kate said.

"Right. I know. Dark as hell, right? But there's a handrail, and then we're in the basement of this old place. Wait till you see it. Like tunnels and caves. But there's light down there."

As if it would force her to move, Tom vanished down the stairway.

"I'm down here," he said.

She heard steps. His voice again, a bit more distant.

"Hey! Come on."

Kate went through the door, found the handrail, and followed the boy down.

Part of the way up, Simon stopped and looked around.

He could see the mountains that surrounded the inn and this mountain, some looking much higher.

But he could actually look down at the inn, still looking so big, still looking like a castle.

But he *was above it.*

"What did I tell you? You can see everything!"

"But can they see us?"

"Duh. If they looked. But I don't think they ever look up here. It's closed, right?"

Joe grinned. He had everything planned out. He had an answer for everything.

Simon supposed that should make him feel good.

But somehow, it didn't.

Joe started up again.

Down the dark staircase, and Kate couldn't even see her hand on the handrail, feeling her way with one foot, then the other, as she navigated the stairs.

"Almost there," the voice from the bottom said.

And then a bit of light as she came to a landing, the darkest place as the stairs turned in the other direction.

But she saw light at the bottom, a hint of an outline of the bottom steps.

She kept on going.

Midway up the stone trail, Simon saw broken rock covering the flat surface of the trail. Big pieces, smaller pieces. Rubble that had broken away from the cliff wall, he guessed.

Slippery to walk on.

He had to look down to be careful of his step.

Joe had slowed as well, also having trouble making his way up.

Then Simon took a step, and his foot gave way. A flat part that looked like it was part of the trail . . . actually a loose stone.

Like it was hiding.

His foot slipped, and then he felt himself tumble forward. His hands went out in front to break his fall.

And as he landed, a stone dug into the palm of his hand.

"Owww," he said.

He slipped a few feet, then, as he fell on his knees, his sneakers dug into the rubble, and he stopped.

"What happened?" Joe said.

"I . . . slipped."

Simon raised his left hand to his face. The stone had broken the skin and his palm was bloody. He wiped it on his pants.

He looked again. The hand still oozed blood. And it stung.

"You're bleeding?"

Simon held up his hand to show the other kid.

"That's nothing. Lick it."

Instead, Simon gave it another wipe on his pants, and this time, though the skin was broken, red, it didn't seem to bleed as much.

It wasn't bad.

"Okay—we're almost there."

"Where's *there?*"

Simon had been keeping his head down, watching his steps on the trail.

He hadn't looked up . . .

To see something he hadn't noticed before.

Something like a little house at the top. With a pointy roof, and tree trunks for timbers.

"*There.* Up there, you can see *everything!*"

Simon felt as if he had already seen plenty. Having fallen, and cut his hand, he just wanted to go back down.

Sneak back into the house.

End this.

Yeah, he thought, *that's what I want to do.*

End this.

But Joe put out a hand to help Simon up. Simon took the hand and struggled to his feet.

He felt where his knees had banged against the stone.

Joe seemed to sense what Simon was thinking.

"We're almost there. A quick look. And down we go."

And Simon nodded.

Kate left the dark stairs and came out into what looked like a stone tunnel.

"It's cool, right? All this stone. They carved these tunnels and rooms out of the mountain!"

"It's chilly," Kate said.

A light bulb protected by a metal cage glowed from the top of the tunnel.

"Let me show you where this leads. Got to be really quiet though. Sometimes the guys like to hang out down here. Away from the Colonel."

He leaned close to Kate.

"Close to the cars and the guns."

Tom took her hand.

She wanted to wriggle free, but he used it to lead her forward as the tunnel curved one way, then the other, and then one more curve, and Tom stopped.

Now she wriggled her fingers and freed her hand.

"See. Look!"

And ahead, the mazelike tunnel opened to a giant cave, filled with cars.

"All the cars are kept here." Tom pointed to the far end of the cave. "Over there, they store the gas, anything people brought with them."

"Oh, yeah." He raised his arm again, pointing again. "And the car keys are in the box, all locked up. Only a few guys have the key to the lock. Same for that room over in the corner with the guns and bullets."

Only then did Kate notice that the boy's arm had stayed up, that he had turned, and then *planted* that arm on the wall of the tunnel.

Right over Kate's shoulder.

He had turned to her.

"But here. This tunnel. It's like a secret place. Away from everyone."

He came closer.

And Kate had the thought.

He's going to try and kiss me.

That, and . . .

His arm is keeping me from moving back into the tunnel, back to the dark staircase, up, and away from here, away from him.

He moved closer.

"We could come here. Anytime we want."

Kate realized the feeling she had.

Trapped. This boy planned this. To get me alone.

Then, as if confirming it, his other arm came up, another hand planted, one hand on either side of her.

"Anytime . . ."

31

Fear

Christie walked out of the bedroom.

Where are they? she thought.

She had expected Kate to be in the room. Maybe reading. Simon . . . usually playing with the other kids, and Christie hoping that they didn't do anything they shouldn't.

That older kid . . . worried her.

Kids got into things.

She saw Helen walking down the hallway to her room, and ran up to her.

"Helen, have you seen my kids?"

She shook her head. "No. Simon's usually with those other boys, isn't he?"

Christie looked up and down the hallway, people milling about, just standing around, waiting for dinner—always the day's big event, this place sometimes more like a prison than a refuge.

She looked up at the top of the main stairs. The Colonel walking down, talking to a group of men, nodding.

He looked up and saw her, and since she didn't know what else to do, she stayed there, waiting.

Until he got to the bottom of the stairs.

"Something wrong, Christie?"

"My kids. Have you—" she scanned the eyes of the other men— "seen them? I don't know—"

"They know the rules, right? Where to go, where not to go?"

Christie nodded.

Then: "You should keep a better eye on them."

The Colonel nodded, and started down the hallway.

Christie turned to Helen.

"I'm scared about this," Christie said.

"Come on," Helen said. "I'll help you look."

Tom nodded as he spoke to Kate.

"You know, we could come down here anytime," he said. "No one would know."

His arms still pinned to the stone wall, now each closing like a trap on both sides of her.

Until he had her head locked between them.

"Anytime . . . for anything . . ."

He started to lean into her, his body pressing close, right into hers.

Which is when she brought her left arm up as hard and fast as she could.

A move her dad had taught her.

"If you are ever cornered, Kate . . . by anyone. Do it fast, do it hard."

The boy, a guard, more of a man, with his strong arms holding her head fast.

Would her arm do anything?

But when her forearm smashed up against his elbow, Tom's right arm slid off the wall, and in that moment, Kate started running.

She thought . . . *did she know the way back to the dark stairs, back up to the hallway, to the inn?*

Running full out as she heard Tom's voice behind her.

"Hey, where are you going? No need to . . ." and he raised his voice on this ". . . run away scared."

Then she heard his laughs.

Her feet made a slapping noise as she ran, an echo off the stone.

I go left here, she thought.

Then straight.

Would Tom chase her, try again to trap her?

He was going to kiss her, Kate thought.

She knew that.

And there was no thrill at that thought.

Would that be all?

Just fear. And now, a desperation to get out of this maze.

Until, another turn and she saw the dark hole of the stairs leading up to the shuttered section of the inn.

She ran in, locking her hand on the rail, and took the stairs as fast as she could.

More rubble, more crumbly rock, every step sending pieces flying down the trail, the angle more steep.

The wooden house, nothing more than a pointy roof like an elf's hat and some logs, lay ahead.

But Simon wanted to turn around.

Head down.

Had to be dinnertime soon.

The air turned cool, the stone cliff that he'd touched trying to find something to hold, now cold.

Joe had gone quiet too, and Simon wondered whether he had been telling the truth.

Had he *really* been all the way up here before?

Because it didn't look like anyone had been up here. Not in a long time, not with all this loose rock.

Another step, and a piece went flying, this time over the side of the stone path, falling off the cliff.

The wooden railing also seemed more wobbly here as Simon grabbed it, the path now too narrow to stay well away from the edge.

We should stop, he thought.

Go down now.

"Joe," he said without turning around to the boy behind him.

When he didn't answer, Simon said it again. "Joe—I think . . . this isn't safe. All this rock."

"Almost there," Joe said. But his voice didn't sound the same.

The voice higher, and shaky. Maybe the chill. Or maybe Joe was a little scared too.

And Simon knew that for Joe, it was important to do this.

Because of what I said I did.

That was it. He had to do something big. Something dangerous.

"Joe, I think—I think I'm going back down. I—"

Another step.

A flat piece of rock. His sneaker on it squarely, carefully. One hand on the wall, another on the shaky log rail.

It would be so easy to pull that rail down, to have no protection from falling off the trail, the cliff.

But this piece of rock, loose like so many others, was exactly the size of his foot, his sneaker floating on the rock as it so quickly began to slide backward.

One hand touching the cliff face, but his other hand, not trusting the rail, had slipped away.

And Simon started to slip, sliding down, falling backward.

"Joe!"

He said the name again, louder this time, yelling, not caring if his voice carried all the way down to the inn, to the guard who hadn't seen them come up here.

Knees onto stone, hands forward, his hurt left hand stinging with the slap, sliding down until he saw that he was moving at an angle that would send him . . . off the trail.

He begged, he pleaded for the fall to somehow stop, but the rocks on the trail all seemed to want to keep rolling on down . . . and off the stone path.

Kate burst out into the musty dark hallway, out of the pitch-black stairwell. Still she kept running, to get out of this place.

Back to where there were people.

Thinking how stupid that was of her. To do that, go down there.

So . . . stupid.

She came to the sliding doors that sealed off this unused end of the inn. *What if it was locked?* she thought. Tom lying about that, and now racing after her.

Another trap, she thought.

Her fingers dug into the sliding latch and turned it.

It gave way, and she slid the door open, and then kept on running.

She didn't bother shutting it behind her.

She just wanted to get to where there were others, to lose the feeling of being down there . . . at first exciting, then—with those arms trapping her—so scary, giving her a sick feeling in her stomach.

Kate ran full out, past offices, the classroom, now dark and closed, the dining hall, and people standing outside.

Slowing her pace as she sucked in gulps of air.

Realizing what she must look like.

Rushing. So scared.

Face flush. Eyes wide. Gasping, her walk more like staggering.

Until she stopped—

Facing her mother.

Her mother looking left, right, all around, until her eyes landed on Kate.

And Kate knew, in that glance, that look, that her mother *knew* something had happened.

And she kept walking to her, her mother's lips tight.

Her face worried.

Kate went to her, and without even thinking, hugged her mom close as Christie did the same thing, hugging her tight.

Then—one leg went off the trail, over the edge.

Fingers digging at the loose rubble.

The other leg, turning, kicking, Simon's foot trying to dig into the stone, trying to stop his slide.

And then quick kicks, not slowing at all.

And one leg now—

(No.)

—over the edge, and Simon trying to get his leg to dig into something, so he could kick up, to stop his slide—

(Please. Please . . .)

—and it did.

His foot digging into a crack, a space in the cliff wall just below the trail. A crack, an opening that his foot slipped into.

Then—his foot . . . jammed into the crack by his weight and the fall.

His fingers still digging at the loose stone.

Except now—he stopped.

He stopped.

For a moment, he didn't move at all.

32

Seeing Them

Christie held her daughter tight, and for a few moments, didn't move.

Then, quietly, as she led her away from the people moving into the dining room, she whispered . . .

"Kate. What *happened*?"

Her daughter looked at her, her face set.

"I—" Kate started, then looked away.

And what was that look? Christie thought. Shame? Guilt? Embarrassment?

She immediately guessed at what might be the cause.

"Did one of the guys . . . did someone . . . do something?"

Kate's eyes returned to her mother's face.

Then, the lightest of nods.

And Christie felt her entire body tense.

"Get up, Simon! Get up!"

Simon looked at his leg hanging over the side, feeling where his foot had stopped his slide, and where it was now wedged.

"You gotta get *out* of there!"

Simon nodded. He felt his heart racing. The stone felt so cold. He wanted to get down from here.

But when he yanked his leg up . . . it didn't move.

Didn't move at all.

"Simon, we gotta—"

"It won't move," Simon said. Then: "It's stuck."

He saw Joe look all around, as if there might be someone who could help them. But they were all alone.

"Help me," Simon said.

Joe didn't move.

Did he think that the same thing might happen to him?

"Maybe if you help me pull on my leg . . . it'll come free."

For another few seconds, Joe didn't move, but then he knelt down beside Simon. A few more stones slid, down the trail, away from the two boys.

Joe very carefully reached over to Simon and wrapped one hand on the ankle of Simon's other leg, his forearm leaning on Simon's sneaker.

"Don't do *that*," Simon said.

It felt as if that bit of weight on his foot could send him sliding again.

Joe moved so that he just held the ankle, his elbow resting on the stone.

"I don't know, Simon. I mean, I don't know if I can do anything."

He tugged at Simon's leg.

Once, again, and then:

"What are you doing?"

Joe stood up, so slowly, the stone seeming more like chunks of ice now.

"I'm going to go get help."

Simon nodded. They'd get in trouble. But he needed an adult to help him.

"Okay. Go do that. And hurry."

Joe nodded back. Simon watched him turn and start down the trail. He moved slowly.

Simon wished he'd race down the trail—but he knew that wouldn't be safe.

So he had to lie there, caught, his face flush against the stone trail as Joe took each careful step back down.

Simon felt the wind blowing around him, the sky losing its color, the stone that had tripped him up making him cold, scared . . .

And then as Joe vanished around a bend . . . alone.

"One of them did something?" Christie said, her fear turning to anger. "Which one?"

Kate shook her head.

Their voices were low, but others heading into the dining room could see them, standing there, talking so seriously.

"Does it matter, Mom? Does it?"

"I'll—talk to someone. God, you're fourteen."

Christie looked away.

Then Kate put a hand on her mother. "Nothing really happened. I went somewhere I shouldn't have. I got scared. I was stupid."

It's this place, Kate thought.

This fortress of guns and people sealed away, hiding.

Then, as if suddenly clear, she thought: *this isn't a good place.*

"Okay. We'll talk more later?"

Kate nodded.

"As long as you're okay."

"I am. I'm . . . okay."

She touched Kate's cheek.

Then put a hand on her shoulder.

"Now, I have to find your brother. You haven't—"

But those words died with the sound of voices coming from the entrance to the inn, shouts—and then she heard her name being called.

She let her hand slip from Kate's shoulder, fear again returning.

The voices shouting, excited, alarmed.

She turned and looked in that direction, to the men, standing, talking to a kid.

Simon's friend.

The older kid.

One of the guards leaning down, nodding.

Another watching as Christie walked—and then ran to them.

Simon looked down at the inn, trying to see Joe, but a jagged tree trunk blocked his view of the big door.

Come on, he thought. *Hurry*!

He felt so alone here. The only sound other than his breathing was the wind making some nearby leafless branches shake and scratch the rock.

Nothing else alive up here, he thought.

He closed his eyes for a moment, thinking it would be better.

Just keep them closed until people showed up and got him out of here.

But when he did that, it seemed worse, with only those two sounds and the cold of the stone against his face, his body feeling the jagged pieces of rock that he lay on.

So he opened them.

And looked to the left, out to the far end of the mountain where the inn ended, and the mountain led to the road down.

He blinked.

He had thought that he was all alone.

That he was the only thing alive here while he waited for people to come. To help him.

But now, looking at the sloping ground far from the inn, he saw . . . *movement*.

His eyes stayed locked on the movement he saw.

What is it? he thought.

Then he noticed that there was movement in a *lot* of different places. Shapes moving among those trees that still had green needles, and also among others, the ones that had died long ago and stood there like . . . like . . .

Skeletons.

His eyes now not even looking down at the trail to see if anyone was coming for him because these moving shapes had him staring *so* hard.

People, he thought.

People coming up the mountain.

Maybe people from the inn? Guards?

Is that who he was seeing? Because, yes, they definitely looked like people as the moving things took on a clearer shape.

He saw legs, heads turning.

None of them using the road.

Sneaking up.

All of them sneaking their way up through the tree trunks, the bushes, and the tall pine trees.

Almost hidden.

Secretly, he thought.

Moving so secretly.

In a way, in a place, that no one would see them.

People moving.

Except he knew, looking at them now, after everything he had seen and done.

He *knew*.

These weren't people at all.

33

Surrounded

Christie leaned down to the boy, his name escaping her for a moment.

"What's going on?" she said. "Where's Simon?"

But one of the guards touched her shoulder.

She didn't take her eyes off the boy.

"He's still up on the trail," the guard said. "We're going now."

Christie pulled back from the boy. "Me too."

"Best you stay—"

Christie's response was to head out the door, pushing it open, the men hurrying to follow her.

The cool air hitting her skin. She hadn't noticed how it had started to darken already, the mountain casting a big shadow, the sun nearly down.

She had to stop for a moment once outside.

Where was the mountain trail; how did Simon and those other kids know how to find it?

The guards ran past her, one of them turning to her, accepting the inevitable.

"This way," he said.

Christie ran full out to keep up with them, circling around the side of the lake, heading toward the sheer wall of the cliff, the mountaintop ahead, and the trail where something had happened to her son.

Simon kept looking.

Suddenly, it seemed to him that no one was coming for him.

He had a bad thought.

What if something had happened to Joe?

What if he never got back to the inn?

And now, down there, all these—

(He let himself think the word.)

—*Can Heads* were coming toward the inn, on the ground, all around it.

He started counting them.

One. Two. Three. There . . . a fourth. Over there—a fifth!

Were there others that he couldn't see? More on the other side?

Then: could they see *him*?

And if they *could* see him, would they come up here, seeing him not moving?

Almost as if he was waiting for them.

Again thinking, begging . . .

Hurry.

He gave another yank with his leg.

But again it didn't budge.

Christie followed the men, climbing over the barrier, scrambling to keep up with them.

The trail was closed. All this shifting rock . . . so dangerous.

Yet Simon had come up here.

She felt angry. How could he do that? Then, angry that the guards, all these men supposedly keeping them safe, had somehow let kids come up here, climb up here, away from the inn where anything . . . *anything* could happen.

And even then she knew that underneath all that anger, there was really only one clear and overwhelmingly powerful feeling. *Fear.*

She slipped once on the smooth rock, sidestepping the rubble that seemed to litter that path all the way up.

How far up was he? Would he be okay, and if not, if not—

The thoughts distracting her from paying attention to the tricky climb up the path, but then a misstep suddenly calling her back to attention.

She started to lose her breath.

The thought: *I should have been doing more exercise inside the inn. You never know when you would need to move fast, to run.*

She wouldn't let that happen again.

Need to stay in shape.

All the time.

She opened her mouth wide to force in as much air as possible.

Simon balled up his fists. His fingers so cold.

The Can Heads below had spread out.

He could see them, almost taking their time as they moved this way and that, as if studying the building.

Monsters looking for a way into the castle, he thought.

That's what they're doing.

And though he had been worried that they would see him . . .

That one of those . . . things . . . would scurry up here, and squat down beside him, and, and . . .

Now he was worried for his mom. For Kate.

Just them.

Neither of them knowing that the Can Heads were there, outside, and getting closer.

There was nothing he could do.

No way he could warn them.

All he could do was watch.

Gasping, yards away behind the men, the trail at this speed, this angle . . . punishing.

But then one of the men's voices.

"I see him!"

She pleaded: *let him be okay*.

The hope—the sweet, elusive hope—that he would be okay.

She would make any deal, any promise to anything, anyone, if he would simply be . . . okay.

Christie ran even harder, stumbling as rocks slipped, tugging on the wooden, splintery handrail until she too could see Simon, lying on the path.

She called out: "Simon!"

And in seconds, she was beside him.

One of the men turned to her.

"He got his foot wedged."

Christie couldn't hug him, but she cradled his head.

"You okay, Simon? You all right?"

She expected him to nod and say he was okay. That he slipped. Got his foot caught.

One of the men already leaning over the edge, looking at how his foot had become trapped.

But he didn't nod.

Didn't smile.

And what he said . . .

What he said . . .

"Mom. They're coming. Right down there."

Then louder as Christie became aware that the men were listening, turning, looking . . . "They're down there and nobody can see them."

Now Christie turned and looked down the mountain, and for a second, she saw nothing.

Then—God—they were so clear.

The bodies moving through the woods, close to the inn, picking their way through the brambles and fallen limbs of dead trees, moving steadily.

One of the men, looking as well, spoke. "Shit."

Then another. "We gotta get going. Gotta warn everyone."

The third man, leaning over the edge, tugging at Simon's leg.

"He really got it jammed in here."

"Come *on*," another man said.

Christie took her eyes away from the figures below, pausing to look at Simon.

Gonna be okay.

Then she said to the man working on the trapped foot:

"Is it—"

But the man turned. "I have to undo the laces, work his damn foot out." Then, almost impatiently, as if telling the others not to rush him. "Hang on."

More moments, and everyone's eyes turned to what was going on outside the inn.

One of the men had gone farther up the trail. "I'm gonna fire a shot. Warn them down there."

But the guard beside him said, "Then they'll see us. Know we're here. They could—Christ—cut us off."

But the man raised his gun and let off three blasts, the sounds of the firing echoing off the sheer cliff wall.

"There. Okay," the man said, helping Simon as his foot sprung free of the sneaker and the crack.

The man turned around, and Christie watched him yank at what had to be the sneaker.

She helped Simon up.

"There. *Damn.*"

The man swung back from the edge, and handed the sneaker to Simon.

"Get that on as fast as you can, son."

Christie watched Simon bend down and slide his foot into the sneaker, doing the laces up quickly, her hand on his shoulder.

"We gotta go," the man who had fired the warning shots said.

"Stupid," his friend said. "Firing—*goddamn.*"

Simon stood up.

"Ready," Simon said.

Christie took his hand, and now they trailed the men who, having freed Simon, acted as though Christie and Simon's getting back to the inn, getting back safely, wasn't their problem at all.

So Christie held Simon's hand tight as they went down the trail.

They hit a point where they couldn't really see the woods that surrounded the inn, that mix of dead trees, bushes, and the few stands of pines that somehow grew in this new world.

Christie knew everyone had to be thinking:

We're running down, off this mountain, right into Can Heads.

And she had this added thought . . .

I don't have my gun.

The weeks of quiet had lulled her.

She kept trying to move Simon as fast as he could, holding his hand, taking care that neither of them slipped on the loose rock, the men so far ahead of them.

Almost abandoning them.

Yeah, she thought. *Fear of Can Heads will do that.*

Who wouldn't *want to get away?*

When things were coming . . . things that wanted to eat you.

Nothing more primal than that.

Not a goddamn thing.

Until finally she saw where the trail ended, level ground. The lake ahead, the path curling around to the inn.

Still moving fast, she leaned down to Simon.

"We have to run, Simon. As fast as you can. Okay?"

He had said nothing since pointing out the Can Heads. Now he just answered, "Okay."

And as soon as Christie hit the level ground of the path, with no more rubble, she started to run, though her lungs still hurt from before, pulling Simon behind her.

Not seeing anyone for a minute.

Though one of the men stopped, and looked back at them, impatiently waving at them to hurry.

Guess it wouldn't look so good to go out and rescue someone, and then lose both him and his mother.

She could see the building, massive, but now with those things moving around it.

Like rats, she thought. *Looking for a way in.*

All the so-called safety of this place vanishing.

Maybe they'd become complacent.

What people do.

Get complacent. Make mistakes. Then pay the price.

The man waving at them, waiting, gun lowered.

"Almost there," she said to Simon between gasps of air.

Until, curving around the small lake, she saw the main entrance to the inn.

Men outside, guns ready.

Reminding her of a painting.

The men with guns, waiting for others to get inside.

Guns ready, attackers coming.

Remembered from a museum trip she took with her high school class, centuries ago.

Last Stand at the Alamo.

She risked a look to the right, to where the jumble of trees and dead limbs ran near the road, near the inn.

And she moaned as she saw two of them, running.

So fast—and bolting right for Simon and her.

34

Kick the Can

The guards positioned by the door saw the two Can Heads, and Christie watched them raise their weapons.

But to hit the Can Heads, the men would need to shoot through her and Simon as they ran to the inn.

They held their fire—and Christie didn't look back.

Until they reached the group of men and she heard someone say, "Now!"

And the guns fired behind Christie and Simon, blast after blast, the sound deafening, the shots echoing off the nearby mountain wall.

They kept on running into the building.

Where mayhem prevailed.

The Colonel stood in the lobby pointing, giving his orders to men, each holding a gun, as they raced up to him.

She also saw Helen, her riot shotgun in hand, standing near him, but her eyes fixed on the entrance.

As soon as Helen saw Christie, she came running over.

Her first words to Simon:

"You okay?"

The boy nodded. Christie held him close, though part of her wanted to yell at him, so angry that he had put himself in so much danger.

So foolish.

But that was overshadowed by the tremendous relief she felt.

He was okay. They were okay.

And then her mind came back to what was happening.

"I—I should get my gun," Christie said.

"Hang on. *You* should go back to your room. Get your gun, sure. But stay there. They got enough guys with guns running around here. You—go up with your kids. I told Kate to wait there."

Kate.

She had forgotten all about Kate, the boy who tried to do something with her.

Her kids suddenly pushing against the limits of this place. This place suddenly not safe at all.

"What are *you* gonna do?"

Helen raised her gun a bit.

"See if they could use some real firepower outside."

"No. Stay with us."

"Look. I think there's only a few of them out there. The shots dying down already. Though, gotta tell you one thing . . ."

Helen came closer so only Christie could hear.

"Seemed like it was kind of a planned attack. Y'know, a surprise. Working together."

Christie nodded. She thought of the people at Paterville.

Who looked so normal.

Were the ones outside like that?

Able to think, plan?

Trying to sneak around the building, find a way in.

In which case—

She gave Simon's shoulder a squeeze.

Simon had given the alert.

He might have made the difference between a bunch of dead Can Heads, and losing people here.

Christie heard the gunshots, now sporadic, the occasional blast in the distance.

"We'll talk later," Helen said.

Christie nodded.

"Be safe."

Then she led Simon upstairs.

The gunshots had ended. Someone had come around to say that there would be no dinner tonight.

But everyone was safe.

No one got hurt.

Hurt.

Guess no one would ever say the word eaten.

You wanted to avoid that image.

After sitting quietly, she decided to talk to her two kids, placing them side by side on the big bed in the guest room. She pulled up a chair so she faced them.

First, she took Simon's hand, then Kate's, who reacted by looking away.

"You hungry, guys? I have some of those crackers they make here."

Both of them shook their heads.

"I guess," Christie said, smiling, "we can wait until breakfast then."

Both nodding.

Then, after a pause: "But I need to talk to you about something. What happened today. With both of you."

Simon started defending himself right away.

"I didn't want to. The other kids made it like . . . like a dare!"

A squeeze of his hand, Kate still looking away.

"I know. It's something boys do. But you see—" Her voice caught on this, remembering her scramble up the hill, the sight of Simon trapped—Can Heads below.

"You *see* how dangerous it could have been . . . how dangerous it was. You see that, don't you?"

She felt that Simon maybe wanted to tell her something about his climb, something she didn't know.

But when he didn't volunteer anything more . . .

"I need you to stay *here*. In only the safe areas. I need to know where you are, all the time, that you're safe. That makes sense, doesn't it?"

She saw in Simon's eyes what looked like the beginning of tears, the light glistening.

"Yes," he said quietly.

"Good." Then a smile for him.

Before she turned to Kate. Another squeeze to indicate that it was her turn.

Christie thinking then . . .

The two of them. Both going where they shouldn't, both having bad things happen.

Would those bad things end today?

Or was it only the beginning?

"Kate, what happened with you? I mean . . . you're not supposed to go down to the basement and garage. Off-limits, right?"

Still looking away, Kate nodded.

Simon had his eyes on her, not knowing what had occurred with his sister. And Christie knowing she wanted to be very careful here.

To warn Kate. About this place. The boys.

The men.

But also to not scare Simon any more than he already was.

So she cut to the chase.

"Kate." Waiting for her daughter to slowly turn and look at her. "I need *you* to promise me that you won't go anywhere you shouldn't. That, like Simon, I'll always, *always*—" her voice rising a bit—"know where you are."

Then looking at the two of them, trying with her gaze to tie her family together after being so scared for them.

Two final squeezes of their hands.

And Christie let her words of concern and caution fade.

She smiled. "How about a few rounds of hearts?"

And Kate, sweet Kate, ever more willing to be by her side, to help her through these terrible and dark days, said, with a touch of forced brightness in her voice, "Sure."

A few hands later, and there was a knock at the door.

Thinking it was Helen, and that it would be great to have a fourth for the card game, she went to the door.

Where the Colonel stood.

"Christie, could I have a word?"

His voice made it sound like more of an order than a request.

And having "a word" with the Colonel was something on her agenda as well.

To talk about today.

The way this place was run.

"Yes, do you want to come in—?"

"Out here, if you don't mind."

Christie looked at her kids, Simon dealing cards.

"I'll be right out here."

And she stepped out into the shadowy hallway.

"You know, Colonel, I wanted—"

He put up a hand.

"Your son broke a very important rule. He endangered the lives of my men."

Ever the military man . . .

"The rules are for safety, and he—"

"Hold on," Kate said, cutting him off. "Other kids were with him."

"Their parents have been spoken to as well."

"And how did your guard, standing right at the front door, miss those kids going out, sneaking off to the—"

"That—will be looked into. But this, for now, is a warning to you."

A warning?

"Make sure your kids stay where they're supposed to. That they, and you, obey the rules."

"And what about your guards?"

Christie wanted to tell the Colonel about Tom, how he lured her daughter down there, and actually tried to pin her in some dark tunnel under the building.

To kiss her. And who knows what else.

Kate. A *kid*.

But that might only trigger more warnings. And maybe it was better that the Colonel didn't know any more about what Kate had done.

How she had seen the subterranean cavern of rooms and the garage under the building. All the things she had told Christie about.

Information.

And sometimes, it was better if people didn't know you had information.

"Are we on the same page?"

Christie nodded.

"Good. Then I'll expect no other incidents like this one."

Christie turned to the door, grabbed the knob.

"Good night," the Colonel said.

"Right," Christie said, going back to the room, to her kids.

To the only two people in the world she gave a damn about.

Night.

The inn quiet.

Simon sleeping on the small couch in the room.

Kate beside her, also already asleep even as Christie stared up at the dark ceiling.

She thought of them, and the responsibility she had. To keep them safe. Yes.

But also—to give them a life.

Could that ever be here?

She closed her eyes again, hoping that would cut off the stream of thoughts, her doubts, her feeling that somehow they were trapped here.

She tried counting backward from 100 in her head.

99 . . . 98 . . .

An image of Kate cornered.

97 . . . 96 . . .

Simon on that ledge, caught by the rock.

95 . . . 94 . . . The sight of Can Heads moving around the grounds missed—

(Missed!)

—by the guards, all those swaggering men with guns running this place as if it was a throwback to some medieval castle. Women kept in their place, and men had guns.

93 . . . 92 . . .

Running into the inn while the Can Heads approached, fast.

91 . . . 90.

And how—

(She opened her eyes.)

How the Can Heads seemed to be acting together. Like someone told them what to do.

She thought of the conversation she'd had with Helen.

Was it changing? Did what happened at Paterville Family Camp mean that there could be different Can Heads, some who still seem human?

Or was it simply, in the end, all about choice?

That choice: how the hell do you survive?

The counting . . . now failed.

When suddenly, there was a noise.

From below, outside, down on the open courtyard to the side of the building.

Christie and Kate's room was at a far right corner, one of the last before reaching a sealed wing of the building.

A laugh.

Another. Mumbled words carrying through the night air.

She got up out of bed and walked to the window.

Christie pushed the curtain aside. A quarter moon hung in the sky, shedding light on the area below.

She saw the path that ran to the front and trailed off to the right. And off to the side, she saw a small courtyard, like a servant's entrance into the building, but with no overhang, nothing to protect it from rain, snow, not that it did much of that anymore.

So she could see and hear.

First—the sounds.

Men standing in a circle, all dark spindly figures. Laughing. Talking. Most of them holding things.

Guns, a few holding their rifles.

But others holding—what?

One man raised the object above his head.

A few hoots from the other men.

Then Christie knew what it was.

A baseball bat.

Waving it over his head, crazy, insane.

Something smaller passed between two men.

Something to drink.

So there is booze here after all.

A secret homemade stash for the medieval men guarding the castle.

The group of men moved a bit, in a circle, weaving this way and that, until Christie could see the rest of the scene.

The men—many with bats, good old baseball bats. The all-American sport.

And a rope that went from one pair of men to the center, and then onto another pair at the opposite side of the circle.

And at the center.

Someone with that rope tied around its neck, staggering this way and that.

Not someone, Christie saw.

A Can Head.

A *live* Can Head.

What the hell was going on?

One man came close to the roped Can Head and, with a great windup, smashed a bat into its body.

The thing doubled up to the laughs and cheers of the men.

The Can Head still stood though.

But now another man came and, making a gesture with his hand—

Some famous baseball gesture.

Pointing up, to the stands, to the bleachers—

He slammed at the thing's head, and the Can Head reeled back onto the ground.

Lying there.

The men's voices, the words indistinguishable, but taunting.

Christie had to watch.

The horror of it, the sickness . . . when she felt a hand on her shoulder.

———

Christie spun around. Her heart racing.

To see:

Kate. Standing there, in the shadows. Not looking out the window.

Not yet.

But looking at her mother.

"Mom. What is it? What's happening?"

She thought of telling her not to look, to go back to bed.

But those days were over.

She nodded in the direction of the window.

And Kate came and stood beside her.

The Can Head had staggered to its feet, swinging its neck left and right, as if it could shake off the nooselike rope that held him.

Another swing of the bat to the thing's midsection, and now when it doubled up, someone else came and performed a golf swing with his bat, sending the thing flying immediately erect.

The laughs so clear. The circle of horror moving as the thing stumbled around, still held by the ropes, as each man came and swung the bat at the thing.

Over and over and over . . .

Christie let the curtain close, put a hand on Kate's shoulder, and gently pulled her away.

As a tidal wave of thoughts, a jumble of concern and doubt and even fear, suddenly became clear.

Suddenly coalesced into one very clear thought.

One idea . . .

We have to get out of here.

the capture

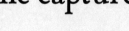

35

Whispers

Christie pulled Kate a few more feet away from the window, the sounds still clear, but now they couldn't see.

Didn't have to see.

"Mom—what were they doing?"

Christie didn't answer right away.

"Mom?"

She looked over at Simon, then making her voice low, modeling the quiet she wanted Kate to pick up on.

"Kate—I don't know. They must have caught a live one. And—"

"Why not kill it?"

"Guess they do that . . . for fun."

Kate's eyes went wide. The horror immediately clear to her.

"They take it out and beat it, over and over?"

Christie nodded.

"Why? Why not just—just *kill* it?"

Christie looked at her daughter.

Killing them . . . yes . . .

That was something they both accepted in this new world.

But what was happening outside, in the courtyard?

What was that?

The thought occurred to Christie . . . if humans do that, then who are the monsters?

And with all the thoughts and doubt, she had turned a corner.

Then Kate confirmed the reaction.

Because part of Christie could think, almost accept . . . after all, they're only Can Heads, *only* monsters that should be destroyed . . . why not have some fun with them?

"It's sick."

She noticed that the laughter had subsided from outside.

Did everyone here know that this was a game the men played, the good old boys with their rifles and grain alcohol?

Did the Colonel know?

Approve?

"It's one thing to kill them, Mom. But that—" Kate pointed to the window.

She shook her head.

"This place. Maybe this whole place is sick."

Christie nodded.

She debated telling Kate her decision, now, when things were still unclear . . . when they would leave, how.

Maybe even . . .

If.

But she raised a hand to her daughter's cheek.

"Yeah. You're right. I'm not feeling . . . so safe anymore."

She didn't say that it was mostly her concern for her kids.

Kate took a breath. "Me either."

"I think we have to leave."

Kate held her mother's gaze even as her hand came away from the smooth skin of her daughter's cheek.

"Leave." Kate nodded. "But where can we—"

Christie cut her off with a shake of her head, reminding herself to keep her voice as low as possible.

It wouldn't make sense to have Simon join this discussion.

"I don't . . . know. I have to think about it. But this, here—it isn't the place for us."

"Okay," Kate said as if getting an order.

"Can't tell anyone—"

"Helen?"

"Maybe Helen. Who knows—she might want to come."

"I like her."

Christie smiled at that.

Now only silence from outside.

"I'll do some thinking. Make a plan." Another smile. "Talk to Helen. Tomorrow. Okay?"

Kate nodded.

And at that end point, Christie led Kate back to her bed, the night turned quiet, a bit of milky white from the moon lighting the window, the curtains.

And Christie doubted she would sleep at all.

Morning.

Everyone had filled into the dining room for breakfast, the noise level loud—Christie figured—as everyone buzzed about what had happened yesterday.

But she didn't see Helen.

Sleeping in? Working? Skipping breakfast?

She felt that first tug of fear.

Like the meal at the camp when the Blairs just didn't show up.

Then she saw her friend hurrying down the hallway, head down, lost in her thoughts.

For a moment, Christie could look at her without being seen, wondering . . . what is this place like for her?

At least I have my kids.

With her husband gone, in this place, this world, she's alone.

But then Christie thought: *no, that's not actually true. It'll be important to tell her that.*

She has us.

Finally, Helen looked up. A smile slowly appeared as whatever thoughts had been preoccupying her vanished.

"Morning," Helen said brightly.

But then that smile faded as she looked at Christie.

Instinctively knowing that something was wrong.

"Helen—you got a few minutes?"

"Sure."

Christie looked over her shoulder.

"Maybe over there."

Helen looked at the open doors leading into the dining room.

A private conversation where no one could see.

"Lead on," she said.

And Christie walked down the hallway to the closed wing of the building until they were well out of earshot of anyone, unlikely to be seen even if someone quickly inhaled their breakfast and came out.

"I need to tell you some things. I don't know who else to tell."

Helen's hand shot out and gently closed on her wrist.

"Anything, Christie. Go on." Another smile. "We're family."

Christie thought: *yes, we are.*

"Okay—last night. I saw something. Kate, too."

Helen nodded.

And Christie told her what she had watched from the window of her room.

Helen nodded, listening.

Christie struggled to keep her voice low. Describing the circle of men bashing away at the Can Head . . . it was hard not to let that memory make her voice rise.

Finally, the question to Helen.

"Have you ever seen that?"

Helen shook her head.

"No. But I've heard the men talk about it."

"It?"

A nod. "Yeah. Something they do. When they capture a live one. They don't just kill it. They do . . . exactly what you saw."

"It's sick."

"They call it 'Kick the Can.' And yes, it is sick."

"I mean, even Kate said it. My own daughter who lost her dad to them. She said . . . 'why not just kill them?' But to do that, smashing it over and over."

Another hand to Christie's arm.

"Easy."

Christie nodded.

"Guess if you've lost friends, maybe it's a release."

She could hear in Helen's voice that she herself didn't buy into that.

"If that's what they do, what we do . . . how are we any different? The so-called normal ones."

"Good question."

"And there's something else."

Helen smiled. "You mean Simon's adventure on the mountain? Colonel wasn't too happy about that, I bet."

"No. Something happened to Kate."

Again, Helen's eyes showed a flash of understanding of words not being said.

"Yes?"

"One of the Colonel's men got her to go down to the basement, those tunnels down there. He cornered her. My little girl."

Helen shook her head. Then:

"I didn't want to worry you. But I gotta tell you. It's something I've been thinking about. Something *I've* been worrying about. She's a beautiful girl."

"A girl! Exactly!"

Helen nodded. "But in this place, these days . . ."

Christie looked away.

Neither said anything for a few moments, and when she turned back to Helen, her mind had been made up.

A decision reached.

And with what had happened to her life over the past few months, once a decision was reached, there was only one way to go.

She looked down the hallway. No one there.

And then she told Helen her plan.

36

Out of the Castle

"I'm going to leave. Me, my family."

Helen waited a moment.

Then: "Where? Where will you go?"

"I don't know. I only know that I can't stay here. Not with my kids. With these humans turning into animals. How long before something really bad happens? And . . . is it even safe here?"

"You mean the attack? Last night? Turned out okay—"

Now it was Christie's turn to reach out and grab Helen's arm.

"Turned out okay . . . maybe because my son, a boy, he sneaked past their guards, nobody saw him go up that mountain, and he saw *them*? That's safe?"

Christie's voice made Helen turn and look back to the dining room.

"I hear you. Maybe all these men, their guns. Place this big. Maybe it's too big."

"And I was thinking. Winter's coming. What do animals do in winter? When food is scarce?"

"Animals. You mean the Can Heads."

Funny question, Christie thought. Obviously . . . yes.

But then.

Standing in this hallway, whispering, maybe not.

"Yeah. Sure."

Unconvinced that it was simply the Can Heads she should worry about.

"But where will you go?"

Christie shook her head.

"I don't know. It's a big country. There have to be places where no matter how bad things got, no matter how long we have to wait until the government does something, discovers *something*, people still live decent lives."

Helen didn't respond.

Which Christie took to mean that she didn't agree.

"I gotta think," Christie went on, "that there are places better than here. Even—" and this thought was new. Terrifying in its implications.

"Even—if we have to live all on our own."

Helen nodded.

Then: "If you do this, if you want, and if—" a smile—"you got room for an old lady . . . you can count me in."

Now Christie smiled, suddenly not feeling all alone.

"Great. I was hoping you'd say that."

"One last question, and then we better get some breakfast before they shut down . . ."

"Yes?"

"When?"

Good question, Christie thought. When indeed?

She'd need to pick a time, get the kids all set to leave. Make sure they had gas for the car, their weapons back, the food they brought.

Would the Colonel do what he said? Simply give her back all their stuff?

"You can leave anytime you want," he had said.

Was that true?

"Soon."

She wondered if Helen was also thinking about the Colonel, whether simply leaving his redoubt—no questions asked—would be easy.

Or even possible.

"Okay. I think sooner rather than later. Like you said—"

And it seemed to Christie that Helen's next words were not just about changing weather, a changing mood in the fortress, but about something larger.

"Winter's coming."

And with that, they both walked into the dining room as people started to stream out, no one paying attention to them as they entered.

But as soon as they sat down with plates of oatmeal like stuff, the dining room nearly empty, Christie felt someone's eye on her.

From the front of the room, the Colonel.

Helen turned to her.

"Steady. I think Captain Crunch noticed our late arrival."

Christie nodded as she dutifully turned back to her bowl of gooey pseudo-cereal.

But out of the corner of her eyes, she saw the Colonel stand up and start walking to their table until he stood beside them.

"Morning, ladies," the Colonel said.

"Morning," Helen said.

Christie nodded.

Then the Colonel pulled a chair from a nearby table and turned it around so he could sit near them.

"I wanted to tell you something. I like letting people know . . . what's happening to their things."

Now Christie looked. It was as if he had read their minds, their talk of leaving.

My things?

"What do you mean?"

"We got a great report from one of our night patrols. They found a place—miles from here, some kind of big warehouse. I guess people stockpiled things and left. Might be a lot of things we'll all need for winter in there."

"Good," Helen said. "Lucky us."

The Colonel paused as if he picked up on the trace of sarcasm.

"Yeah. Still, we have to go get the stuff . . . while it's still there, before anyone else comes along looking for it. Things will get pretty desperate this winter."

The Colonel looked at Christie.

"So we're doing a *big* run tonight, every vehicle we can trust. Grab everything we can and get it back here."

The car, Christie thought. *He's talking about the* car!

"You're asking to use my car?"

The Colonel shook his head. "Not asking. I told you when you came here, everything is communal—unless you leave. And we'd need to plan that. Just like I told you."

Christie didn't react to that. Helen took in a spoon of cereal.

"But I only wanted to *inform* you of what we'd be doing. That's all."

Christie held his gaze, her mind racing.

The possibilities . . . racing through her head. What if something happened to that car? What if it blew a tire, broke down, whatever?

Then they would truly be trapped here.

Options . . . gone.

She took a breath, nodded.

"No."

The Colonel's eyebrows shot up.

"Look, Christie—you don't—"

"You can use the car. But I go. *I* drive."

The Colonel made a small laugh.

"I don't think you want to be driving all that way, over those dark roads at night. Miles from here, in the dark. No telling what the men will face. And—"

"I've killed more of them than most of your men. Maybe—all your men. You can use my car to get whatever is there and bring it back. But I go. I drive."

And all the time, Christie was thinking—

That way—I'm with the car. I'll see how they park them down below, where they keep the keys, the gas, the guns—

Yes. It was the only way.

Still, the Colonel could say no.

He started shaking his head.

"It's dangerous. You should stay with your kids."

Then Christie saw a card to play.

"But they'll be here. You'll have guards staying here, yes? They'll be safe."

Helen cleared her throat.

"I'm going too, then. Because I *know* I've killed more of those things than most of your men. Besides—"

She reached over and patted Christie's forearm.

"—we're a team. I watch her back, and vice versa."

The Colonel didn't say anything; he didn't look convinced.

Christie lowered her voice and leaned across the table closer to him.

"You don't want me making noise about this, Colonel. Just take the car, and me with it—"

"And me," Helen added.

The Colonel looked away as if checking who might be within earshot of this standoff. But except for a few people cleaning up near the large serving table up front . . . nobody.

"Okay. Against my better judgment. Everyone leaves tonight a little before sunset. In a caravan. You head down below later and Sam will get your keys—"

"And my guns?"

"You have a gun."

"The rest of them. You did say you didn't know what to expect."

"Right."

The Colonel stood up.

He stood there for a second as if searching for something to say.

But having lost this battle, he walked away.

And when the Colonel was gone, Helen turned to her.

"That—was amazing. You got balls, girlfriend."

Christie smiled at that.

She herself didn't know where she got the will to pull that off.

Jack would have been proud.

"I had to do it. If we lose the car—"

"I know. We're stuck. Still, you sure you're up for a road trip miles away? Got to be prime Can Head country out there."

Christie smiled. "Thought you said you'd have my back?"

"That I did."

"And . . ." Another look around . . . "after tonight, we can leave. Whether we get the Colonel's permission or just take the damn car, the guns, the gas."

"Guess when you make up your mind, you make up your mind."

"Yeah." She took a breath. "I had a good teacher."

She was about to add that it was easy to do when you had kids. When you worried about your kids.

When their survival was your *job.*

Instead—

"Thanks for coming with me."

"As if I'd let you go out there on your own . . ."

Christie nodded.

This, she thought, might be her last day—last night—in this building, this cloistered castle of men and guns and growing fear.

Something inside her . . . told her that *that* feeling was indeed true.

37

The Caravan

"You two okay?" Christie said to Kate and Simon.

Simon nodded, still so quiet after his time on the mountain.

But Kate had a question.

"I don't get why you have to go?"

Kate knew about her decision. To leave.

But neither of them had told Simon. Best, she thought, that he find out at the last minute.

"I want to make sure that the car is okay. That it comes back. It's our car, right?"

As soon as she said it, she knew how wrong that sounded.

Our car.

Actually . . . the Blairs' car.

Our *car blew up in the Adirondacks.*

Kate didn't ask any more questions.

Good girl, Christie thought.

Stay with me.

"Now, they say it's only about fifteen . . . twenty miles away. Imagine we'll load all the cars, the trucks, and get back, real fast. A couple of hours at most."

She paused, for a moment questioning her own decision to leave.

Was there any right thing to do here?

Stay with her kids and let whatever happened to the damn car . . . happen?

But she knew . . . if they had a future, it wasn't here.

"I want you to stay in here, in the room."

Simon rolled his eyes.

"I know. Bor-ing. But a few hours. Just do it for me."

"Okay," Kate said quietly.

She saw Simon's eyes dart to the lower drawer. Another decision she had made.

"And leave those exactly where they are, okay?"

Should she take the guns? Or trust them to leave them untouched?

For a moment—she felt immobilized.

Then: "Okay, I gotta go down to the garage. Won't be long."

She pulled them both close, hugged them so tight, then a kiss to each.

She let them go.

"Love you," she said.

She waited for the words she wanted to hear.

Needed to hear.

"Love you, too," they said together.

And then she turned and hurried down to the underground area below the inn.

Christie stood with Helen off to the side, watching as men brought the cars around to a narrow driveway that led up and out of the subterranean garage.

She felt Helen give a nudge.

"Check over there."

In the back, a storeroom with large double doors, a padlock dangling, that door now open as men carried guns out.

"There are your weapons. In there."

Not far from the storeroom, Christie had already spotted a wooden chest on the wall, also open, with rows of keys like an NYC parking lot.

She looked around . . .

The gas. Where the hell do they keep the gas?

But when another car was moved into position in the line leading out, she saw rows of mismatched plastic and metal containers piled at the back, dozens of them, stacked two, three high.

Guess, she figured, *they don't worry about protecting the gas if the car keys are locked up.*

She saw her car being jockeyed out of its space, the smell of so much exhaust, so many cars in the closed area making her sick.

Then the driver moved her car into position behind a pickup.

She saw someone get out. A kid, only a little older than Kate. He didn't make eye contact.

Was he the one who had cornered her daughter?

Could have been any of them.

"Got a full tank," the kid said, walking away.

Another man, an older guy, walked over with guns in one hand and boxes in the other.

"Here you go," he said.

Christie shook her head.

"I had *more*. Another handgun, a lot more ammo."

Someone handed Helen a few boxes of shells for her shotgun.

"Me, too," she said.

"This is plenty," the man said.

Christie thought of demanding it all—all the guns she brought in, Jack's armory. The ammo.

But would that tip them off that she may be planning to leave?

Come back. Get Kate, Simon . . . and leave.

So she kept quiet.

She took the guns and walked over to the car, sliding the rifle and a handgun onto the backseat, pushing the ammo boxes toward the back of the seat.

Helen got into the passenger side.

"If you don't mind, I'll keep mine with me. Up front."

"Don't mind at all," Christie said, sliding into the driver's seat.

Then they waited for the night patrol to get rolling.

Loud shouts from up front, the sound of doors grinding open, car engines revving.

"Here we go," said Helen.

With the engines started, everyone turned on their lights, making the dust motes that filled the dank air down here look like snow.

The heavy-duty pickup truck in front of Christie sat high, cutting off the view of the cars in front.

In the rearview mirror, Christie could see another four or five cars.

We're in the middle, she thought.

Maybe for safety.

The sound of the pickup's diesel engine in front roaring as it slipped into gear.

And then the line of vehicles—SUVs, trucks, cars—began rolling up the stone driveway and out of the underground garage, out into the night air where the sky—laced with a hint of blue and purple to the west—had already turned dark.

———

The line moved slowly.

"You'd think they'd hurry. Just get there, grab whatever's there, and get the hell back."

Christie had her hands locked on the steering wheel.

"Seriously. And why do it at night?"

"I'm guessing they don't want any of the locals, the normal or otherwise locals, trailing along. This way the loot is all theirs."

Christie nodded.

Daytime, and anyone who lived in the nearby towns, in the woods, who still hung on, would see them, wonder what the hell was going on.

Could have people coming from everywhere to see what was up.

"You okay?" Helen said.

"Yeah. I'll be glad when this is over and we get back."

"Me, too."

And then they both sat quietly as the caravan winded its way down the mountain road, and then toward the town of Wawarsing, where the warehouse waited.

Fifteen minutes into the journey, the line stopped.

Then, from the front, the sound of gunfire.

"That sounds bad," Christie said.

She sat listening. More shots.

The door to the pickup ahead opened, and a short man in a flannel shirt hopped down from the high cab of the truck.

He walked back to Christie.

"A few of them came out of the woods," he said. "I got my two-way radio so they let me know. No problem. They got 'em."

He moved down the line of cars, telling everyone the short news update.

"*No problem*," Helen said. "Right. I think we need to keep our eyes open. And I best keep checking the side of the road."

She shifted her gun so instead of pointing straight down, the shotgun now lay level on her lap.

The caravan started moving again.

More time.

Another fifteen, twenty minutes, the journey feeling like it was taking forever.

From here, Christie had been told, the caravan was to take a back way to the warehouse, avoiding the actual town. A narrow two-lane road.

Occasional shots rang out from the front, and then once from behind them.

But the encounters—whether Can Heads or just desperate people— didn't stop the cars.

"Got to be getting there soon," Helen said.

Even Helen's voice, Christie thought, sounded wary, tight, tense.

Out of place for a woman who always seemed to be confident, strong.

Then the woman said: "Oh, God."

On the right side of the road, a pile of two, three Can Heads— hard to tell—their clothes worn away, jutting pieces of exposed bone, the blood turned a near blackish color as it picked up the headlights from the line of cars.

A pile of them.

Killed a while ago.

Then—farther on—Christie had to follow other cars, moving around a body that lay in the right lane.

Face down.

Fully dressed.

Perhaps killed by the men in the cars ahead.

She saw Helen look at the body as she swerved to avoid running over it.

"That's one well-dressed Can Head," she said.

Christie hesitated.

As if what she was about to say might make the idea, the question real.

Letting fear grow.

"If . . . if it *is* a Can Head."

Helen turned to her as she got back to the center of the right lane.

"You mean, might be one of those . . . like you had at Paterville?"

A nod.

"God, Christie. Can't tell you how that shit . . . really disturbs me. If we can't tell the difference anymore . . ."

The next words left unsaid.

What the hell will we do?

Finally, they saw a sign.

Dotted with bullet holes. Titled at a strange angle.

But the words could be read, the white letters reflecting back the milky glare of the headlights.

WAWARSING—TWO MILES

Helen shifted in her seat. Christie heard a click. The safety of her gun being released.

"We're here," she said to Christie. "Let's hope we do this fast."

38

Night

"Why do we have to stay here?" Simon asked, standing by the window.

"Looks like everyone's gone somewhere. And we have to stay in the room?"

He turned to Kate.

"I want to go see where my friends are."

"Mom said to stay here till she got back."

Simon nodded. "It's boring here."

"We can play more spit. Or Monopoly."

In truth, Kate didn't want to do either.

But she also knew something that Simon didn't.

That soon they were going to leave this "boring" place for good.

He started for the door that led out of the room.

"I'm going to walk around."

"Simon!" Kate said. "You're not going anywhere."

"Oh yeah?" Then: "You going to stop me?"

She wanted to say that he had caused enough trouble for one day, but attacking her brother didn't seem like the right thing to do.

And—it *was* boring just sitting in the room.

All those cars, people leaving the inn. The place had to be empty.

"Okay. You can go walk around—but I'm coming with you."

Simon rolled his eyes. "Why—are you my babysitter?"

Kate stood up. "Actually, yes, I am."

He turned to the door, and she hurried to catch up to her brother.

And as he walked out . . . "Yeah, well, I don't *need* a babysitter."

Wawarsing.

Probably one of those beautiful mountain towns, Christie thought.

Before things changed, and made towns like this so dangerous, towns that couldn't afford the police, or the fences, or the weapons.

Most people left.

A few stayed. But how many of those could hang on, doors locked, guns ready?

The red brake lights of the pickup in front flashed once, then again, and the caravan again stopped.

"What's up?" Christie said.

Absolutely impossible to see anything with that pickup in front.

"I don't know. Maybe we're there. But looks to me like we're still outside the town."

Someone honked a horn from the back.

Like a traffic jam in midtown Manhattan at rush hour.

Helen turned to her.

"Want me to go look?"

Christie sat there. Hands locked on the steering wheel.

Then—a feeling.

This seemed *wrong*. The cars stopped. Something about it . . . all wrong.

"No," she said to Helen.

"I could just go walk up, see what's what."

Christie shook her head.

She turned to her door lock.

It was up.

Unlocked.

What did Jack say? *Always* said?

Windows up.

Doors locked.

Always . . . goddamned locked.

She turned to Helen.

"Just . . . lock your door."

Helen looked at her as if confused by the order, the tone of voice, the tense, strained sound, engine still idling, still burning precious gas.

Helen turned and pushed down her door lock as well.

"There we go. You expecting—?"

And then the reason for the feeling became clear.

Ahead, they came out from both sides of the narrow road, holding things in their hands.

"Oh, God," Helen said.

She raised her shotgun as Christie reached to the backseat to grab whatever gun her fingers first touched.

"Okay. *Enough* walking around. Looks like your friends are grounded."

"I bet they're probably doing something fun," Simon said. "With everyone away."

Kate looked around.

Usually, at night, there'd be a guard at this end of the building, where the locked doors sealed off the other building attached to the main part of the inn.

But tonight there was no guard.

Some of the rooms they passed were open.

She saw a woman reading who smiled at them as they walked by. Then a couple sitting together while some music played quietly, the woman holding the only baby here.

Other rooms closed.

So quiet, with so many people away.

"Let's go back, Simon."

Then she confessed her own fear.

"I don't like this. It's too quiet."

He turned to her.

Was he trying to prove he was brave? she wondered. After what had happened? Is that what boys did? One dumb thing after another?

"But that's why it's good to explore."

Would he just go off on his own if she said no?

"All right. A bit more. But I want to be back in the room well before Mom comes back."

"Sure."

They turned away from the shut doors, the sealed wing, and Kate followed Simon as he wandered back to the main staircase, wishing there were more voices down here, more open rooms, more people . . .

Things happened so quickly that Christie had no time to react, to think, to do anything.

She saw Can Heads—though the dark made them just blackish figures erupting from both sides of the road—bolting toward all the vehicles.

Gun blasts.

People in the vehicles shooting. Can Heads holding things over their heads and then smashing down on the cars.

Just the quickest of glimpses—and then she turned and looked to her left, and one of the things' faces came flush to her window, using its head . . .

God—using its head!

—to smash against Christie's window.

She heard a noise to the right. A smash, a crack.

But she didn't turn away from the thing trying to smack its way in to look at what that might be.

Then: another cracking noise from the right.

"Helen," she said. "Are you—"

The window, she thought. That was the noise. Had to be.

But not broken.

The electric window sliding down.

She wanted to yell at Helen, "No!"

But the sight and sound of the Can Head beside her, inches away, eyes a criss-cross of red lines, the reflected light of the dashboard making the thing look like an alien.

Still, only seconds had passed.

The pickup truck in front reared backward.

Like a rodeo bull, bucking, nearly rising from the ground with its massive tires.

Smashing right into her small Honda and sending Christie jerking forward, her head smacking into the steering wheel.

But with that bump, the Can Head slipped away from the window.

She had the thought: *the driver's panicking, trying to get the hell away.*

She heard a blast. Deafening, the sound an explosion in the car.

Quick turn.

Helen had lowered the window.

And she now fired the shotgun into the darkness outside.

The truck reared into them again, as if it could bulldoze the entire line of cars backward.

Christie held the steering wheel in one hand, a revolver in the other.

Was the safety off?

She'd have to take her hand from the steering wheel to check.

Ahead, the spill of milky light from her too-low headlights cast enough light to show that a Can Head now stood on the running board, near the cab of the pickup truck, *reaching in*.

Then—a horrible moment, the door to the truck popped open.

"Christie—we've got to get the hell out of here."

More blasts. Helen's gun a cannon in the car; Christie's ears ringing after each blast.

"*Christie!*" Helen yelled.

The Can Head on the truck pulled back, yanking out the driver; Christie heard his screams.

Christie's headlights caught the driver clawing, clutching on to the steering wheel, then the door, the plump driver no match for the monster that pulled at him.

Until finally, the driver rolled to the ground, and the thing literally leaped into the air to pounce on the driver, bringing its head down fast into the driver's midsection.

Christie felt bile gather at the bottom of her throat, ready to throw up.

She thought:

I'm not moving. I'm frozen.

I'm not doing anything here.

Then Helen again: "It's a trap. Christie—we have to get the hell out of here. *Now.*"

She saw two other Can Heads race past the one feeding off the truck driver. A hesitation as they looked down.

But then they both looked up and saw Christie's car.

Their eyes—in her mind—locking on hers.

Another blast from Helen's gun, like a ticking clock counting off the seconds of Christie's indecision, her immobilization.

"Wait."

Simon stood at the staircase that led down to the garage.

"I bet we could go down there now—and nobody would see."

"We're not doing that. We're going back upstairs. And—"

As if to dare Kate, Simon took a step down the staircase to the garage, his eyes on Kate.

Then another step, as Kate remembered being down there, with that boy trapping her.

I don't want to go down there, she thought.

"Simon!"

He had a big grin on.

"You can try . . . to catch me."

Another step, and as Kate finally stopped standing and started moving toward him, down the staircase, his smile so big now as he bolted and disappeared down the stairs.

"Simon," she said again, taking care not to yell.

There were still a few people milling about in the dining room. And more people down at the other end where the Colonel had his office.

I don't need to get in any more trouble, Kate thought.

But she did what she had to.

She raced after Simon.

39

Escape

The Can Heads near the one squatting on the trucker now began a crazy, loping run toward Christie and the car.

Helen leaned out her window and fired, but Christie could see that without stepping out, her angle was no good.

And Helen would have to be crazy to get out—with who knew how many more of them out there.

A look to the left.

The narrow two-lane road sloping down an incline.

But the other lane was blocked.

The cars behind her had tried to turn, but it was so narrow that they all seemed locked together, nobody going anywhere.

While Can Heads went from one to the next.

On either side of the road, trees . . . most of them dead, a few pines, and lots of scrubby brush.

But as she looked left again, Christie saw a possibility.

An insane possibility.

But the only possibility.

She threw the car into reverse and backed up, smacking into the car behind her.

Was that driver gone? Had they been able to pry him out, someone else to be turned into their version of road kill?

Forward, and then another lurch backward.

Helen kept shooting and not once asked . . . *what the hell are you doing?*

Until Christie thought she had enough space, with the two Can Heads racing toward her now splitting up, one moving to her side, the other to Helen's open window.

But that one's head suddenly disappeared as Helen finally had a good shot.

The car in drive, Christie now cut the wheel hard to the left.

There was an opening amidst those trees and the brush.

Maybe—she thought—just wide enough.

Who knew what was ahead? What kind of hidden rocks, branches, tree limbs. Anything and everything that could stop her car.

But whatever it was, it had to be better than sitting in that line, mired, waiting to be attacked.

She pressed her foot down hard. With the steering wheel cut so hard, the tires screeched, and she moved into and then over the Can Head beside her window, its scream merging with the shriek and squeal of the tires.

She had the thought:

They don't even sound *human.*

And this—as the car literally rocketed into the woody brush to the left:

Is what those men were doing to the Can Head so bad after all?

They're not human.

They're not even animals.

Monsters.

But even as she had that thought, her eyes wide, trying to avoid anything that could bring the Honda to a dead stop, she realized the real reason it was wrong.

If we do that.

If that's how we act . . .

Then we're no better.

The front of the car nosedived into the depression, then rose up, a ship bucking on angry waves.

"Hang on," she said to Helen.

"Oh, I am," Helen said, her rifle and head back in the car, barrel pointed down.

Christie thought . . . *we might only go a few yards and then get stuck. Just delaying the inevitable.*

Nowhere to go.

Committed, she had no choice but to keep the accelerator down, hands locked, and eyes looking dead ahead.

Kate took the staircase, fast, risking a look back to see whether anyone had heard her and followed them here.

Until she got to the bottom, and again saw the mammoth cavern of the garage.

Unlike before, only a few cars down here. Older cars. Maybe wrecks.

Most of the cars gone with all the others.

She couldn't see Simon.

Playing hide and seek.

Idiot boy, she thought.

She looked around to see if there were any guards down here. Maybe Simon had already been seen by one of them, told to get out.

And they could both go back to the room, the adventure over.

But there was no one.

The place so quiet.

Giant overhead lights made the center of the cavernous garage bright, the corners getting no light whatsoever.

To the left, she saw the entrance to the tunnel—where she had stood with that boy.

The tunnels . . . a maze.

Would Simon go in there?

Why won't he do what he's told?

She had no choice but to play his game, and she began walking slowly through the garage, needing to walk around each car, this damn game of hide and seek that she didn't want to play at all.

The car hit something—a branch, inches thick, four, five feet long— and it flew over the hood, sliding over the windshield onto the roof, and off the back of the car.

The bushes and trees on the sides created a constant scratching sound as if screaming about an impending disaster ahead.

Then the right front tire hit something hard—maybe a boulder, a stray rock jutting up—and the car rose on one side and tilted sharply to the right.

Then the rear tire hit the same rock, and the car repeated the movement.

But then the trees and stumps that had seemed to wall the car in so tightly . . . thinned out, creating more room for Christie to maneuver.

The car still bucked up and down, the movement constant now, but it was easier to dodge the obstacles.

And even when the car dug into another depression, the front of the vehicle jerked quickly out of the hole.

Christie was going fast.

Damn good car, she thought.

But then Helen said: "Oh, shit."

This open area led to a hill, a steep angle down, with nowhere else to go.

Unless she wanted to stop and go back the way they came.

She took her foot off the accelerator, but she'd still be hitting the slope at a great speed.

Foot moving to the brake.

But braking only made the car start to slide wobbly to the left, then right, veering out of control.

Foot off the brake.

And now she could at least attempt to steer it as the car rolled down the hill, bumping up and down.

Christie felt herself rise out of her seat with each bump, only the steering wheel helping her stay in place.

Hands locked, the car halfway down the hill.

A quick look up, to see beyond the hill.

To see what was ahead.

Then: what she saw—

There was only one word for it.

Hope.

Kate walked around one car.

She looked at the back of the car and wondered if Simon might have crawled under it.

So annoying!

"Simon," she said quietly. "This game is *over.* Come out now . . . and I won't tell Mom."

Then she thought . . . *maybe Mom should have told him.*

That we're going to leave.

As soon as we can.

Maybe then he wouldn't be doing this.

"Simon. Did you hear me?"

Still taking care to keep her voice low.

"Stop it now—and I won't tell Mom."

Nothing.

She moved to walk around another car, listening so carefully as she took each step for any telltale sign of where her annoying brother might be.

It was a road.

A dirt road, right where the hill flattened out.

Beyond it, another hill down. Bigger, the angle steeper, a hill that surely would have the car tumbling end over end, out of control.

She had to hit that flat area just right, so she could turn the car into it and not roll over.

Get onto that road and stop.

She also registered—just barely—what was beyond that second hill. Sitting on the outskirts of the town, which looked dark, abandoned.

But a building, and grounds.

A warehouse, with lights, a parking lot with cars and trucks, and an open area.

All taken in so quickly before her eyes had to go back to keeping the car from turning into a rolling disaster.

Helen freed a hand from the dash where she had planted an arm to keep herself in place.

The hand gently touched Christie's right arm.

Just a touch.

Support, human contact.

Christie turned the wheel to the right, just a bit, so as the car went down, it now slid as well.

She'd have to try the brake even if that made the car slide.

It was just going too damn fast.

Christie felt herself sucking in air, gasping, hyperventilating from the craziness.

Back to the brake, the flat dirt road yards away.

Just a touch.

One, two. Which made the car veer more to the right, too much. The worst angle to be hitting the flat dirt road.

She turned the wheel to the left.

Now with the combination of tapping the brake and adjusting the steering wheel, she had a better angle for hitting the flat area.

No guarantee that the car wouldn't continue moving, sliding, ultimately rolling over the edge and down the hill.

Then the front right tire finally hit the flat dirt road, and it made the car pivot, a jerking near stop. The other front tire followed.

Another so-quick tap of the brake.

A slide onto the dirt road.

Then the right rear tire hit the road. Another lurch due to the sudden change of angle.

Until the last rear tire hit the flat, and the car began moving on the road, but Christie knew, with enough momentum that might still carry it over the edge if she didn't have control of the car.

But Christie didn't know what to do, how to arrest the inevitable slide.

Helen finally spoke.

"Gas." The word shot out. Then, quickly, as it registered: "Give it *gas.*"

Christie had held her foot suspended over the brake to give those quick taps as she aimed the car down.

Now she moved her foot over the accelerator pedal, making sure that the wheels were turned the slightest way in, toward the hill that they had just come down.

And then—

Then . . .

The car moved along the dirt road as if nothing strange had just happened at *all*.

The dirt road curving a bit as it circled the hill.

Christie had to stop.

If she didn't stop . . . she'd scream.

Or break down.

Had to stop.

If only for a moment.

And as she let the vehicle slow down, she kept repeating to herself, in her mind . . .

We're safe, we're safe, we're safe . . .

40

The Farm

Kate took one more look at the giant cavern that was the garage.

Either Simon went back upstairs while she wasn't looking or he had hidden in one of the openings that led to the stone tunnels that ran under the building.

She didn't want to go in there.

And for a moment, she was frozen, standing in the chill of the underground area, growing more irritated and also wanting more than anything to get out of there.

But she had to look in the tunnels.

Maybe he wouldn't have gone far. He couldn't want to get in trouble again, and Mom would be coming back soon.

She walked toward the closest entrance, which looked like a cave, the opening surrounded with giant stones.

Frightening. But she had to take a look.

Thinking that when she found her brother, she'd like to smack him . . .

All she could hear were her own steps as she moved to the entrance, and then, with just the slightest hesitation, inside.

"You okay, Christie?"

Christie had stopped the car, hands still locked on the steering wheel, not believing what she had just done, that somehow they had survived the crazy careening down the hill.

"I'm—yeah—I'm okay."

"Don't think . . . we should stay here. We're not that far away. From the road. Some of them . . . could have followed."

Christie looked up at the rearview mirror.

She thought of the line of cars. How many others did what she did, were somehow able to pull out of the line, get away?

The narrow two-lane road clogged in all the panic . . .

No way to turn around.

Then a question: Why did we come that way?

It was as if—it had been planned.

"Right. We better leave. Okay."

She took a breath. Her head tingling, as if an overdose of adrenaline still rampaged through it, a narcotic.

Nothing had felt like this. Even that night in the camp.

Then: she remembered that she had quickly looked straight ahead, over the crest of the next hill, down to a small valley.

Saw a building.

No—a complex.

So close.

A quick roll down the hill and they would have been *there*. Smashing into the warehouse.

Was that the place? Where all that food was supposed to be that they had come for?

She looked at the building.

Lights on outside.

She tried to understand what she was seeing, the meaning so slow to come.

Just the images, taking them in.

Then, she understood what she saw.

"Christie, we going?"

Men with guns at one end as a line of people were led in, under guard, into the warehouse.

The men guarding them.

All the men, shadowy figures. No telling who any of them could be. No way at all.

Off to the side, other figures—these now recognizable if only by how they walked, how they gathered together.

You face enough Can Heads and you begin to sense how they act, that jerky, feral way they moved.

Like clumsy cats, crazed tigers whose hunting movements are marred by spasms, shaking.

Almost as if they had an electric prod buried in them and every few seconds—as they moved—someone gave them a nerve-twisting jolt.

"Helen—look down there. What's that?"

She waited.

"What?" Helen said.

Seconds of quiet.

Then: "Jesus. I—I—"

"Those are Can Heads to the side, and the guys with guns, those people . . . they're marching into that—"

(*Factory. Warehouse. Farm.*)

"The men. The guards. From the inn. What the *hell*."

Christie said nothing for a second. But she reached down and shut off the car's lights, suddenly worried that she had sat up here so long with the lights on.

She turned to Helen.

"It was a trap. The Can Heads. Working with those men—controlled by them."

"That can't be," Helen said.

"Look."

They both could see.

The line of captured men disappeared into the giant building.

The horde of Can Heads, like rabid dogs, milled about outside.

One of the men with a gun fired a shot into the air.

Another door opened at the back.

Christie couldn't move, couldn't simply drive away.

Not yet.

She had to watch.

Had to.

Into the cave.

Overhead lights made it so she could see part of the way into the tunnel.

But the small pool of light would end, and then before the next ceiling light, Kate had to cross some shadows, totally dark.

She still kept her voice low, even though there didn't seem to be anyone down here at all.

"Simon." A bit louder now. "Simon, where the hell are you?"

Walking deeper into the tunnels.

Until she knew she couldn't go any farther into this lonely scary place.

Even if her dumb brother was in here.

Just a few more steps and she would turn around.

Back upstairs, to where he was probably hiding in the closet.

Laughing his stupid head off.

Idiot . . .

Christie watched the warehouse door open and two men tolled out a large wheelbarrow as the Can Heads, weaving and bobbing but not attacking anyone, waited.

Something in the wheelbarrow.

Impossible to tell.

Could be anything.

Just something in a wheelbarrow.

The two men moving the wheelbarrow stopped by the man who had fired the gun.

The Can Heads still standing away.

Until they dumped the wheelbarrow and something went sloshing onto the ground.

The men with the wheelbarrow quickly pulled back, now joined by a man with the gun.

As the Can Heads matched the men's retreat, and now approached the pile of whatever had been dumped on the ground.

"Oh my God," Helen said.

She turned to Christie.

"We have to get out of here *now*. And keep the headlights off."

Christie still watched the scene.

Something inside her said she needed to understand this, so she kept watching.

Kate stopped.

She pressed her back against the wall, the stone cold, feeling damp even through her clothes.

She heard voices.

Two men. The voices deep, echoing in the outer garage, filtering in here, their words not clear at all.

Almost like barks.

Like dogs, quietly growling, making sounds at each other. Grunts.

She didn't move.

If Simon was here, would they find him and they'd get in more trouble?

Maybe . . . yes, maybe—she thought—she should just come out.

Be honest. Tell them that she was just looking for her dumb brother.

And they'd say: *You mean, that brat one who went up the mountain and almost got people killed?*

Yeah.

That one.

Her hands still pressed against the stone. Feeling the indented areas, the smooth curve of the stone blocks, cool, wet. Time to walk out of this tunnel.

When she heard, from outside, from far away . . . a gunshot.

Then another.

And suddenly moving didn't seem like such a good idea.

41

The Prisoners

At the far end of the warehouse, whatever this building was, doors flew open.

A pool of light from inside spilled into an open area, surrounded by fences.

"Christie, we'd better go."

"Hang on. Just a minute—"

Something happening here.

Somehow—she knew it was important. To see this, understand this.

The open doors. People being led out.

No.

More like *herded*.

The men with the guns surrounding them, making sure they stayed together, that they didn't move.

And Christie felt that it was all wrong before she could really understand it. Some instinct kicked in as her mind raced to catch up.

To see, then to *understand* that the men with guns weren't herding people, that these *weren't* the men from the inn that had come here to raid food and supplies that clearly didn't exist.

Into this trap.

That the people she was looking at, in the fenced-in area, were actually children.

Her fist went to her mouth, the understanding kicking in, as sick and twisted as it could be.

Then, one bit more of understanding.

A terrible clarity.

She moaned in the car: "Oh, please, no . . ."

Gunfire around the building.

Kate's palms pressing flat against the stone.

Why would anyone be firing guns?

Most of the men, the guards who kept this place safe, had gone with the others, with her mother.

Just a few left.

Now this shooting?

It could mean—the thought registering clearly now—only one thing.

We're being attacked.

Only this time, with so many of the others away.

Kate removed her hands from the stone as if prying them away, freeing herself from the curves of the cool stone wall.

The men in the garage began shouting. No gunfire there yet.

Were the men shooting from the house or—?

And: what should she do?

Then, from behind, the slightest sound echoing from behind her down the twisting tunnel that must lead to the distant back of the property.

Other noises.

A clattering sound.

Things being pushed, moved, and not too far away.

Kate started looking around the tunnel, where she was trying to quickly figure out what her options were.

Thinking . . . *do I even* have *any options?*

"What is it?" Helen asked.

Christie released one hand from the steering wheel to point at the far end of the warehouse, to the open area, the pen surrounded by fences, the men with guns.

She could barely say the word: *Children.*

It took Helen only a moment to see, then, "Oh, sweet Jesus."

In those moments, Christie had taken the images in, and now understood what she saw.

"They've captured children. They're keeping *children.*"

Helen shook her head. "No. They can't. That can't—"

Christie threw the car into reverse to pull back from the edge. Then the Honda rocketed back, stopped by a sharp brake.

Then, she threw the car into drive and they started moving ahead.

"What are they doing?" Helen asked.

Did she really not understand, or was it just too unbelievable for the woman to grasp?

"They've captured *children.* Holding them there. Under guard."

Christie didn't say the obvious.

"But why children? They just captured a bunch of our men. I don't—"

The dirt road curved around, and in a moment the car vanished into a wooded area, on this road she hoped led somewhere.

"Like . . ." Christie said, so obvious now . . . "livestock. Growing them. Maybe they're easier to move, to control. I don't know."

"We have to do something."

The dirt road straight, and now running away from the hill over-looking the warehouse.

Christie threw on the headlights.

"For them?" Christie said.

"We can't just let—"

She didn't get it, Christie thought. Didn't really understand at all.

The rest of the horror.

She was tempted to floor the accelerator, but the road was narrow, with branches still to be skirted, rocks to be passed.

She could only go so fast.

"This was a trap, Helen. A trap! The news about all that food in-side a warehouse? Just to get our people here."

Helen got it.

"Oh, God. The inn."

"Right. The inn, left almost defenseless. All our kids there, all the young people. For them to capture."

Christie couldn't believe the words she was saying as she pictured her own two kids, the only two people in the world her mind would let her think about, worry about.

Back there.

On their own.

Helen's next words were spoken quietly, calmly, filled with the grim meaning of their journey back to the inn.

"Drive as fast as you can."

Kate looked to where one pool of light ended, just catching the curve of another tunnel that split off from the main passage here.

The sounds seemed to be coming from straight down the tunnel.

The jangling, crashing noises had stopped.

The thought:

They're in.

Whoever was trying to get in . . . was.

She would have only seconds to do something.

Kate looked at a smaller tunnel that led off to the side.

If she ran to the garage, she would be between the guards and whoever was coming inside.

And so—though going into the small tunnel meant moving away from the men with guns, from the garage—she moved as fast as she could.

Thinking that every step had to be so quiet as she entered the smaller tunnel and started looking for a place to hide.

Simon stood at the window of the room and looked out.

Just below the window, men from the inn had guns out, and started shooting—but they didn't seem to know what they were shooting at, turning left and right, pointing.

Their heads also turning, looking out to the nearby woods, over to the other side of the lake.

He heard their voices.

But with the window shut, he couldn't understand what they were saying.

Simon thought . . . *almost everyone is gone.*

Not a lot of guards here.

It had seemed like a fun idea to run away from Kate, but now he wished she'd come back to the room.

He didn't like being alone here, not with the men outside looking around, their guns out, taking shots at nothing.

The door to the room was open.

He looked at it.

Was that a good thing? To have it open?

He was torn between looking out the window and going to the door and closing it quietly.

Somehow—it seemed important to shut the door quietly.

Outside, another gunshot, but this one sounded as though it came from far away.

He quickly turned back to the window.

One of the men had fallen to his knees, still holding his gun.

Then he fell forward.

And Simon raced to the door as fast as he could.

"Does this damn road go *anywhere*?" Christie said.

"It has to," Helen answered, her voice low. Then repeating it, more of a wish. "Has to . . ."

For a moment, neither spoke as the low tree branches and bushes brushed the car, reaching out for it, trying to hold it back.

The car hit a rock and went bumping up, and then it hit a patch of the road pockmarked with depressions that kept the Honda bucking up and down.

"Shit," Christie said. "Damn road—"

Then, as the road turned left, she saw an actual paved road ahead, barely visible under the light from the stars and the crescent moon low in the clear night sky.

"There you go," Helen said.

The Honda's lights hit the pavement, and Christie was ready for anything—Can Heads waiting there, men with guns, a barrier of some kind.

But the dirt road simply deposited them onto the paved road, which she took as fast as she could, the car turning and fishtailing as she now gunned it.

Only then did she turn and risk a look at Helen.

"They're not going to get my kids."

She nodded at her own words, the strength of her resolve making her entire body tighten, tense and coiled.

She would do anything, she knew.

She brought her eyes back to the road, where she was doing close to double the forty-miles-an-hour speed limit.

"No way they will *ever* get my kids."

And though she sounded strange, crazed, she kept repeating the words over and over until it became clear that they didn't need repeating.

42

The Trap

This narrow tunnel to the side passed small locked rooms, with tiny doors, all held shut with heavy latches and padlocks, and Kate wondered if she had wandered into a dead end.

Maybe she should go back the other way, back to the sounds that filtered from the far end of the inn, out to the garage.

At least some guards were out there.

But then she saw one of the small rooms without a door, open and exposed. Inside, not much bigger than a low closet, an empty storeroom. But the space was out of the light.

She could sneak in there, sit quietly, and wait till the sounds passed.

Then—Simon. She'd have to go find Simon.

She ducked into the room and quickly sat down on the floor, pulling her knees up close.

And as she sat there breathing as quietly as she could, straining to hear whatever sounds she could, thinking . . .

That something bad was happening out there, and Simon was alone.

So that in the darkness, she felt two things equally strong—alternating, dizzyingly swinging one to the other—from her terrible fear to an equally terrible guilt.

Simon shut the door and then stood there, looking at it.

More gunshots from outside.

People outside shooting at the few guards left.

Trying to break into the building.

That's what was happening . . .

What did they want?

That last question made him feel very cold.

Only now did he turn and see the old-fashioned bureau that faced his mother's big bed.

He reached out and slowly turned the latch that locked the door.

It clicked much too loudly he thought, the metallic *click* seeming so loud.

But it was done; the door locked.

He heard a yell from outside. Maybe one of the guards needing help. But where would that help come from if everyone was away?

And when would they come back, the men in the cars with all their guns, his mom?

He started to back away from the door. The floorboards creaked even though they were covered with the dark maroon rug, each step producing a bunch of squeaks.

He didn't let the sounds stop him.

Instead, he just kept moving until he stood beside the bureau, about to do something his mother said to never ever do.

He crouched down and, again concerned about the noise, slowly pulled open the drawer.

Two guns there. His mother had taken hers.

Simon's gun the smallest. One that had been his dad's.

Kate had shown him how to shoot it. It wasn't hard. Just have to throw a switch, and he'd be ready.

Important to hold your arm out straight, look at where the gun was pointing, and, and—

He took a breath.

Then he reached down and took the gun.

Had his father ever used it to shoot someone? Had his father . . . ever killed a Can Head with it?

Then, still crouched, one more thought.

I have. I've killed one of them with it.

His hand tightened around the handgun.

Then, he slowly stood up in the cold room.

"Careful," Helen said. "We nearly lost it on that curve."

After a few wrong turns, Christie had gotten them back to the county road. At this speed, the inn was only ten minutes away.

"What are we going to do?" Helen asked.

Christie nodded, amazed and happy at Helen's *we*.

"It's so obvious. They lured everyone away into a trap. But the real goal was everyone left in the inn."

A look at the woman sitting next to her.

"The children."

"I don't get it."

"No?" Christie nodded her head; she had finally started to understand. What had happened back in the camp, what was happening here, in the city, what the hell was happening everywhere in the world.

"They get kids, and they can control kids, move them around—Jesus—herd them. You see—"

She tilted her head, the insane logic of it clear.

"—that way they have a . . . have a—"

(The words too hard to say. But she had to.)

"—food supply. They can't just depend on finding people, killing them."

"God."

"Christie. We don't know what we're going to face. What might've happened to our people back there. Did anyone else escape that trap at the warehouse? I mean, if it's just us—"

Christie's voice low, steady as she worked to keep herself level, calm.

"If it's just us, we'll have to be enough."

Nothing for a moment.

"Okay. If it's just us then—yes. We'll be enough."

The road became straight here, and Christie could hold the accelerator nearly flush to the floor.

The inn, her kids, whatever lay ahead . . . only minutes away.

Simon heard noises in the hallway.

Yells, screams. A woman, making a big howling noise.

Then a gunshot.

And nothing.

Kids voices, crying. But no gunshots answered those cries.

But Simon noticed how the sounds stopped after a few minutes. Had something been done to quiet them? Or had they been taken away?

Where would they take them?

Simon realized: I can't move.

Thinking: *it's impossible to move.*

The gun, feeling like a toy, dangling from his hand, pointing to the ground. His eyes, though, were locked on the door to the room.

Locked door, he reminded himself.

The sudden burst of cries and yells and screams had ended.

But he could still hear the squeaks of the wooden floor outside as people moved about.

Squeaks growing closer.

Mumbling sounds. Men speaking.

Simon, a statue with a gun.

When—eyes on that door—he watched the doorknob twist left, right, and left again.

And all Simon wanted to do was cry.

Kate raised her head. Sounds from the other tunnel. Steps, people hurrying.

No talking.

Rushing to the garage where she could still hear the voices of the men there, waiting, unsuspecting of these people running toward them.

Would they turn and come down this tunnel?

Just to check it?

Try all the small locked doors and then come to the room that had no door, the dark stone storeroom where she sat, curled up, totally defenseless.

She kept her head up, eyes blinking in the darkness.

No, she begged. Just keep on going.

She started to formulate a plan if the people kept going. What she could do.

To get out of here.

To get back to Simon.

Because she knew more than anything that she had to do that. There was no choice.

It has to be done, she told herself.

No matter what. No matter the risk.

But for now . . . she waited.

———

Christie started up the long curving road to the inn, still driving crazily fast.

"Easy, Christie. Don't want to go flying off the edge."

She nodded. The edge of the road had a small stone wall to stop cars from going over the side, rolling down the hill of the mountain.

But at this speed?

The car could easily roll right over the stone barrier.

And as the Honda weaved its way up the mountain, Christie tried to see the inn.

First, the top of the buildings came into view, a few windows dotted with lights.

Maybe it's all okay, she thought.

But she quickly pulled away from that thought.

Can't let myself hope.

Have to be *prepared*.

Another curve, and the tires squealed, but Helen didn't try to get her to slow down.

"So stupid," Christie said.

More of the building came into view.

She turned to Helen.

"I'm out here . . . because I came to protect this damn car. When I should have protected my kids."

"And without a car? You want to be here, in this world, with no way to . . . get away?" The woman sitting beside her took a breath. "You made a decision."

Christie dared looking over at her. "And if my kids pay a price for that?"

There was no answer to that.

Not for Helen, she knew.

And certainly not for her.

She came to the last section of the road, a straight section before a last curve up to the inn and the lake.

And they both heard the *popping* sounds.

Gunshots.

And Christie slowed the car.

Another rattle of the doorknob. A voice on the other side.

Simon looked around the room; he saw the bathroom nearby. A closet near the bed. A big chair that sat in the corner of the room facing his mother's bed.

He stood there with the gun still dangling.

And then, the only idea that came to him finally allowed him to move as if he was released from a spell, like in one of his old video games.

He could *move*!

And he ran to the bed, slid to the floor, and being careful to keep the gun pointing away from him, he *rolled* under the bed, fully to the middle, barely room for his head, his face now looking up at springs, lips nearly touching them.

A bang at the door.

Then louder, something hard smashing against the doorknob.

Simon heard the door fly open, smacking against the inside wall.

Someone said: "Check it out."

He didn't dare move his head to look as someone came into the room.

All he did was force his breathing to stay steady. Slow, in and out, as quiet as he could while—nearby—the floorboards creaked.

"They're here," Christie said.

Now she could make out, just ahead, cars and trucks pulled off to the side of the road.

The back of the trucks open.

Ready.

The popping noises sporadic.

"We can't just go up there," Helen said.

Christie nodded. As much as she wanted to race up to the inn, grab her kids and get the hell out of there, she knew she couldn't.

"Look," Helen said, nodding to the left. "There's a driveway to the back of the inn. Probably used for supplies. It must go somewhere. Maybe we can get in that way."

Christie turned.

The narrow driveway did appear to lead to the back of the inn.

A snap decision was needed.

It all seeming so hopeless.

"Won't be long before whoever came in those cars ... leaves. And—if what you think they're doing is true—they'll already have the kids with them."

Helen reached out and patted Christie's hand.

"It's the only way."

Christie nodded and killed the lights. Maybe someone had already seen them.

Maybe they'd think it was some of the raiding party.

The people from the warehouse.

The farm.

The place where they keep children.

She started down the driveway to the back of the inn, slowly. Eyes straining to follow the path in the darkness.

43

Family

Gunshots began exploding from the garage.

Kate could guess what was happening. The men there had been surprised by whoever had just come from the tunnels.

What did they want? she wondered.

Why did they come here?

She also knew that if she was going to move, to get out of there before the attackers started exploring, she had to do it now.

Kate put her palms on the ground, and pushed herself to a crouch, and then up.

She took a breath.

And quickly moved out of her hiding place.

———

The man walked around the room, each step making a loud creaking noise.

The sounds seemed so loud to Simon. First on the left side of his head, then, as the man moved around the bed, to the right side of his head.

He heard the man move a chair, a different noise as the legs of the chair pulled at the rug.

Next to the chair, the closet, open when Simon had rolled under the bed. The sound of clothes on hangers being pushed around, rattling.

Then the feet walked away from the bed.

Simon's eyes open.

Looking straight up.

Barely . . . breathing.

The man walked away.

From the noises, he moved into the bathroom where, for a few moments, the sounds stopped.

A new noise, as the shower curtain was pulled back fast.

Then a word: "Damn."

Simon knew he'd look under here.

Had to.

It was the one place he hadn't looked.

A hiding place everyone knew about.

There was nothing he could do, Simon knew.

Then a voice from the hall: "Hey! Get the hell out here. Bring these ones outside now!"

The steps near the bed stopped, hesitating.

Simon imagined that the man was thinking. The voice calling him, but maybe wondering if he missed anything.

But then the feet turned and now, more quickly, moved away from the bed, to the door, and finally out into the hallway.

And Simon stayed right where he was.

With the car lights killed, Christie opened her car door as quietly as she could, doing it slowly to minimize any squeak of the door swinging open.

Helen did the same thing.

And when outside, Christie did a quick look around. But back here, in the darkness, it seemed quiet, all the noises coming from the front of the inn.

She turned to Helen and whispered.

"You don't have to come. You could stay here, by the car, and if—"

Helen touched her shoulder.

"You're kidding, right? Let's go get your kids."

They began walking up a gravel path to the back of the inn.

Kate edged out of the tunnel.

The safe way was to go out the other tunnel, make her way to the deserted side of the building.

Maybe even get out of here.

But Simon was somewhere. And with her mom gone, it was her job.

I have to do this, she told herself.

No choice . . . no choice at all.

She kept moving to the open cave that was the garage.

The gravel path led to a back door, locked and with a board over the glass panels, hiding what was on the other side.

Helen gave the knob another twist, and then brought the butt of her rifle down on the knob. No choice but to make some noise if they wanted to get in. On the third smack of the rifle butt, the knob fell to the ground as Christie kept looking around.

But still—all quiet here.

The door opened, and they were back inside the inn.

The tunnel curved around, Kate still walking slowly.

Then, voices ahead.

It sounded like a man crying.

She couldn't make out the words, but people were ahead.

A man *crying*.

Then a word she understood.

"Please." Then another sob. "Please, you don't have to—"

A gunshot, the sound seeming so close as it echoed in this tunnel.

The crying, the words stopped.

And Kate remained frozen, thinking *I can't go back . . . I can't go forward.*

Nearly impossible to see as Christie moved with Helen down a totally dark hallway.

This must have been the place where the staff of the hotel lived, a wing of rooms well away from the main building.

But with no lights, no windows, they moved in total darkness.

"You okay?" Helen asked.

"Yes. I—"

Helen took her hand.

"This way if one of us trips, maybe we can hold each other up."

The fact that they were whispering in this total darkness only made the walk more terrifying.

At the same time, Christie knew that she had to hurry.

Every minute could mean that something had happened to Simon, to Kate.

Even here, they could hear the gunshots, though they too had grown more sporadic.

Maybe the attack had failed.

Maybe everything was okay.

But she knew that depending on *maybes* was dangerous.

"We need to find stairs up. There has to be some stairs that go up to all the floors," Christie said.

"If we could *see* them."

Then, a few steps farther, they came to an opening, a dark hole to their right.

But as Christie's eyes adjusted, she could see the barest outline of a staircase.

"There!" Christie said.

She pulled Helen forward.

The sounds from the garage stopped.

Got to move, Kate thought.

Then, a command, as if her body was a machine that she struggled to control.

Move!

One step at a time, Christie told herself, using her feet to feel the steps, finally reaching the landing where the steps turned.

And somehow, they reached a door that must have led to the second floor.

Still so dark, but at last a door in front of them.

"This is it," Christie whispered.

Helen let go of her hand, and Christie heard the sound of Helen's gun being readied, the click of the safety, checking the chamber.

Christie withdrew the gun from under her belt.

And together, they pushed on the fire door in front of them, and it swung open to another empty, dark corridor.

But this she knew led to the main wing of the house, to lights, to her room. To Simon. To Kate.

She started walking more quickly, Helen right behind her, as the total darkness changed to scant light from the outline of another fire door ahead.

Simon wondered if he should stick his head out.

See if everything was okay.

See if—

What was it Dad used to say?

"If the coast is clear."

He hadn't thought of him for a while now.

But now, when he wished so hard that his father was here, it felt like he only lost him yesterday.

Simon's fingers dug into the rug, holding on.

He used them to pull himself forward, crawling, dragging his belly across the rug like an animal.

Until he came out from under the bed.

44

Leaving

The doorknob from this wing to the main building turned in Christie's hand.

Is it locked?

She didn't say anything to Helen, not without knowing what might be on the other side.

The woman's face caught some of the light.

She's worried too.

With the knob turned all the way to the right, she gave it a push, and the door opened and both of them were instantly bathed in what seemed brilliant light.

Christie blinked, her eyes having grown accustomed to the dark.

She held her gun out. Helen had her shotgun up as well.

Both ready.

But the hallway was empty.

A ghost hotel. Totally deserted.

Christie held her breath, her heart sinking, a physical feeling, then a whisper. "No."

"Come on," Helen said.

Resuming their march to the bedroom, now only seconds away, Christie's fear near total.

A few feet away, Christie ran to the open door.

She took in the doorknob, blown away, pieces of wood and the metal on the floor.

And a fear that had seemed immeasurable grew into horror.

She couldn't bear to look in the room.

What could be an empty room.

When she saw movement on the floor.

Right *there*. At the bed. Then a head popped out, a voice:

"Mom! Mom!!"

Simon finished scrambling out from under the bed and sprang to his feet, a rocket, throwing himself at Christie.

Wrapping himself around his mother.

And for a few brief moments, everything seemed all right.

With Simon's arms around her, Christie also felt the gun in his hand, and she knew that they had no time.

She pulled him away.

"Simon—where's your sister? Where's Kate?"

His eyes looked hollow. They darted away and then returned to her.

"I don't know. We were downstairs."

"Downstairs? Where?"

"The garage place. And I hid from her. Came back here."

What he did—so dangerous.

That could be talked about later.

Let there be a later . . .

"She didn't come up here?"

"No. People came. Then I heard guns. I—I—"

She pulled him close again.

"Okay," she whispered. "Okay, Simon."

Just a few seconds to get the boy steady, but her eyes were on Helen, standing at the doorway, looking at them, but also looking at the hallway.

Christie broke the embrace and led her son over to Helen.

"Helen. Can you take Simon to the car?"

Working hard to keep her voice steady.

"Shouldn't we both go down—"

Christie shook her head. "We have Simon. We need to . . ."

Get him someplace safe. Get him out of here. Where he'll be okay.

Simon's okay. But what about Kate?

All unsaid.

Instead: "Can you take him to the car? And I'll go get Kate—"

As if it was easy.

A simple matter. Just go get her daughter. Downstairs. Sure.

If she was even still there.

"I need you to watch out for him. While I get Kate."

Helen's eyes were locked on hers. A woman smart enough to know everything that wasn't being said.

Knowing that they had Simon; he was okay. But everything else was unknown.

"Okay. I'll do that. Then we better get going. You too."

Christie nodded. "Go back the way we came." To her son. "Simon, it's dark—but we came up that way. Goes out the back. Nobody will see you."

I hope, I hope, I hope.

"Okay Simon," Helen said, putting a hand on his shoulder. Helen looked down to the boy's hand holding a gun, then up to Christie, as if checking . . . that okay?

A boy with a gun.

Christie didn't say anything.

"I'll be with you in a bit," she said. "With Kate."

Knowing that both statements could turn out to be completely false as Helen quickly led Simon away.

But before she left the room, Christie ran over and got the other gun, the small revolver that Kate used.

(And how she wished Kate had it with her now . . .)

The two boxes of bullets. A quick check that both handguns were loaded.

Then, one gun in each hand, she ran full out from the room.

To the empty hallway.

Noting that the gunshots had completely stopped.

She ran as fast as she could to the main staircase, hitting the steps two at a time, nearly tripping, flying so fast.

She heard sounds from below, noises, cries, moans.

She told herself that nothing could matter, nothing could stop her no matter what she saw.

She hit the bottom of the stairs, and quickly ran right to the stairs that led to the basement.

But as she did, she saw:

Two men on their knees by the Colonel's office.

One of them could have been the Colonel. Hard to tell. The heads of the kneeling men all bloody, looking blurry and out of focus, as she saw a man ram a rifle butt at one man, then at the other.

And at the front door to the inn, other people.

She recognized a few of them from the inn, standing there. Ropes around their necks, tied together.

With their kids—also tied with them.

Huddled together.

One of the men watching the beating turned and saw Christie.

He yelled.

"You! Stop!"

And though Christie was close to the stairs—she wasn't close enough.

Not to risk the man shooting at her.

So Christie had no choice.

Got to fucking do this, she told herself.

Coming to a near instantaneous stop.

Had they not seen what was in her hands?

She raised both guns.

The men raising their rifles as they stood beside the bloody bodies kneeling on the deep maroon rug.

She pulled the triggers.

Again, and again, the first shots missing, then adjusting up, and over to the left, as one man took a shot in his shoulder and spun around, wounded.

The other man taking aim with his rifle wasn't as lucky as Christie's unaimed shot blew right into the very top of his head.

A brief glance at the huddled people, tied up.

Had to be more men outside, the invaders.

She had seen the trucks.

There was no time to help them do anything.

It's all about choices, she thought.

And she quickly turned, not bothering to lower the guns as she now reached the stairwell down to the garage, where Kate had to be.

Had to be.

Please.

Racing down the stairs and not letting herself think of the impossibility of what she was trying to do.

Kate entered the garage.

A few cars here. The lights bright.

And in the center of the garage, a man face down. A bloody pool oozed out from under him.

But there didn't seem to be anyone else.

No one else here.

But then—

With noises coming from behind, from the tunnels, Kate knew she was wrong about that.

Men with guns had been here.

But now, following them, maybe planned . . .

. . . other things came.

And she turned, helpless, hopeless, to watch three Can Heads race into the room, ready to—she knew—feast on whatever they'd find.

Any dead bodies they'd find . . .

Kate started backing up, literally running backward because the only thing she could do was watch the Can Heads run toward her, ignoring the fresh body on the floor.

Targeting—instead—*her.*

Christie now raced into the garage, her head and body spinning wildly around looking for Kate, about to shout her daughter's name, terrified beyond anything she had ever experienced that her cry would go unanswered.

But in that wild spinning, she saw *her*—off to the side of the mammoth cave, near the rooms with the guns, the gas.

About to say her name—since Kate didn't look over at her.

But then seeing why.

Kate had her eyes locked straight ahead, looking across the room.

The three Can Heads charging her, running so fast.

Is this how it works? Christie had a flash of a thought.

The Can Heads, the real animals, work with these people, these human monsters, get to come here, and have what's left?

Is that what this world is now?

With the Can Heads moving so fast that she couldn't trust her aim from here.

And she wondered—do I need to reload? How many bullets left?

Every second precious.

Like the Can Heads, she ran toward her daughter.

Until one of them noticed her, and slowed a bit, dumbly calculating what was happening.

Kate had turned, and she too ran to her mother, all of them three points on a deadly triangle.

But the Can Heads had—by what . . . instinct?—separated. No longer an easy cluster of targets.

Christie had to measure her shots. There would be no chance to reload.

She watched them carefully as they bobbed and weaved like feral animals.

And fired two shots.

Neither hit, both wide misses.

Kate called: "Mom!"

Christie struggled to retain her focus.

Two more shots. The smoke from the pistols hanging like a cloud in the room.

Kate still racing to her, now trailed by a Can Head.

This time, after the blasts, one of them stopped and reached for its chest.

A hit, but would it stop it? The other shot another miss.

Two more shots from each gun. How many more were left?

But at least the Can Heads converged. She brought her arms together. Took a breath. Pulled the triggers.

45

The Car

So dark here, Simon thought. This was worse than hiding under the bed.

But then the woman, Helen, a good friend—Simon knew that—gave his hand a squeeze.

Like she could tell what he was feeling.

Then in a quiet voice, sounding *so* quiet in this dark hallway.

"We're almost there, Simon."

Then:

"You okay?"

He nodded, then realized that like everything else here, he couldn't be seen. "Yeah. I'm okay."

"Good boy. Just a bit ahead. And then we're out, near the car. And we can wait for your mom."

But Simon had to wonder, couldn't *not* think about it . . . was Kate okay? Would Mom find her? Could they both get back okay?

He held Helen's hand tighter.

One gun fired, and one Can Head was close enough that the shot blew a hole in its throat, and it landed to the right of Christie.

But she also heard the sickening sound of the other gun firing on an empty chamber, and then the last Can Head, with a shoulder wound, fell on her.

She saw the thing's mouth open as it aimed its teeth like a weapon right at the area above her knee.

Christie smashed at it with the empty gun, but the weapon seemed to bounce off its head, and then fly away across the floor.

The teeth bit down.

She screamed.

She pointed the other gun at it, the one that had fired. But now, with another click, she knew that gun was empty as well.

The thing had put one of its claw hands on her chest to pin her down. The pain—so intense—spread from her thigh to fill her body. The bright white lights in the ceiling turning molten, sparks shooting out of them.

Her cries constant as though she was listening to someone else make them.

But then, backlit by those lights, standing over her and with the thing attached to her leg, she saw a shadow.

Amidst the screams, something *eclipsed* those lights.

She remembered what she was doing down here. How she had seen Kate.

Kate was still okay.

A beautiful thought amidst the horror of the thing's hand pushing her back, its mouth pulling back on—

(Yes, tearing back . . .)
—on skin, muscle.
But there was the shadow.
And the shadow moved.

Helen turned into a room, still holding Simon's hand.

There was a bit more light, he saw. Just a bit—but enough to see a door ahead.

It had windows. Light from outside. From the moon maybe, or the stars.

"See—we're here," Helen said.

Simon didn't say anything.

"The car is just outside."

But Simon noticed that the woman had slowed.

His right hand tightened on the gun that felt so heavy during this walk in the darkness.

Helen let go of his hand and he could see her pull back the door. It wasn't locked. They could get out.

He wished she hadn't had to let go of his hand.

Even for those seconds.

He waited for her to take it again.

But she held the door open, and said, "Hold on a sec."

She went out first. He saw her holding her gun up, looking left and right. Then again.

She turned back to him, the woman's round face making a tiny smile.

"Okay. Let's go."

She turned, and he followed her out of the inn.

Christie heard a *thwack*.

And the thing that had just torn a piece out of her right leg went flying to one side.

It reared back.

It took its hand off her chest, and turned to see what had hit it.

Which is when the shadow, Kate, used the butt of the gun again on the thing's head.

Christie could see her daughter pull her arm all the way back and then let it fly right at its head.

This time, the blow—straight to the Can Head's skull again—knocked it right off of her.

Christie tried to sit up, but the leg wound sent more mad spears of pain shooting through her body.

So she got to see Kate, still over the thing, hitting it again, and again, and again.

Until it was clear from the holes that now pockmarked the thing's skull that it wouldn't be getting up.

Wouldn't be attacking anyone ever again.

"Mom," Kate said.

And it was enough.

And Christie fought past the pain, seeing the hole in her leg, blood everywhere. Not good.

But she fought past the pain to sit up, and say:

"We have to go. We have to get out of here."

Then, using her good leg to get up to a half-crouch.

"Give me a hand."

And Kate reached down and pulled her mother up.

Simon saw the car, parked under trees, sitting on the dirt, waiting for them.

Helen spoke, keeping her voice low.

"We're going to get inside, and wait. They won't—"

But then in that darkness, with the trees so still, a few bushes with leaves surrounding them.

Nothing moving . . .

Until something *did*.

He turned. He felt Helen let go of his hand.

She had seen it too.

They were so close.

So close, he thought.

And what happened next, he didn't understand at all.

Christie turned to the main staircase out of the garage.

"No, Mom. There are stairs back through the tunnel. No one will see."

Christie looked at her daughter. They both held guns.

"Okay. Go get some bullets. From the room. Anything else they left."

For a moment, Kate didn't move.

"Go!"

Kate turned and ran over to the room, while Christie started to hobble toward the tunnel.

She went as fast as she could, as fast as the agony would allow.

Still so excruciatingly slow.

And with every step, she moaned.

Men popped up from behind bushes, from behind trees, even from the corner of the building.

They all had guns.

And at first Simon thought they were the guards from the inn.

But he didn't recognize any of the faces.

And as he watched, they began to lower their guns.

Helen had stopped moving, and before she could get her big rifle up, a bullet hit her.

She turned to Simon, eyes wide.

He knew what to do.

He didn't have to think.

He raised his gun and looked away from Helen.

Which is when one of the men had come close and smacked at his hand with the butt end of his rifle.

His gun fell to the ground.

Another shot.

And this time he turned to see Helen doubled over.

No, no, no, he kept thinking.

She's a friend. Why would these men do this?

They're *not* Can Heads.

Helen fell to her knees, and she was barely able to get her head up.

Simon took a step backward.

He'd be next, he knew that.

But then he felt something slip over his head. A loop of rope that went right over his head just as he was about to start for Helen.

And it tightened.

So tight that he couldn't move at all.

As Christie hobbled, Kate loaded one gun, then the other.

Christie didn't look at the trail of blood she was leaving as they moved through this tunnel, then up the stairs that would take them close to the back entrance.

To the car.

To a way out of here.

If—

If, she thought.

—I don't bleed to death before I get there.

She kept one hand on the wound, applying as much pressure as she could to stem the flow.

But it needed to be bandaged.

And after that, who knew what it would be like.

Each step brought insane waves of pain crashing into her.

"Mom, you—"

"Shhh," Christie said.

Who knew what was ahead.

Best they do this journey in silence.

Step after step after step.

Simon's hand went to the rope, tugging at it. He could see that one of the men held a long stick that was attached to the rope. Almost like . . . a fishing rod. Or . . . something you would use at a rodeo.

Simon tried to jerk his head, but that only made the rope tighter.

Another man came to the side, picked up Simon's gun.

"Easy, boy. Easy, and you will be all right."

Simon started struggling.

Then the man laughed.

"Look. He even had a gun."

The man turned back to Simon.

"You were going to shoot us boy? *Kill* us?"

Simon didn't move. Didn't say anything.

The man slapped him with the backside of his hand.

"From now on, you better do exactly what we say."

The man paused.

"Got that?"

The rope tightened a bit.

Simon nodded.

Then the man turned to the others.

"Okay, we got to catch up to the others. Let's get the hell out of here."

And the man with the stick and rope used it to guide Simon, choking and coughing, up the path.

One last thing he did, even though it made the rope pull at his throat . . . he looked at Helen, on the ground, face down.

But then all his mind could think of was . . .

Mom and Kate. Mom and Kate.

Mom.

Kate.

46

The Discovery

The pain grew with every step, and Christie could feel how the blood oozed through her fingers with her hand pressed flush to the wound.

She fought hard not to whimper.

Kate had taken her arm, and Christie struggled to not let all her weight fall on her daughter.

When they reached the upper floor, and started toward the back, Christie heard the sounds of cars moving, then truck engines.

Whatever had happened here, at the inn, was ending.

How long had Helen and Simon been waiting? she wondered.

Was the car still safe, undiscovered?

She wanted to hurry, but this was the fastest speed she could manage.

"Almost there," she whispered hoarsely to Kate.

"Good."

Then they came to the end of the dark hallway. The outside, the car, and escape were only minutes away.

Christie turned to her daughter.

"But be ready."

Christie held her gun up a bit. And she knew she didn't have to tell Kate what to be ready for.

Out the door, and Christie started to think of next steps.

How they'd back out, lights off, secretly slip down off the mountain.

Get away.

That was the first thing.

Then her wound. She needed to do something about that fast. She didn't feel dizzy, wasn't losing consciousness yet, but that couldn't be far away.

Steps on the dirt ground.

She stumbled a bit and Kate was barely able to hold her up.

Recovering, she looked ahead, making out the car in the shadows. Still here.

Still *safe.*

Soon she'd see Simon and Helen inside, waiting.

More steps.

And then, with such amazing slow speed, the horror hit her like a breeze that gradually builds and builds, rising to the force of a hurricane.

The car was empty.

Kate spoke quickly.

"Where are they? Where's Simon? And Helen? I thought you said—"

First thoughts: *they hadn't made it back here. Somehow they had been caught.*

Christie looked around, as if the two of them might be hiding in the woods. A few cars and trucks could still be out front.

So quiet here, the night sickeningly still, and all Christie had were the slowly unfolding thoughts, the revelations that left her so confused.

It was Kate who saw it.

Christie about to call her son's name.

Her lips open, knowing that saying anything, calling out, was a bad idea. But she had to.

Kate again.

"Mom . . ."

And Christie turned to her daughter.

All she had to do was look where Kate was staring.

Follow the angle of her head.

Something on the ground.

Her heart sinking, actually feeling as if it would fall right out of her, as if in that moment she stood in an elevator plummeting straight down, racing to smash down on some personal ground zero.

"No," Christie muttered.

Thinking the worst.

Pulling away from Kate, hobbling as fast as she could to the shape.

Then, torturously falling to one knee, the only knee she could use, her other leg screaming in pain.

To see what the lump, the shape prostrate on the ground, could be.

Fearing the worst.

———

Then, crouched next to it, she saw . . . *Helen.*

Head down, short brown hair catching light.

"Helen," Christie whispered.

A hand to the back of the woman's neck.

The skin cold.

Then seeing around the body the signs of the wounds that couldn't be seen.

The gunshots that had killed her.

Kate came and crouched beside her.

Put her arm around her as Christie stroked Helen's hair once, then again before she turned and looked at Kate.

Eyes wide.

The terror.

Simon.

"Kate—"

Kate said nothing.

But the same question was roaring through both their minds.

Where's . . . Simon?

There was no more time for mourning.

"They got him," Christie said. "God, Kate—they got *Simon.*"

And feeling crazed, she struggled to her feet.

"Here, help me. Help me *up.*"

Kate hurried to prop up one side, and Christie was ready to find her son.

And when she began her hobbling walk, she started talking quickly, near manic.

"W-we have to hurry. This just happened. He's still here. We can—"

But Kate put a hand on each of her mother's shoulders.

"No."

"What do you mean? We have to hurry, Simon could—"

"No," Kate said quietly. Her voice icy in the night. Determined. "Not *you*. Me. I can run."

Christie shook her head back and forth, while Kate stood perfectly still.

And then:

"Let me take the guns." Then, as if Christie was too befuddled from her wound, from this night, to understand anything . . . "I can run fast."

And Christie nodded.

She gave her daughter the two guns.

Then a whisper, "Hurry Kate."

Please.

And in an instant, her daughter turned, and sprinted through the woods, to the front of the inn as Christie stood there, wound oozing, unable to breathe, unable to cry but—somehow—still able to hope.

47

Sister and Brother

Kate stopped.

Running so fast now that, with her jerky stop just outside the pool of light at the inn's entrance, she thought she'd fall.

Sucking in air so quickly.

And looking.

To see:

A truck pull away, and thinking . . . *I'm too late.*

But then—as if it was a gift—she saw two men standing with a boy.

A boy!

Simon.

One of them removed something from around Simon's neck. The car door was open. Only seconds left to do anything. A quick look around to see if there was anyone else here, anyone she wasn't seeing . . . that might see her, stop her.

But only the two men.

One pushing Simon toward the car, using the end of a rifle as if herding him.

Kate ran out of the shadows, and into the light. At the same time, she raised her guns, running straight at them.

Knowing that she couldn't simply shoot—not with Simon there.

A few steps closer to getting him in the car.

Time . . . up.

"Simon!" she yelled. "Simon—run!"

Her voice as loud as she could make it, a scream that echoed off the stone buildings.

And again: "Run!"

And her brother looked over at her, taking in what she was doing. The men, now moving, getting their rifles up.

He has to move, she thought.

And as if an answer to a prayer, he bolted to the side.

Leaving the two men turning to her, ready to shoot her, but hesitating—perhaps wondering . . . should one of them go get Simon, bring their captive back?

And with each step into the courtyard, feeling tears in her eyes, thinking . . . *this is so insane* . . .

Kate fired. And again. And again.

Her aim wobbly with all the running, her mind reeling.

But first one, then the other man, recoiled backward into their car.

Kate stopped running. Stood there.

One man fired a shot, but wounded, he missed Kate.

The sound of ricochet off the stone wall.

So—standing there, where she could now take aim—she fired again.

One gun clicked, signaling an empty chamber. But the other kept firing.

And as if they were melting, the men slowly slid to their knees, and then forward.

These men who thought they could take her brother.

Her breathing still fast.

The thought:

Take my brother?

No fucking way!

Then: one last bellow.

"Simon!"

She held him close, one gun still up and ready.

Neither said anything, but Simon matched her speed walking back. She thought of all the things he had seen. And even though she could easily say the same thing about herself, she thought . . .

He's so young.

Into the darkness around the side of the house.

She felt Simon stiffen.

Of course.

I'm taking him back, back to where he just saw what happened to Helen.

She had to speak.

"The car, Simon. Mom's there."

She felt him once again fall in line with her pace.

Until they finally reached the back of the inn.

Kate saw her mother in the car. The passenger door popped open.

"Simon!" her mother said.

Kate released her hand on her brother's back and watched him run to his mother.

Kate stood back while she hugged him, crying, saying words, so fast.

Babbling.

"You're okay, God, you're okay. Now . . . now get in and we—we—"

She looked up at Kate as Simon opened the back door.

Her mother in the passenger seat.

Confusing.

Why . . . would she be in the passenger seat?

"Kate—"

She held out the denim jacket she had been wearing.

"Tie this around me. Around the wound, tight as you can. I can't reach."

Kate took the jacket, holding out the two arms of the jacket to make it as long as possible. She bent down to wrap it around the wound.

Her mother made a small groan with the contact of the material on the open gash.

Then, wound bandaged—

"Kate—get in. Over there."

The driver's side.

"Mom, what are you doing? Why are you—"

Her mother looked up.

"I can't drive, Kate. Not with my leg. *You* have to drive."

And Kate just looked at her.

Christie looked back at Simon, sitting in the shadows of the backseat.

Then to Kate's hands on the wheel.

Her daughter shook her head.

"I don't know, Mom. I don't think—"

"Kate. You have to do this. You've seen your dad drive, me drive. I—I'm right here. You *have* to . . . do this."

Kate still shook her head.

But then stopped.

"Turn the car on. The ignition."

Crazy. Insane. Someone who had never driven a car.

Kate took her eyes away from the windshield. Down to the ignition. She grabbed the key.

"Okay, turn it."

The car started.

"Good," Christie said, her voice strained.

So hard to talk.

"Now, we're going to leave the lights off. Okay?"

Kate was back looking at the windshield.

"See the two side mirrors, and the rearview right above you?"

"Yes."

Kate's voice sounded totally hollow.

"Put your foot on the brake."

The engine revved.

"No. The pedal to the *left* of the accelerator. You have to be careful."

Kate banged the steering wheel. "I am!"

"I know. I know you are. Okay. Okay, Kate. Foot on the brake now?"

"Yes."

"Okay, now move the shift so that it's on *R*."

Christie watched the dashboard go from a brightly lit *N* to *R*.

"Now . . . you have to use the mirrors, and look back if you need to. Steer the car back out of here, all the way down."

Kate turned and looked at her.

"Backward?"

"There's no place to turn it around. But if you go slowly, it's wide enough. We can get back to the road."

She watched Kate look at the left and right mirrors, locking their location in.

Then she felt the brake release.

"Now—just a bit. Slowly. On the accelerator."

Kate's first press on the accelerator made the car lurch backward.

But the tires were still aimed straight so the car stayed on the dirt driveway.

Christie didn't say anything to Kate about the too-heavy step on the gas.

She's smart. She'll adjust.

And sure enough, the next time Kate barely gave it any gas at all, and her head whipped from one side mirror to the other, then up to the rearview.

At one point, she turned around to look back and see the road.

"Good, Kate. You're doing good."

A glance back at Simon.

So much to talk to him about.

But not now.

The car edged down.

Once, Christie heard the sound of some branches on the side of the road scraping the left side of the car.

She remembered how hard it could be to get a sense of where the car was when you first began driving.

Could Kate get them out of here?

Then what? Where would they go?

Kate kept backing the car down the dirt road.

Until . . . they were on the highway, and Christie told her to put the car into drive, and get it pointed straight on the road that led down the mountain.

"You're doing good, Kate. So good."

Her daughter said nothing, her hands locked on the wheel, and the speed . . . so slow.

But that was okay.

And Christie started to think of a plan.

Had to be a plan, didn't there?

Kate looked straight ahead. And with a gentle touch, she gave the car gas, and they started down the mountain road.

epilogue: family

Christie held on to just a few thoughts . . .

They needed to get away. From this area, whatever was going on here.

And . . . she needed to get the wound treated. And fast. It still oozed blood, even through the tightly tied denim jacket.

Then?

Then . . . indeed.

"You okay?"

"It's not so hard," Kate said. "Getting the hang of it."

Christie nodded. She winced as the pain of putting her leg into a sitting position stretched her wound.

Then silence for a few moments.

Maybe both of them thinking about what comes next.

"We have to find a town, something with a hospital. I—I can't stay like this."

Then from the back. A voice. Low and flat.

Almost, Christie thought, *ghostly*.

"I can look for one of those signs."

Christie couldn't turn fully around to face Simon. That would have caused too much pain.

But a tilt of the head, trying to keep her voice light.

"What, honey?"

"A big *H*. For *hospital*."

Christie smiled.

"Right. We can keep our eyes open for a sign like that. Have to be hospitals around here."

Though she didn't add her worry that they too would be closed up, relics of a time when people helped people.

Instead of . . . what went on now.

Then Kate: "We'll find one."

She patted her daughter's leg.

Christie had the thought . . . *my family will get me through*.

And if the leg gets treated, what do we do then?

This family?

She didn't know. But she did know a few things.

That they couldn't hide from this.

That if there were good people like Helen, like—sweet God—her own two kids, then there had to be others.

And the others would be trying to stop this.

Not just hide. Not find someplace that's supposedly safe and just wait.

And if that meant that they—the three of them—would have to live a different way, then that's what it would be.

Reality.

Anything else, an illusion.

The time for running and hiding had ended.

There had to be good people working to stop this, willing to risk everything to do that.

That's who we need to find.

That's who we will *find.*

One last thought . . . as she, like her kids, scanned the signs, looking for the big *H.*

More of a hope.

There has to be more of us . . . than them.

Has to be.

And with that, she went back to monitoring her pain, trying to breathe through the agonizing spasms, thinking that's enough of a plan for now.

We'll deal with tomorrow when it comes. It's enough to simply know that for all of us, there will be a tomorrow.

Simon kept his eyes wide open.

Thinking: *Mom needs me.*

Have to get her help.

And then:

We need each other.

They'd be okay as long as they were together.

And now . . .

Simon thought.

He let himself think of what had just happened.

His stomach tightened as he remembered seeing the shadowy figure of Helen shot, the sounds so loud. The way she fell forward. Then, the rope around his neck.

Where were they taking me?

To the same place they took the other kids?

Took Joe, his friend?

Why?

He didn't let himself think about an answer to that.

And Kate saving him.

He looked at her driving—like she was an adult. *Driving!*

The two men who had caught him, trapped him, too slow as Kate shot them.

And again:

She saved me.

Now they had left that place, the castlelike inn, and were going somewhere else.

We'll get Mom some help.

Kate drove slowly. Plenty of time to look for signs.

We'll find a hospital. Everything will be okay.

When the men took him away, he'd thought he'd never see his mother again.

All he could think was . . .

This is bad.

That was enough.

Because he'd have to tell them—his mom, Kate—sometime, let them know . . . that he realized something then.

Thinking about the others, where they had been taken, what would happen to them . . . thinking so clearly that it made him cold.

He actually shivered.

Thinking: *I would have fought until they had to kill me.*

At one point, Kate stopped.

Ahead, the sign . . . a big *H*, and an arrow pointing toward a small town.

Maybe it will be open, maybe it won't, Simon thought. *If it's not, we'll look for another.*

No, that wasn't something he worried about. Because he was with his family again.

Kate turned the car, nearly coming too close to the curb, a dead tree trunk.

"Sorry," she said.

And Simon added quickly: "You're doing really good, Kate."

In her mirror, he saw her smile.

"Yes, honey. Great," Christie said.

And Simon realized something else. About this night, about *now*.

Something strange, even . . . scary.

I didn't cry, he thought. *And I'm not going to. Never again.*

Somehow that was important.

Crying would do nothing. Nothing at all.

And something else now as he kept his eyes open, seeing a big building ahead. Lights on, guards at a fence.

"It's open!" Kate said.

He thought of other kids, maybe taken away. Or those still in their warm beds, safe for tonight.

I've done things, he thought.

Things that none of those kids have ever done.

And seen things.

He told himself something, as if reminding himself.

I've fired a gun.

I've shot them.

Crying would do nothing.

But maybe, he could do things.

He just needed to remember what he'd done.

How he was different now.

The car slowed. Guards opening the gate. Giant letters, all lit up, glowing so brightly: EMERGENCY ROOM.

Simon didn't know what was ahead for them; he didn't even want to think about what was ahead. It didn't matter. As long as he was with his family, he was home.

He was sure, though . . .

He and Kate and his mom would figure it out.

We'll plan. We'll survive.

Together.

And whatever came next, he and his family would be ready.